SCENT
To Her
GRAVE

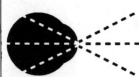 This Large Print Book carries the
Seal of Approval of N.A.V.H.

SCENT To Her GRAVE

A Bath and Body Mystery
India Ink

Thorndike Press • Waterville, Maine

Published in 2006 by arrangement with the Berkley Publishing Group, a division of Penguin Group (USA) Inc.

Thorndike Press® Large Print Mystery.

The tree indicium is a trademark of Thorndike Press.

The text of this Large Print edition is unabridged.
Other aspects of the book may vary from the original edition.

Set in 16 pt. Plantin.

Printed in the United States on permanent paper.

Library of Congress Cataloging-in-Publication Data

Ink, India, 1961–
    Scent to her grave : a bath and body mystery / by India Ink.
        p. cm. — (Thorndike Press large print mystery)
    ISBN 0-7862-8405-6 (lg. print : hc : alk. paper)
    1. Beauty contestants — Crimes against — Fiction.
2. Beauty shops — Fiction.   3. Women detectives — Fiction.   4. Washington (State) — Fiction.   5. Large type books.   I. Title.   II. Thorndike Press large print mystery series.
    PS3609.N57S28 2006
    813'.6—dc22   2005033826

"It's the friends you can call up at 4 am that matter."

— Marlene Dietrich

With that thought in mind,
I dedicate this book to
Alexandra Ash.

As the Founder/CEO of NAVH, the only national health agency solely devoted to those who, although not totally blind, have an eye disease which could lead to serious visual impairment, I am pleased to recognize Thorndike Press* as one of the leading publishers in the large print field.

Founded in 1954 in San Francisco to prepare large print textbooks for partially seeing children, NAVH became the pioneer and standard setting agency in the preparation of large type.

Today, those publishers who meet our standards carry the prestigious "Seal of Approval" indicating high quality large print. We are delighted that Thorndike Press is one of the publishers whose titles meet these standards. We are also pleased to recognize the significant contribution Thorndike Press is making in this important and growing field.

Lorraine H. Marchi, L.H.D.
Founder/CEO
NAVH

* Thorndike Press encompasses the following imprints: Thorndike, Wheeler, Walker and Large Print Press.

Acknowledgments

As always, I owe so much to my beloved Samwise, who, through the years, has proved a stalwart, loving, and faithful friend and husband, giving me the best encouragement that I could hope for. I love you, don't you ever forget that. And a fuzzy thank-you to my four "gurlz," who purr me to sleep, meow me awake, and generally make life livable.

Thank-yous go out to: my critique partner, Carolyn Agosta; my agent, Meredith Bernstein; my editor, Christine Zika; all my beloved WWBW Warpies; and friends who have encouraged and supported my efforts.

And lest I forget, thank you and a gentle nod to Aphrodite and Venus, who embody the essence of Beauty and all that it encompasses. And as always, to my beloved Mielikki, Tapio, Rauni, and Ukko.

To my readers: I hope you enjoy this new series, and though I write it under an "alter ego," India Ink is just another mask of mine. You can reach me via my Web site: www.galenorn.com.

~the Painted Panther~
Yasmine Galenorn, a.k.a. India Ink

Foreword

The recipes in this book are my own concoctions. I've spent many years blending magical oils, and here I give you — perhaps not magical recipes — but ones to heighten your senses, and bring new experiences into your lives.

Essential oils can be expensive, so yes, you may use synthetics if you can't afford the pure ones, but bear in mind the fragrance may end up differing slightly. However, this should not be a significant problem. Also, some oils may irritate the skin, so if I make a note to the effect of "do not get on your skin," I mean it. Cinnamon can irritate the skin. Black pepper and other oils can burn delicate tissue.

The oil and other bath recipes are obviously not for consumption, but I am stating it here to clear up any potential miscommunications: *Don't eat them or drink them.* They're meant to be used as fragrances, for dreaming pillows, sachets, potpourris, and the like.

". . . thou who hast the fatal gift of beauty . . ."

— Lord Byron, 1788–1824

Lite Dreams Oil

Created a great blend for a relaxation oil this week. Works like a charm and invigorates the spirit while calming the nerves. My insomnia has decreased ever since I started using it. I've been using Lite Dreams oil to scent dreaming pillows, homemade bath salts, unscented soap, sachets, potpourri. Aunt Florence thinks it will go over big, so we're marketing it with a checklist of hints for restful sleep:

- Change your sheets and pillowcases and add a vase of fresh flowers to your nightstand.
- Dot your dreaming pillow or a sachet with Lite Dreams Oil and let set for an hour to absorb the oil. Tuck inside your pillowcase.
- Take a long, warm bath in lavender bubble bath.
- Spend ten minutes on slow, even stretching to relax the muscles in your body.
- Read a soothing book or magazine

while sipping a cup of lemon tea.
- Cover closed eyes with slices of chilled cucumber for ten minutes.
- Slip into bed before midnight, to allow your body to catch the most restful hours of sleep.

Blend and store this oil (as with all oils) in a small, dark bottle. You will need a bottle and stopper or lid, an eyedropper, and the following:

> $^{1}/_{4}$ ounce almond or apricot kernel
>   oil (a good unscented base)
> 25 drops sandalwood oil
> 25 drops lilac oil
> 10 drops lavender oil
> 12 drops lemon oil
> 8 drops carnation oil

> OPTIONAL:
> dried lemongrass clippings (5-10
>   pieces, about $^{1}/_{4}$ inch in length)
> a small piece of rose quartz or
>   amethyst (you can use chips off
>   a gemstone chip necklace)

Using an eyedropper, add each fragrance oil to the almond oil, gently swirling after each addition to blend the scent. After adding all the oils, cap and shake gently. At this time, add a few clippings of dried lemongrass and/or a piece of rose quartz or amethyst to the bottle for added energy, if so desired.

Rose quartz crystals promote peace, happiness, and love. Amethyst promotes healing. The lemongrass clippings will intensify the scent and add a decorative touch. Keep oil in a cool, dark place — if left in the sun it will lose potency. As always, remind customers to avoid eating or drinking this oil, and to keep it out of the reach of children and animals.

Chapter One

When I found myself flat on my back, staring up at the ceiling with the edge of a stair jutting into my shoulder blades, a premonition told me that the week was about to be shot to hell, but I never expected to end up embroiled in the middle of a murder case.

My lack of foresight was probably a good thing, considering my tendency to jump in feet first, damn the torpedoes, full steam ahead. After all, my nickname when I was a little girl was Imp, short for "impetuous." Over the years, I've learned the hard way that there's no escaping your destiny, and if the fates want to roast you over a fire and serve you on a platter, you might as well just open your mouth for the apple. So when destiny comes knocking, I yank open the door and invite her in, suitcases and all.

"What the heck do you think you're doing?" I leaned my head back to stare at Delilah, who flicked her tail at me from her perch on the landing above.

She'd darted under my legs as I headed down the stairs, then looped around back up to the landing. At least I hadn't gone tumbling down the entire flight. Instead, when I tripped, I flailed, regained enough balance to grab hold of the railing, then toppled backward, like tall timber, rather than face first to the waiting hall below. Yeah, a typical Monday, all right.

The inky spot on her squashed-in nose seemed to pulsate with a life of its own in stark contrast to the rest of her white fluffball of a body. Sixteen years old and well on her way to senility, Delilah had considered me "the enemy" ever since I'd moved back home. She was certain I was trying to usurp her place in Aunt Florence's heart and I couldn't convince her otherwise.

I pushed myself to a sitting position. My lower back popped and I grimaced. That sore spot hadn't been there before. I glanced over my shoulder at Delilah, whose eyes were positively sparkling.

"You're crazy as a bedbug. You know that, cat?"

With a thwap, her tail smacked the floor and she turned to sashay up the stairs to my aunt's room, her work for the day complete, her bloomers swaying with every delicate paw-step.

16

I tested myself for any broken bones. Nope, none that I could find. I had a background in Aikido and Tai Chi, but neither had left me prepared for the machinations of a jealous cat. Moving my shoulder again, I decided that the only damage done was a couple of bruises from where I'd managed to catch myself on the railing. At least I didn't break my neck. I'd live. Yeah, Mondays sucked rocks.

With a quick shake to scatter the dust bunnies that now complemented my black jeans and tank top, I dashed down to the kitchen. I was running late and didn't have time for breakfast. As I yanked open the refrigerator, a sandwich in a Tupperware container caught my eye. Yay! Auntie had left me a sandwich. She knew that without food I'd be a basket case by midmorning. Grateful, I snagged up the ham and cheese along with my purse and hit the door. Twenty minutes late and counting. Not good. Not good form to keep customers waiting. Not good business *juju*.

I edged the odometer up a notch, running through my to-do list for the day. Tawny had scheduled four appointments for me at Venus Envy, my aunt's bath and beauty shop. And we were out of Lite Dreams oil; I needed to whip up a new bottle. That in lf wouldn't take long, but blending it ...., the lotions, soaps, and bath salts we sold in the Dream-Song line, well, that required a little more skill. Maybe I could snare — oh, shit. I hit the brakes and swerved over to the shoulder of the road.

As I fumbled through my tote bag, my stomach twisted. I'd lost the lesson plan I'd written up for the self-defense class I had recently began teaching at the local community college on Sunday evenings. I knew that I'd put it in my tote bag yesterday, and I didn't remember taking it out.

I closed my eyes, trying to recall the last time I'd seen it. An image of lamb chops drifted through my mind, distracting me briefly. Yum, I could go for a lamb chop, grilled medium rare with rosemary and garlic.

With a shake of my head, I brought my attention back to the matter at hand. The image of the lamb chops reminded me where I'd left my notes. Last night, I had dinner with Barb at the BookWich. While searching for my credit card, I placed the lesson plan next to me on the seat of our booth and forgot to put it back in my purse. Since the BookWich ran a barebones lost-and-found box, chances were good that it had been recycled. Anything that looked like a pile of papers had probably ended up in the trash.

With a sigh, I pulled back onto the road and shifted into high gear. That lesson plan would take me a good two hours to reconstruct and, like an idiot, I'd also left the handouts on the table. To add insult to injury, I hadn't bothered to save it on my laptop after printing it out. Aunt Florence had warned me, and I'd laughed her off. *I printed it out, why should I bother saving it?* Stupid, but par for the course.

Thoroughly ticked, I didn't notice the cruiser hiding behind the blue spruce at the corner of Oakwood Avenue and Lake Park Boulevard. The siren startled me out of my thoughts and, with a groan, I pulled over to the shoulder again, brushing the hair off my face where the wind had blown it into my eyes.

A glance in the rearview mirror confirmed that today was indeed the day from hell. Kyle Laughlin, Gull Harbor's ever vigilant chief of police, swaggered over to my Sebring. Joy, joy, and more joy. Kyle and I had never been on the best of terms. When I was in seventh grade, Kyle had developed a crush on me, but I'd been after his cousin Jared, who was in my homeroom class. And when I accepted

19

Jared's invitation to the Gull Harbor Harvest Dance after turning down Kyle, it caused a rift that had lasted until I left for college.

Six months ago, when I'd returned to Gull Harbor, I'd hoped that the intervening years might have taken the edge off their rivalry, but apparently I'd been wrong. Even though his cousin had come out of the closet, Kyle still acted like I'd refused him yesterday. He was still playing king of the hill with Jared, who now worked over at Gull Harbor Community College. Jared and I had rekindled our friendship when I moved back to town, but Kyle had remained as sour and prudish as he'd been when we were kids.

"Well, hello Leadfoot," he said, leaning down to peer in my window. "You taking lessons from your aunt? With her, I look the other way because Miss Florence is an institution in this town, but I'm afraid I just can't do that with you. Come on, out of the car."

Grumbling, I grabbed my registration and insurance card, and dug through my purse for my license. I handed them to him as I stepped out of the car and leaned against the Sebring, wondering how much this little faux pas was going to cost me.

He glanced at them and then grinned. "I'll just call these in and be right back. Don't go anywhere."

"Call them in? You know who I am, Kyle!" I squelched an impulse to wipe that smirk off his face. He didn't have to call in my info! Everybody who owned a police scanner would hear the call and I'd be the talk of the town as far as gossip went, especially if old Heddy Latherton got wind of it. She'd make Auntie miserable, gloating over the fact that *her* nieces never got ticketed.

Kyle shrugged and sauntered over to his cruiser, where he got busy on the radio. Within less than a minute he returned, thumbed open his ticket pad and commenced writing me up. A gleeful look spread over his face. "The speed limit on this stretch is forty. You were zipping along at fifty-five."

I flashed him a cold stare. "Kyle, you are two years older than me, so quit playing Big Daddy and wipe away that smug look. You aren't funny and this isn't an episode of *Cops*."

"Feisty as always, aren't you?" His eyes narrowed and his voice took on an unpleasant tone. "You might want to remember that I'm the law on this island. Maybe you can find a touch of respect somewhere in it jaded little heart of yours?" He leaned toward me and waggled his finger in my face. "That snot-nosed attitude might have worked in Seattle, but around here? I don't think so."

If there's one thing I hated, it was having some local yokel patronize me. Without thinking, I snapped at his finger and he yanked it back just in time to prevent my teeth from making contact. Oh shit! I swallowed and glanced at his startled face, wondering what the punishment was for trying to bite a cop. Not exactly a bright idea, even though we had been schoolmates.

"Uh . . . Kyle?" Was he going to throw me in jail for attempted assault? I wouldn't put it past him.

He cleared his throat and examined his finger. I sucked in a deep breath, waiting for the fallout, but he just slowly tore the paper off the pad. "You know, next time you're running late, you should plan ahead."

Not waiting around for him to change his mind, I grabbed the ticket out of his hand and jumped back in my car.

"Gotta dash. Later!" I threw her into drive, swung back onto the road, and made tracks. A glance in the rearview mirror showed him staring at my retreating dust, scratching his head. Good. He'd have some-thing to think about next time he decided to get in my face.

As I reached the center of town, I slowed down and turned onto Island Drive, Gull Harbor's main drag. I eased into my parking spot in front of Venus Envy, leaned back, inhaled slowly, then gathered my purse and tote bag. Over ten minutes late for my first appointment. Couldn't ask for a better start to the week. Nowhere to go from here but up.

Tawny motioned to me frantically as I raced through the door. "Your appointment is here," she said, her voice low. Her short spiky hair was strawberry today. Yesterday it'd been platinum. And the gemstone stud adorning her nose now matched her hair. At least she was color-coordinated.

I grinned at her and whispered, "Why all the secrecy?"

"She's pissed because you're late, and I don't want to attract her attention." She jabbed her finger in the direction of the fragrance section. I peeked at the figure standing there and my heart sank. Lydia Wang? Oh, delightful. How had I conveniently managed to forget that she was my appointment? Selective memory was a wonderful thing. After all, ignorance is bliss, they say, and apparently my sub-conscious preferred to remain as blissful as possible.

I groaned. "Oh God. Miss Beauty Queen, herself." The hot new find by Radiance Cosmetics, Lydia was twenty-three years old, with a personality hard enough to cut diamonds.

Tawny popped her gum. "Yeah, she's a real snot, all right. We were in the same class in high school. I hear she's gotten worse since then, though it's hard to believe." She rolled her eyes and gave me a sympathetic look as I mutely shook my head.

I glanced at the clock. Couldn't put it off any longer, so might as well get it over with. I squared my shoulders, plastered a smile on my face, and marched over to do battle with the dragon lady.

My name is Persia. Persia Rose Vanderbilt, to be precise. I'm thirty-one years old and single, which is fine by me because the thought of marriage scares the hell out of me and I skirt bridal shops and gift registries like they're infected with Ebola. The idea of marching down the aisle sits right up there with that of major surgery or participating in one of those TV reality shows. Not in a million years.

I've never particularly been drawn to one specific career, but I'd finally lined up several jobs that I could enjoy and feel good about doing, and I'd managed to find a nice boyfriend who was on the same relationship page as me. All good, right? We moved in together, into his penthouse condo, and life was peaches-and-cream as far as I was concerned. That is, until whoever deals out destiny decided to pull the rug out from under me.

First, Elliot got arrested. Yes, my nice-if-a-little-boring accountant boyfriend turned out to be an embezzler who, over the course of three years, siphoned off a quarter of a million dollars from the coffers of his company. The company caught him and started to put the squeeze on when the feds found out. They took over the investigation, which led to the discovery that his accounting firm had been laundering money for a local drug runner. The cops offered Elliot a chance to cut a deal in return for squealing on the owners and, since he didn't want to spend a full twenty years behind bars with his former colleagues, he agreed.

Elliot had told me that his grandmother died and left him a trust fund. When I found out the truth, I felt totally duped. While he wasn't the most adventuresome man in the world, Elliot had always struck me as stable, secure in himself, and fun to be with. So much for women's intuition.

When the bust went down, it occurred to me that some of his rather unsavory co-workers he'd ratted on might decide to take out their frustrations on Elliot's close acquaintances. Chances were good that I'd be singled out for some unwanted attention, so I decided the best idea would be to lay low and make myself invisible for awhile. Time to scram and leave no forwarding address.

As Auntie says, the universe works in mysterious ways. Just as they carted Elliot off to jail, the Alternative Life Center where I'd been teaching classes in aromatherapy, yoga, and self-defense went bust, and with it went my livelihood. All signs now pointed to the desirability of removing myself from Seattle proper. I stifled my pride and called my Aunt Florence to ask if she'd mind if I moved back to Gull Harbor.

When I asked her if I could stay with her for awhile, she snorted. "Quit whining and get your butt back here. It's time to put that education of yours to good use. You can come work at Venus Envy. I'll put you in charge of our fragrance lines — with that nose of yours, you'll make us a fortune. You can still teach your classes, and you can also oversee the gardens for me. With you in charge of mixing up signature lines of bath salts, oils, and soaps, my bet is that our business will double within six months."

Now, Aunt Florence is a lot like King Midas — she has a golden touch, but unlike the greedy king, she also has a heart of gold. When my mother died and my skunk of a father abandoned me — at four years old — on her doorstep, Auntie took me in and raised me like I was her own daughter.

I remember watching as the wheels turned in her brain whenever she came up with a new project. Never married and independently wealthy, Auntie could have retired any time she wanted, but the idle life was not for her, so when she got bored with playing the world traveler, she settled down in our old house in Gull Harbor and opened Venus Envy, a bath and beauty shop.

Venus Envy offered Gull Harbor's stressed-out yuppies and artists all sorts of marvelous things used to make the body and soul feel good. Lotions, powders, bath gels, soaps, shampoos and conditioners, all sorts of loofahs and scrubbies . . . the shop was a mecca for customers in need of a little pampering.

Aunt Florence also sold dried herbs in bulk, essential oils, exotic scarves, a few trinkets like crystals, and several lines of intricate handmade jewelry from local artisans. After the shop had been open for a year or two, she added in a day spa, serving up facials, manicures, pedicures, and skin-care consultations on an appointment-only basis. Venus Envy was thriving, and I had no doubt that she'd crunched the numbers to make sure that I'd end up an asset rather than a liability.

"In fact," she said, "while you're at it, why don't you just move in with me? You can take over the third floor and use it for an apartment. Might as well put the rooms to use. I never go up there."

I jumped at the opportunity. I loved that old house, and living with Aunt Florence had always been a blast. By ten years old, I'd seen a good share of the world thanks to her wanderlust and with the help of my nanny, who was also my private tutor. But the day I turned ten, Auntie decided it was time to settle me into a routine. She bought the hundred-year old house and enrolled me in the local school. By the time I was fourteen, I'd skipped two grades ahead.

Eva — my nanny — took charge of running the household. Auntie came and went, still under the spell of the travel bug, but Eva was a constant in my life, and when she finally married her sweetheart and moved into her own home, I cried for weeks. Shortly thereafter, I turned sixteen, graduated, and left for college with Auntie's permission.

Moss Rose Cottage was brooding and gothic, as weatherworn as it looked. The three-story monstrosity sat on a thirty-acre estate overlooking the inlet. When we bought it, the neighbors told us that the house was haunted. Oh, no overt ghosts coming screaming out of the closet, but footsteps in the middle of the night, and a blast of cold wind here or there. They said that the original owner, a retired captain from the navy, still walked the halls, making sure all was well in his beloved home.

Once, when I was eleven, I thought I caught a glimpse of the Cap'n, as we called him, in the mirror, but he just smiled and faded from sight. I hadn't been afraid of him, though. In fact, on nights when I found myself unable to sleep, wishing for my mother and wondering why my father abandoned me, I'd crawl out of bed and sneak up into the attic. There, I'd curl up in a comfortable old rocking chair and watch the waters of the sound under the moonlight through a window shaped like a porthole.

I'd pull an afghan over me and rock back and forth while having a quiet chat with the Cap'n. I used to tell him all my troubles, the way some little girls talk to their teddy bears. I talked to him about missing my mother, who I could barely remember, and I'd ask him why my father had tossed me aside like a piece of trash after her death. Even though I never heard a peep out of him, I had the feeling the Cap'n was listening. Most nights I'd be back in bed in twenty minutes, but once in awhile I'd fall asleep up there, listening as the wind scraped tree branches across the roof, and I'd wake up when Auntie or Eva would check on me and see that I wasn't in my bed. One or the other — sometimes both — would trudge up to the attic and bundle me back to bed.

While the house seemed unchanged on the exterior, upon my return to Gull Harbor, I found that Auntie had been busy inside. "I've got DSL, digital cable, and I've redecorated from top to bottom," she announced.

"You didn't get rid of that gorgeous old coppery paper in the East Bedroom, did you?" I'd always loved that room.

She laughed. "No, but I made sure it was in good condition, and had all the floors refinished, and painted the rooms that needed it. What do you say? Will you give it a try? Come home to live for awhile? It's just me and the Menagerie here."

Over the years, Auntie had opened her home to a variety of stray animals. Currently, she had eight cats, three dogs, and a TV-watching rooster named Hoffman. Other members of the pet brigade had passed through over the years, eventually finding their way over the Rainbow Bridge, but the Menagerie, as she called the pack of critters, was now firmly entrenched in her life.

With a readymade job staring me in the face, along with the prospect of moving back into the only childhood home I'd ever really known, how could I resist? I was desperate to drop out of sight for awhile, opportunity had come knocking, and, as Auntie always said, "The boat won't wait at the docks forever, so you'd better get on

31

board while you have the chance."

So I packed up my Chrysler Sebring, said good-bye to Seattle, and hopped the ferry for Gull Harbor.

My fragrance counter sat to the far right of the shop, next to the hall leading to Auntie's office. We'd planned it so that I'd be out in the open, to encourage clients to ask about custom-blended fragrances. From where I sat, I had a good view of Venus Envy.

Lydia was waiting, impatiently tapping her foot. I sighed as I slipped into my chair. Blending specific fragrances wasn't simply a matter of dumping several oils into a bottle, giving it a shake, and then slapping a name on it. No, a delicate inter-action had to take place between the body and scent. I found the process fascinating — a dance of scent and reaction. It was up to me to make certain that the fragrances worked in rhythm with both my client's body chemistry and personality, not always an easy task when I was working with someone who was abrasive. Considering Lydia's character, I'd have to be careful or I'd end up with a fragrance that smelled like skunk cabbage. Or maybe just the skunk itself.

Lydia Wang was Gull Harbor's latest *celebrity raison d'être*. The *GH Weekly Digest*, a local paper, had wasted two entire pages on her when she won the Radiance Cosmetics Beauty Contest. Being a connoisseur of local gossip, Aunt Florence had read every word to me. Being the good niece I am, I listened, feigning enthusiasm. But regardless of her fame, Lydia's reputation was already firmly entrenched. She used people like Kleenex and tossed them in the garbage after blowing her nose on them. No surprise that I'd rather take a trip to the dentist than participate in our little adventure through perfume land.

As I quickly organized my materials, I noticed a strange fragrance wafting off of her. Spicy, it had a definite oriental scent, but it wasn't any perfume I recognized, and I kept up with them all. I took a discreet whiff. Masculine, whatever it was. The foundation note ran strong, and though I couldn't quite place the source, it smelled familiar.

"Lydia, would you go wash off your perfume? It will interfere with how this new one reacts on your skin."

She looked at me as if I were crazy. "I'm not wearing perfume."

"Then it must be your bath gel or soap. Please, just go rinse off your wrists." I finally got her moving and set to work. After I'd mixed up three batches, all of which Lydia dismissed with the wave of an expensively manicured hand, I was ready to tear her hair out. I'd give it one more try and then tell her to forget it. I wasn't a masochist, for God's sake.

"Shall we see if this one works?" I tried to keep the sarcasm out of my voice as I made a few adjustments to the fragrance and motioned for her to hold out her freshly washed wrist. I sprayed on a light mist. "Go walk around for five minutes. Don't touch anything else until you come back."

As she wandered off, I leaned back and let out a long sigh. Each fragrance had suited her body chemistry perfectly, but she had nixed them all. The first had been "too cloying," the second "too faint," and the third was "too retro." If she didn't like this one, she could shimmy her scrawny butt over to Donatello's Department Store and they could deal with her.

When she returned a few minutes later, I took a whiff of her wrist and smiled. Intoxication. Sheer intoxication. If I didn't know who she was, I'd want to cozy up and start talking to her right away, she smelled so good. Satisfied, I forced a smile to my lips.

"What do you think?" I asked, holding my breath.

The willowy young woman lifted her wrist to her nose and a smile filtered over her face. Hallelujah! I knew that look — she liked it.

"I love it! What do you call it?"

I let out a sigh of relief. "What else? Beauty Queen." I jotted the name on a label and slapped it on the bottle. I'd transfer my notes with the recipe over to my customer journal as soon as she left. I handed her the invoice and cologne.

She stepped to one side to examine a display of bath lotion as the shop bells chimed and Trevor Wilson strode in. The head gardener out at Moss Rose Cottage, he was in his early twenties and gorgeous. Eye candy for sure, even if he was a few years too young for me. From what I heard, he and Lydia were head over heels in love.

"Persia, when do you want me to start harvesting the lilacs? They'll peak in a few days, and if Miss Florence wants them to be fresh enough to dry properly, we're going to need to get on it right away."

When Auntie assigned me to oversee the

gardens, it was because she knew how much I loved being outside, growing and nurturing plants from seed to full bloom. I had a green thumb that wouldn't quit and had minored in horticulture. All it took to entice me into a ten-mile hike into the back country was a promise of a field full of wildflowers. I'd taken one look at the ragged state of Auntie's gardens and set about organizing a list of priorities to bring them into full bloom.

I jotted a note in my Day-Timer. "Got it. Did you finish replanting the checkerboard garden?"

"Yep, finished with it yesterday. I went over to Home Depot and picked up the marble stones. They're all ready to set in place."

I'd immediately envisioned what could be an ideal checkerboard garden of blue and white phlox and ordered two dozen round marble stepping stones, twelve in black, twelve in white. They would become the checkers, completing the now tidy garden, and then we'd put in a fence that ran just under a foot high — tall enough to contain the phlox but not tall enough to block the view.

Trev opened his mouth to say something else, but at that moment he and Lydia noticed each other. As their eyes met, the dragon lady morphed into a shrieking harpy.

"Trevor Wilson, what the hell do you think you're doing here?" Hands on her hips, she leaned forward, eyes narrowed. "I warned you to quit following me or I'll call the cops, you pervert!"

Oh hell. What now? Had the cozy couple gone belly up?

Trevor paled and stumbled back a few steps. "I had no idea you were here. I just came in to talk to Persia. I wasn't following you." His stricken look answered my question.

"Lower your voices." I pushed my way between them. "If you two have to mix it up, then keep it out of the shop."

Lydia shot me a scathing look. "I have no intention of fighting with this asshole —"

"I said, take it outside! We're supposed to be an oasis from stress, not an arena for a mudslinging contest."

Neither one was listening to me. Not a good thing.

Trevor straightened his shoulders. "I may be an ass, but damn it, what do you expect?" He seemed to have found his voice and it carried through the store. A few heads turned our way. "I can't believe you told all your friends that I'm stalking you. Are you that desperate for attention? All I wanted to do was to find out why you broke up with me, but no — I had to hear about it through the grapevine. You said you loved me!"

Lydia lunged around me to poke Trevor's chest with one bright-red nail. Startled, I hastily backed out of the way.

"And I was a fool to say it," she said. "You're a nothing, a nobody. When I won the contest, all you could do was whine about me going to New York! Can't you take it like a man? Grow up! You're such a loser."

Trevor raised his hand as if he meant to slap her and, gathering my wits, I shoved them apart. "Do I have to throw both of you out of here? I said *enough*."

Trevor lowered his arm and stared at the floor. Maybe there was still a chance that I could prevent bloodshed. "Lydia, take your perfume up to the counter. Tawny will cash you out." I gave her a little shove toward the front of the store.

She let out a huff. "Obviously, customers come second in your shop. Your aunt will hear about this, I can tell you that much."

I stared her down. Beauty queen or not,

Ms. Wang had overstepped her boundaries. "Be my guest. She'll tell you the same thing I'm telling you: When I'm in charge, *I* make the rules."

Trevor apparently couldn't restrain himself. "You'd better watch yourself, Lydia. One of these days, someone's going to take you down a notch. I just hope you don't get hurt in the process because, sweetheart, right now Persia is the only one who's keeping me from wiping that fucking smile off your face. A lot of people around town don't like you, and not all of them have the self-control that I do." His voice dropped as he added, "You know what I'm talking about."

Lydia got in a parting shot. "You've got it all wrong. You don't know a damned thing, even though you think you do! Just leave me alone, Trevor, or you'll be sorry."

By now, we had attracted a gaggle of onlookers. Time for détente. I shoved Trevor toward the back of the shop. "In the office. *Now.* Go cool your jets and wait for me."

His mouth set in a bitter line, he turned on his heel and stomped off. I glanced back to Lydia. "You need to leave."

"Fine. But you'd better keep an eye on Trevor there." Her voice echoed through the store. "He's not very good at listening to reason." She waltzed up to the counter, tossed a fifty at Tawny, and pranced her way to the door. As it closed behind her, I met a line of expectant faces staring at me.

I coughed. "Just a minor difference of opinions, folks. I'm sorry we disrupted your shopping. Tawny, give everyone a ten percent discount today."

Tawny nodded. Maybe a little well-placed bribery would slow down the local gossip mill, though I had my doubts. Small towns fed on gossip like flies on honey. Now I just had to deal with Trevor.

Chapter Two

Trevor had slung himself into the chair and was staring sullenly at the floor. I eased into the room and perched on the corner of the desk. He was a good kid and I'd grown to like him, but he carried a real chip on his shoulder, as if the world owed him a living and it wasn't paying up. I played with Auntie's stapler for a moment, mulling over what to say and how to say it. Aunt Florence expected me to deal with these matters when I was in charge, and I wasn't going to let her down.

"Big screw up, Trev. You're part of the staff and that means you have absolutely no leeway with regards to situations like this." He rolled his eyes. I reached over and tapped him on the shoulder. "Get real, dude. This is a business. You know you can't act like that in front of our customers. I don't give a rat's ass who they are or how much you don't like them. My aunt would have chewed you up one side and down the other if she'd been here instead of me."

He stared at his sneakers, his shoulders drooping as the defiance drained out of his posture. "Yeah, yeah. I know. Look, I'm sorry, okay? It's just that seeing Lydia took me by surprise. I should have just ignored her, but that look on her face sent me over the edge. She makes me so mad, sometimes I just want to . . . to make her hurt as much as she hurt me."

I jammed my hands in my pockets and slid into Auntie's chair, propping my feet on the top of the desk. "So tell me what happened. Do you want to talk about it?"

He shrugged. "You rock, Persia, but just leave it alone, okay? We were an item. I fell for her, she duped me, end of story." He was obviously trying to blow it off, but the pain in his voice was too raw. Lydia had struck a nerve when she confronted him. I wondered just what Trevor had seen in her. She was so shallow and insensitive that a blind man would have read her without blinking.

Trev glanced at me and snorted. "I know what you're thinking. Don't bother asking me why I hooked up with her, because I can't tell you, other than the fact that she's hot. I don't even know why she gave me the time of day, but even though she treated me like dirt, you get used to being

42

around somebody, you know? Even though she thinks I'm crap, I still miss her." He looked like he'd been dumped overboard and left for dead on the rocky shore.

I decided that he just needed some time to cool off. "Okay. Don't let this happen again. Go on back to Moss Rose Cottage and put in a couple hours of hard work to get rid of some of that tension."

"Sounds good, but first I think I'll run over to the BookWich and grab a sandwich. I forgot my lunch." Flashing me a grateful smile, he took off out the back entrance. As I watched him go, I hoped that he'd find someone new, and soon. Trev was a good guy. He deserved a girl who would treat him right.

The intercom buzzed and I flipped the switch. Tawny's voice echoed over the speaker. "Can you come out here? Ms. Wang has a question."

Oh great. Lydia was back? Now what?

"I'll be there in a moment," I said, grimacing. The last thing I wanted to do was to tangle with Snarling Beauty again. With a sigh, I pushed my way out of the office and headed for the counter.

Venus Envy was dedicated to offering customers an oasis of tropical harmony, with soothing sea green walls and muted mauve and gold trim. One entire wall was taken up by a mural-sized reproduction of Botticelli's *The Birth of Venus*, only Aunt Florence had hired Tim Reese, a local artist, to paint it and he'd noticeably enhanced some of Venus's endowments and given her an uncanny resemblance to Sharon Wellstone, a woman on whom he had a crush. A few of the town matrons had been scandalized by the naked woman on the clam shell, but after awhile talk died down, and now people pointed it out as a local artistic must-see.

Cushioned wicker and mahogany benches offered respite to tired shoppers and potted *ficus benjamina* trees — ornamental fig trees — stood sentinel, guarding either side of the door. They towered a good ten feet into the air, still well under the sixteen-foot ceiling near the front of the shop. A large window over the entryway flooded the main store with light, and Auntie's displays were filled with baskets of lotions and soaps, scrubbing puffs, and scented oils.

With so many scents competing with one another, we opted for a fragrance-free, three-foot white pillar candle on the counter, protected by the largest hurricane lampshade I'd ever seen. Tawny lit it every morning when she opened the shop, and the flame flickered all day, dancing around the wick. When I closed my eyes, I could imagine I was in Key West or on some tropical island.

Lydia was standing in front of Aphrodite's Mirror, or Aphrodite's Looking Glass, as Barb had called it. Barbara Konstantinos, my best friend and the owner of the Baklava or Bust Bakery, had brought it back from a recent trip to Greece, where she and her husband had visited his family. She'd given it to me, and I loaned it to the shop, thinking it might be a good draw. I'd been right.

Some twenty-four inches in diameter, the frame was exquisitely hand-carved and painted with gold leaf. Center-top, Aphrodite danced in a field as nymphs cavorted joyfully around both sides of the looking glass. Pan crouched bottom-center, playing on his pipes. The mirror sparkled, and every time I glanced in it, my mood perked up.

Lydia pointed to the mirror. "How much?" She pulled out her checkbook.

Incredulous, I pointed to the note tacked on the wall next to the mirror. In large bold letters, it read, "Not For Sale."

"Read the sign. The mirror isn't for sale."

"Ridiculous," she said. "Name a price and I'll pay it. I want that mirror, and I get what I want."

Growing more ticked by the minute, I said, "I will only tell you this once again: The mirror isn't for sale. Deal with it." Refusing to waste any more time on her, I turned and started toward the office. The next thing I knew, Lydia swung around in front of me. We were nearly the same height, and I found myself staring into her brilliant, fuming eyes. Her nostrils flared. Apparently, she wasn't used to be dismissed.

"I have more than enough money. Don't make this difficult."

I leaned toward her, out of patience. "That mirror was a personal gift to me from a friend. I offered to let my aunt hang it in the store. Read my lips: there's no way in hell anybody's going to get their hands on it."

The anger in her eyes turned to astonishment. Before she could continue the argument, I walked away, leaving her standing in the middle of the aisle. I slipped in back of the counter to help Tawny just in case Lydia decided to get belligerent. Lydia looked around uncertainly. I had the feeling very few people ever talked to her the way I had and no doubt she'd try to find some way to take revenge, but we'd weather the storm. From what I understood, she was due to leave for New York in a few weeks anyway.

She flashed me a cold stare, but I just shrugged and stood my ground. After a moment, she stuck her nose in the air and headed for the door. I watched her retreating figure, shaking my head. Annoying *and* a drain on the psyche.

As she neared the door, two young women who had been browsing through the bath gels swept in to block her path. One, a red-headed beauty bordering on anorexic, looked like she had a bone to pick with our beauty queen. The other girl, a little on the plump side, was truly lovely. Or she would have been, if she hadn't been staring at the ground, her shoulders rounded and slumped as if she carried the weight of the world on them.

Uh oh. Did I sense yet another showdown in the offing? Lydia had no lack of adversaries, apparently. I casually wandered over to the candle section near where they were standing and began to organize the shelves.

"Well, well, well. If it isn't Lydia Wang," the redhead said with a snarky look. "I thought you'd be in New York by now. Better run along to your photo shoot before your Botox wears off."

Lydia inclined her head ever so slightly. "So lovely to see you, too. By the way, I meant to tell you how *sorry* I am that you only placed second, but then again, you've always been second-rate, haven't you, Colleen?" Her laughter tinkled through the shop, unpleasantly light and aloof.

Colleen. That would be Colleen Murkins, the second-place winner. Sponsored by Radiance Cosmetics, a natural cosmetics line out of Seattle, the contest had been open to young women living in western Washington and offered the winner sweet rewards. Not only did the winner receive a substantial cash prize, but she also got her pick from among several SUVs, along with a lucrative two-year contract to be Radiance's new face model and spokeswoman.

Second-place winner, if I remembered right, won a measly thousand dollars. But from what I'd heard, the competition between the two women went a long ways back, years before the Radiance contest.

Colleen bared her teeth. They were a little too white. "At least I didn't screw the judges in order to win."

Zing! Yep, no holds barred. I was about to stroll over and break things up when Lydia turned to the other girl, who cringed and glanced around nervously.

"And you — what a joke! Why did you even bother to enter?" Lydia pushed past them, continuing on her way to the door where, without missing a beat, she turned back to say, "By the way, Debbie, if you get that lard ass in gear, you should waddle over to Trevor's. You might be able to interest him now that I'm out of the way. I know you like him. Although, he's not into pork, so maybe you shouldn't bother." The sound of the door slamming echoed behind her.

Always a sucker for the underdog, I leaned against the shelves, wishing that I could chase after Lydia and smack her a good one. But I flashed back to the speeding ticket in my purse and nixed the idea. Harassment charges weren't my idea of fun.

Poor Debbie turned bright red and looked ready to burst into tears. Colleen wrapped her arm around the girl's shoulders and started to lead her away, but Debbie stopped, staring at her reflection in Aphrodite's Mirror. The crimson slowly drained from her cheeks. She took a deep breath.

"I hate her. I'm not hideous. I'm not that fat!" Her voice faltered as she turned to Colleen. "Am I?" A desperate desire for approval played over her face. I wanted to rush up, shake her by the shoulders and say, *"You're a lovely young woman! Don't rely on others to make you feel better. You have to believe in yourself."* But I didn't. I just stood there, pretending not to watch.

Colleen forced a smile. "Of course you aren't. Don't let her get to you, Deb. She's not worth it. You and I both know she screwed her way to first place. C'mon, let's go pick out some bath salts and lotions."

"Go on ahead, I'll be there in a minute." Debbie leaned against the shelf as Colleen moved off. I could see her fighting to keep the tears down. That did it. I'd had enough of Lydia's carnage.

I cleared my throat. "Debbie?"

She sniffed and looked up at me, swallowing. I knew that swallow — she was trying to gain her composure. "Yeah?"

"I just wanted to . . . well, you really are pretty. You have such classic features, and a figure to die for — men like curvy women, you know?"

I could tell she was trying to decide whether I was mocking her. After a moment, she broke into a shy smile. "Thanks. I wish

I could believe you, but I know you mean well, so thank you."

Before she could head off I added, "I mean it, Debbie. I'm not just trying to make you feel better. I wish you could see yourself the way I see you. I think you'd be a lot happier."

She flicked her hair back from her eyes and gave Aphrodite's Looking Glass a hesitant glance. After a moment, she straightened her shoulders, flashed me a bewildered smile, and followed Colleen down the aisle. As they began to sniff different packets of bath salts, I returned to my station. Lydia had her own little hate club, that was for sure, and I'd happily add myself to the roster.

My stomach rumbled and I glanced at the clock. Time for lunch. I grabbed my purse and pawed through it, searching for my wallet. "Tawny, I'm headed over to the BookWich for lunch. I'll be back in an hour or so."

She waved me off.

Venus Envy was located smack in the middle of downtown Gull Harbor, nestled between the Baklava or Bust Bakery and a Starbucks. The rest of the block consisted of Trader Joe's, the Mahi-mahi Fish Market, a Michael's arts and crafts store, the Pizza-Ria, Longs Drugs, and several small boutiques, including Marianne's Closet, and the BookWich, a wonderful little bookstore-slash-café.

Downtown Gull Harbor was a good place to open up a business, with plenty of foot traffic, especially when the city held Art Walks and other civic events. Unlike a number of other growing communities in the northwest, Gull Harbor's business district remained intact, alive and thriving. Even though the big chains had moved in, the shopping malls and strip malls hadn't been able to usurp the small shops and businesses that made up the quirky heart of the city.

I stepped out into the rain-swept day and cringed as a gust of icy wind blasted my face. Wishing I'd remembered my jacket, I shivered and slipped through the door into the bakery, immediately succumbing to the heavenly aroma of fresh bread and pastries.

Display cases sparkled with jewel-colored cakes, frosted with glazes and heavy butter cream icing. Doughnuts hit the shelves still sizzling from the oil in which they were fried, and fat loaves of rye and pumpernickel dotted the shelves, along with tangy-smelling sourdough rounds and crusty

French baguettes, fresh from the oven. I stepped up to the counter.

Dorian, Barbara's husband, winked at me. "Barbara!" he called, his rich baritone thick with a Greek accent. "Persia's here!"

I smiled broadly at him. Dorian was the kind of man who would come over and fix your car on a Sunday afternoon if you even hinted that you were having trouble with it. He'd also bring a dozen doughnuts with him and a pot of his famous hot chocolate, which he concocted from some secret recipe that he never showed to anybody. Barbara said he wouldn't even let her see it.

"She'll be out in a few minutes. Meanwhile, how about a cookie?"

I shook my head. "No, but I'll take one of those sourdough rolls. Lots of butter." I handed him a dollar and he dropped a quarter and a nickel in my hand. I wandered over to one of the small tables and took a seat.

"So, what are you up to, girl? We haven't had a chance to talk since Barbara and I returned from Greece." He set my plate on the table and I saw that he'd tucked a cookie on the side. Dorian firmly believed in the power of baking to make everything okay.

I eyed the roll, planning my attack. "Working up the classes on aromatherapy and herb-crafts for the shop this autumn."

"Didn't Barbara tell me you're teaching a self-defense class now?"

I licked my hand where the melting butter drizzled down from the bread. "Yeah, over at Gulls Harbor Community College. I've agreed to teach one per quarter. Barbara should sign up for it — every woman needs to know how to defend herself."

"I'll put a bug in her ear." He wiped his hands on his apron. "So you work for your aunt and you teach . . . that's good, Persia. Work is good for the soul. Keep the body busy, keep the mind busy, and God will smile on you. Maybe he'll even find you a husband."

Coughing, I said, "Let's hope not. I've got enough problems without that!" I winked at him and, with a wave and a laugh, he disappeared around the counter again to help another customer.

Hungry, I bit into the roll. Cursed with the appetite of a horse, I focused most of my intake on healthy food, so that the amount I ate wouldn't make a dent in my metabolism. All my years at the gym had paid off — the muscle I'd built through Tai

Chi, weight workouts, Aikido, Pilates, and yoga burned calories faster than I ate them.

Barbara wandered out, pulling off her voluminous apron. Even though she had a decade on me, we'd been friends since I was ten years old. Barb was petite in a way I would never be. Standing exactly five feet tall, soaking wet she couldn't possibly tip the scales at a hundred. I towered over her at five-foot ten and a solid one fifty-five. My wavy black hair hit my butt, while she sported a short, sleek, coppery bob. Looking barely thirty, let alone forty-one, she had more energy than most of the teenagers I knew.

She waved toward the door. "Let's go. I'm starving and want an omelet." I popped the last bite of the roll in my mouth, grabbed my wallet and the cookie, and followed.

The BookWich, on the corner of Island Drive and Barrow Way, consisted of two stories, with an elevator for those who couldn't manage the stairs. The café was on the bottom floor next to the periodicals, with parking around back. We hustled through the crowds, managing to secure a table next to a window that overlooked the parking lot and the alley beyond.

Instead of serving yuppie health food like so many small specialty cafés, the BookWich dished up homemade soups so thick they needed a fork, roast beef sandwiches layered with Swiss and dotted with cracked black pepper, and plump frankfurters covered with chili or sauerkraut or cheese. Food you could really sink your teeth into.

Our waitress bustled over with water and menus and pulled out a menu pad from her pocket. Barb ordered coffee. I went with my usual. "A cup of black tea with lemon, please, and could you check to see if somebody found my lesson plan that I left here last night?"

She grimaced. "Do you remember who was on shift, honey?"

"No, but I was sitting in the back booth."

"That would be Tilda, then. Child, if she was waiting on you, I wouldn't get my hopes up. I'll go check for you though, right after I bring your drinks."

I thanked her. While she was gone, we skimmed the lunch specials, but I already knew what I wanted. So did Barb, apparently, for she folded her menu and tossed it back on the table.

"So, tell me about Greece." We hadn't

had a chance to dish since she and Dorian had returned.

Barb broke into a grin, but I could tell that her mood didn't match her expression. "Oh, the trip was just peachy. You have to come with us next time we go — I could use the support, though you'd have to put up with Mama Konstantinos."

I grinned. "I'd love to go and you know it. Don't tempt me. I was in Greece once, when I was nine. Auntie took me to the Parthenon in Athens and then we visited some of the islands. After that, we swung into Egypt for a look at the pyramids. I've always wanted to go back." Auntie may have conquered her travel bug, but mine was still alive and kicking. "So, how was Dorian's mother? She still think you stole her son?"

A flicker ran through her eyes and she shrugged, growing sober. "Yeah. She isn't getting any better. She refuses to move over here to live with us, so his brother Nikola is moving back home to take care of her. Niki's wife isn't happy about the decision. She'd rather stay in Athens, but I don't think her feelings matter in the issue. That's one hell of a close-knit family. Even though Dorian and I've been married almost eighteen years, I still feel like an outsider."

The rivalry between Barb and her mother-in-law proved to be the one hitch in her otherwise fairytale-like marriage. Barb loved Dorian to pieces, but his family constantly criticized her because she hadn't joined the church, because she dyed her hair, and because she and Dorian had chosen not to have children. Their opinions were particularly harsh whenever the subject of Dorian's decision to stay in the United States came up. Mama Konstantinos blamed Barb even though Dorian often said that he never wanted to move back. Dorian defended his wife, but most of his family proved deaf.

"Do you think they'll ever come to their senses?" I asked.

"Probably not. Dorian says not to worry, but it's hard when your in-laws treat you like a second-class citizen." She stopped when the waitress appeared at the table with our drinks.

"I looked all over the back room but there's nothing there that remotely resembles your paperwork. I'm sorry, honey."

I sighed. "That's okay. Thank you for checking anyway. Let me see, I want the clam chowder and a plate of calamari."

Barbara asked for a Denver omelet and a salad. After June wrote down our requests and left, Barb continued. "So, what's going on with you?"

I filled her in on the morning's adventures. "Lydia's going to get herself in trouble one of these days," I said. "After awhile, she'll meet her match. I just hope that Trevor gets over his heartache. It's never easy, but broken hearts seem especially rough when you're young and your hormones are still raging."

Barbara nodded. "I had a run-in with her a year or so ago. We were working together in a production of *Into the Woods* that the Gull Harbor Community Theatre put on. She was furious because I got the lead and she was stuck as a bit player. The truth is, she can't act. And she can't sing worth a damn. She tried to organize a boycott of the bakery, said she saw a rat in there one day. It started to cut into our business until the health inspector checked it out and gave us a green light. You'd better watch out or she'll try the same thing with Venus Envy now that you've made an enemy out of her."

Just then, our meals arrived and we dove in, punctuating our lunch with snippets of talk.

When I returned to the shop, I dropped my wallet back inside my purse and got back to work. Luckily, my afternoon clients were far more pleasant than Lydia had been, and the last one decided to sign up for my upcoming Bath Rituals workshop. She also took a brochure for my self-defense class and said she'd hurry over to Gull Harbor Community College and register for the summer course, which would start at the beginning of July. Two hours later, I looked up to see that it was almost time to close up shop. I still needed to blend the Lite Dreams oil, so decided to stay late.

"Tawny, go ahead and leave for the day. I'll finish here." I put up the Closed sign so nobody would wander in by mistake.

I flipped through my journal of recipes and pulled out my oils. When I first arrived at Venus Envy, the selection had been sparse. Now we carried several fragrance lines that I'd concocted. Every few weeks, we added a new line and kept an eye on how fast it took off. So far, each blend I'd come up with had sold like hotcakes, and people were clamoring for more.

I readied a sterilized bottle that would hold four ounces of the concentrated oil. When first developing a new scent, I created it drop by drop until I found just the right proportions. Sometimes I had to start over but that was okay. After all, I was searching for perfection, for just the right scent to capture a mood, evoke a response, intoxicate the senses. Alchemy at its most fragrant. Once I worked out the recipe, it was a simple matter to translate it into larger measurements to cut down on time.

Selecting lemongrass, sandalwood, and lilac oil, I measured them out, pouring them carefully into the bottle. After each addition, I swirled gently to blend. Once the foundation had settled, I added a top note — carnation — and then tossed in a few small pieces of rose quartz and capped it. Sitting back in my chair, I grasped the bottle between my hands and focused my thoughts on restful sleep and sweet dreams to wake up the elemental essences of the oils with which I was working. A little extra touch that might or might not do anything, but I felt like it tapped into the core of the energy I was attempting to reach with the fragrance.

As I jotted "Lite Dreams Concentrate" on a label, I glanced at the clock. Almost nine o'clock. Auntie had called and asked me to pick up a few groceries on the way home at the Shoreline Foods Pavilion. I tucked the oil away in the bottom drawer and yawned as I shrugged on my jacket and zipped up.

Something jangled in my pocket. I slid my hand in — my keys? What were they doing there? I was sure that I'd dropped them in my purse this morning. After a fruitless moment trying to remember, I gave up, shrugged, and headed out, turning off the lights and locking the door firmly behind me.

All the shops along the street were closed with the exception of the BookWich and Trader Joe's, and the empty street was damp as mist began to rise. In an hour or so, it would roll low along the ground, a shroud to cloak the pavement. Raindrops on the sidewalk shimmered under the streetlights, looking for all the world like liquid diamonds that had been splashed from the heavens.

I took a deep breath, inhaling the salty tang of moist air that drifted in off the inlet. Gull Harbor was the only real home I'd ever known, and I was thrilled to be out of Seattle, back in the island community that had become my safe haven when I was young. As I headed for the car, my skin tingled and I could feel the hairs stand up on my arms as a shiver raced up my spine. A storm was brewing, heading in off the water, I could feel it. And it was going to be a monster. As I slid behind the wheel, I thought I caught a whiff of danger on the wind.

Chapter Three

By the time I found a parking place in the Shoreline Foods Pavilion and fought my way through the aisles, I realized I'd left the list at the shop. If I remembered right, Auntie had asked for sliced roast beef and French bread, and either chicken or ice cream — something with C in it, but I couldn't recall which one, so I bought both. I knew there had to be more on the list. After debating whether or not to call her from the pay phone — since I'd left my cell in my car — I decided what the hell, why not just pile the cart full of anything that looked reasonably good to eat? Chances were I'd get at least some of what she wanted. Fifteen minutes later I was tired, hungry, and had over sixty dollars worth of munchies in the cart.

The Mohawk-clipped nitwit behind the counter double-charged me for an item and it took yet another ten minutes to get it through his head that no, I was only buying one jar of sun-dried tomatoes in basil olive oil. I ended up proving I was right by taking everything out of the bags and piling it on the counter. If the overcharge had only been a quarter, I would have let it go, but at $4.59 a bottle, I wasn't going to just suck up the loss. By the time we'd haggled it out, it was almost nine-forty. I debated on calling home, but since I'd be there within ten minutes, I decided not to bother. Aunt Florence could reach me on my cell phone if she was really worried.

I parked in the driveway, stepping out of the car at the same time that a huge squall gusted off the bay. The sky cracked open with a dazzling array of thunder and lighting. Soaked by the sudden cloudburst, I grabbed the groceries and raced into the house, only seconds before the lights flickered and went out.

"Jeezuz!" Both grocery bags went flying, spilling oranges and cookies and packets of sliced deli meat every which way as a stab of pain spread through my foot. Great, my toe had decided to play full-body contact with the heavy wooden frame of the sofa. I hopped, holding my injured foot off the ground, trying to maintain my balance, but a rush of fur blazed past and knocked me to the ground amid the scattered groceries. Yep, Monday all right. The day was ending on the same note on which it had begun.

Forks of white-hot lightning flashed across the inlet, putting on the light show of the century. Excited by the storm and the sudden feast, Beauty and Beast barked with joy as they bounded over to help themselves to the food. Still on my hands and knees, I grabbed one end of the roast beef package that was hanging out of Beast's mouth. He promptly decided we were playing tug-of-war and began to growl, shaking his head, the beef, and me with it.

"This — is — not — your — sock!" I said, giving one last yank as he opened his mouth and sent me tumbling back. Good God, the dog was a brute. Auntie didn't know what breed he was, but I bet his parents had been from opposite sides of the tracks. His head was too big for his body and his legs were too short and skinny. However, butt-ugly or not, the Beast was one of those lick-your-face, sit-in-your-lap, good-natured pooches, if a bit on the dopey side. He promptly rested on his haunches and began to howl as another crack of thunder split the sky.

Beauty, on the other hand, was a gorgeous black cocker spaniel who adored everybody and everything. Not only was she good natured, but she was smart as a whip and let the cats walk all over her. She eyed the food in my hand and then looked at me, big brown eyes dripping with love. I sighed and ripped open the slobber-drenched package.

"Here, you moochers." I handed them each a slice. Of course, all the cats came running when they heard Beauty's excited yips, and so did Pete, the oldest of the dogs — an eight-year-old golden retriever. I passed out slices of roast beef left and right, managing to stuff the last one in my mouth. The ache in my toe had slowed to a dull throb, and I was about to get off the floor and pick up the rest of the groceries when Aunt Florence bustled downstairs, holding a candle. She took one look at me and snorted.

"I thought I told you to put the groceries away before you play with the dogs," she said, a grin creeping across her face as she offered me a hand. As wide as she was tall, my aunt was a formidable figure to contend with. She had a strength belied by her soft, rounded body. "I'll go fire up the generator and then we'll have some dinner." She was about to pull her rain poncho over her head when the lights flickered and came back on. "Well, good enough, though

I don't know how long they'll last."

We picked up the groceries and took them into the kitchen. "The radio says we're in for a week of bad weather, if not more. Why don't we just heat up some tomato soup tonight, and toast French bread with parmesan and butter? And we can break out that venison sausage I've got tucked away for a rainy day," she added.

I was starving, and anything hot sounded good, but venison sausage set my mouth watering. While I sliced and buttered the bread, my aunt heated the soup, stirring in a few bacon bits and some leftover broccoli and a handful of grated cheddar. She whistled while she cooked, and as she glanced up to catch me watching her, she winked.

Feeling more at home than I had in many years, I impulsively threw my arms around her waist and leaned over to kiss the top of her head. "I sure missed you all these years, and never realized how much until I came back. The past six months have been wonderful. You've been mom to me ever since I can remember. I guess living in Seattle sometimes made me forget that. I'm sorry."

"Don't worry yourself, Imp. I know you love me, and that's what matters."

Auntie was a driving force directly out of the "when I am old I shall wear purple" crowd, except at sixty-three she wasn't really old. Clad in flowing Hawaiian mu'umu'us, when she went out she always wore a wide-brimmed fuchsia straw hat that sported a stuffed parakeet balancing precariously on one side. A *real* stuffed parakeet. The bird — Squeaky — had been part of the Menagerie until he bit into a faulty wire by mistake and electrocuted himself. She'd taken Squeaky to a taxidermist and had him stuffed and shellacked, and now he went with her wherever she took a notion to go.

Aunt Florence had taken me in when her sister — my mother — died. My father was listed on my birth certificate, but he and Virginia hadn't been married and he didn't want anything to do with me once she was gone. Auntie had become mother, father, and family, all rolled into one. I could barely remember what Virginia had looked like — I'd been so young.

Now my aunt paused and smiled, as if reading my mind. "I wish she could see you now. You've turned out so pretty, and so smart."

I didn't say anything. There was nothing really to say. Virginia had died in Iran,

68

where I was born. She had followed my father there, when he was transferred overseas to the GEO Oil Company's foreign offices.

Passionately in love with the idea of living happily ever after, she'd envisioned life as a long series of days basking in the sunset of the desert, but once she got there he decided that he didn't want to get married. They moved into a small apartment, she got pregnant with me, and that ended her hopes of matrimony for good. He only took care of her because Virginia threatened to sue him with palimony if he didn't face up to his responsibilities. After she died, he petitioned his company for a transfer back to the U.S. and dropped me on Aunt Florence's doorstep on his way to Alaska, signing away his parental rights. Auntie gave me her own last name and formally adopted me.

I was a Vanderbilt, but exactly what that meant, I hadn't quite fully figured out. I'd met my maternal grandparents, Grandmother Dakota and Grandfather William, but we hadn't taken to each other. I was too headstrong for them, and they were too stuffy for me. I wasn't interested in country clubs and debutante balls, and they didn't approve of Auntie gallivanting

69

me around the planet.

When I was seventeen, I spent a week with them in their home in Virginia. They offered to pay for the rest of my college, but Auntie assured me that she had plenty of money and I knew that her support came with no strings attached. But I did accept the box of trinkets and jewelry that had belonged to my mother. My grandparents had carefully chosen the pieces that they thought would mean the most to me, and now I constantly wore my mother's sweet-sixteen diamond ring on my right index finger. It made me feel closer to her.

Every Christmas and birthday until I was eighteen, they sent me presents, and then the presents turned into checks. Each year, I wrote them the obligatory yearly update letter, and called them on major holidays, and we were all content to leave it at that.

My father, on the other had, had been a silent shadow since the day he abandoned me. I knew his name but had never gone to the bother of tracking him down. Why should I, when he hadn't wanted me? I could barely remember him, and whatever love I'd felt for him was buried in the dust of his footsteps. Auntie had done her best to raise me, taught me the difference between right and wrong, and showed me how to make my own way in the world. Everything I'd learned, I owed to her, and I wanted to make her proud.

When dinner was ready, we lit a fire in the fireplace and settled down in front of the crackling flames with our soup and bread and sliced sausage. I told her about the day, going easy on Trevor's part. She nodded and reached for the remote.

"You handled it fine, Persia. You know that eventually I'm going to get bored of this business, and if you decide to put down roots here in the town, I'll just sign it over to you. So I'm glad you're taking the initiative on these matters." She channel-surfed until she found a rerun of *Magnum P.I.*

As usual, Hoffman decided to make his move. The twelfth and final member of the Menagerie, the rooster had no qualms about climbing up on the sofa and settling in on my lap to watch television. It had taken me awhile to get used to him, the little bugger liked to peck me when I wasn't being quick enough in handing out his chicken treats, but over the months he'd clucked his way right into my heart. Aunt Florence had even managed to

71

house-train him, to an extent, and I secretly admired the plucky old cock of the walk. I asked her where he'd come from and she said he'd just shown up in the backyard one day after a big windstorm, and that was that. Hoffman was home.

Auntie flipped the channel to A&E. *"Cold Case Files* is on tonight." A murder-mystery buff, she'd turned me into one too and I'd picked up the habit of watching late-night TV with her. After scaring ourselves silly over an episode about a serial killer who specialized in drowning his wives, we headed for bed, carrying flashlights just in case the power went out again. Florence kissed me on the cheek as we reached the second floor and said goodnight.

As I trudged up to the third floor, the wind howled outside, shaking the trees and knocking fir cones and branches onto the roof. It would be the perfect night for the Cap'n to show himself, but by the time I was ready for bed, I decided he was going to remain in whatever shadowy realm he lived in. Suddenly nostalgic, I whispered, "Goodnight, Cap'n. Sleep well," as I crawled into bed.

The windows rattled and rain lashed the windowsill, but I fell into a deep sleep as soon as my head hit the pillow. At some point, I woke to hear the sound of a fog horn from some boat passing by, or perhaps I dreamed it, but after that, my slumber was uneasy, and images of arguing beauty queens and angry young men filled my dreams.

I woke up to find Delilah sitting on the pillow next to me, staring down at my face with a bemused look. As I struggled to sit up, still caught between my dreams and the waking world, I pushed back the hand-sewn Hawaiian quilt that covered the rich walnut sleigh bed and swung my feet over the edge. The cat watched me cautiously, reaching up to pat my face with her claws barely sheathed. I waited until she withdrew her tufted toes from my cheek before stumbling out of bed. Squinting in the dim light that peeked from between the curtains, I reached out to give Delilah a few scritches behind the ears.

"You're not so tough," I cooed to her. "Not really." She started to bite, but then — teeth poised on my finger — stopped, purred, and thwapped her tail against the vanity. Laughing at the smug, self-satisfied look that filled her eyes, I chased her out of the room.

I opened the drapes. The weatherman was right for once. More clouds were on the way in, ponderous and rain-filled. Nothing new for western Washington during the month of May, but after my dreams the heavy sky felt ominous, almost claustrophobic.

Leaning out into the cool air, I inhaled deeply, watching as a patch of mist rolled along the ground, swirling up from a low-lying part of the backyard. The raucous call of a family of Steller's jays echoed through the morning. The birds made their home in a large fir tree in the back-yard and they set up a stink every time it was going to rain.

As the first splatter of drops hit my face, I closed the sash, fastening it tightly. Maybe I should take my chances and stroll along Lighthouse Spit. Sure, it was raining, but I wouldn't melt, and I could watch the waves cresting in, maybe have breakfast at the Lighthouse Café. But a glance at the clock showed me that I didn't have time for any of that. I needed to start getting up earlier if I wanted to get in a walk every morning before breakfast.

I dressed quickly. Black jeans that fit my curves, hunter green turtleneck that slipped over my head, masking my tattoos.

A brilliant spray of roses embracing my mother's name adorned my lower back, and, for Christmas, I'd treated myself to an exotic faerie hiding among a spray of bluebells that twined around my left forearm and up to my shoulder. My belly button and left nipple were pierced, but few people knew about those little gems until summer hit and I started wearing crop tops and swimsuits. My body art startled a lot of people when they first noticed it, but I figured that if people were going to stereotype me because of the way I looked, then they could find somebody else to talk to. Blanket generalizations irked me to no end. Some of the most ethical people I knew looked the roughest.

I clattered downstairs, whipped up a quick smoothie, chugged it down, and headed for the shop, keeping within the speed limit all the way. Kyle could go suck a lemon; he wouldn't be giving me any more tickets.

The drive to Venus Envy wound along Beachcomber's Drive. I hugged the curves overlooking the ocean for a mile or two until the road headed east, directly into the heart of the town.

Gull Harbor was nestled on Port Samanish Island, one of several little islands making their home in Puget Sound between Seattle and the Kitsap Peninsula. The island was connected on the west side to Kitsap County by a floating bridge, and on the east side, ferry service provided transit across Puget Sound to Seattle.

The town had grown quickly over the past ten years from its roots as a tiny tourist attraction, housing sightseeing boats for the summer trade. Now Gull Harbor had a thriving economy thanks to both the high tech and tourism industries. In the early 1960s, a cooperative of artists and writers decided to make their headquarters here. One by one, they moved in, bringing with them their arts and crafts. Then, ten years ago, Sand Bar Software opened up, along with Red Oak Technology Services, which provided computer consultant contracts along the inland peninsula coastline, as well as over in the Seattle-Bellevue-Redmond area. Though still small, new businesses were beginning to look over to Port Samanish Island instead of Seattle proper when they relocated to Washington State.

The locals were an eclectic — if relatively harmless — mix of stubborn Northwest individualism and quirky artistic vision. But along with the growing population and the java-jive mentality, the natural beauty of the area was indisputable, and still pristine.

As I reached the shop, I pulled into my parking space and absently turned off the ignition. Aunt Florence was spending the morning with her accountant, so I'd be in charge till she arrived after lunch. I had three appointments scheduled, and also wanted to get cracking on a new blend — something to inspire energy and vitality.

I hadn't decided what I was going to call it yet; maybe something along the lines of Juniper Girl or Mountain Maiden. Whatever the name, I wanted to get right to work. Tawny wouldn't be in for another hour and I worked better when nobody else was around.

As I unlocked the door and entered the shop, I noticed a strange scent. Something almost metallic — sickly sweet and cloying. I flipped on the lights and all thoughts of perfume and bath salts and clients went flying out the door. There, on the floor next to the front counter, lay Lydia Wang, her dark hair matted with blood, a stunned look on her face.

Everything registered in slow motion for a moment until my instincts kicked in and I rushed over to her side, knelt, and even though I knew it was futile, felt for a pulse.

Her delicate hand was cool to the touch; she'd been dead long enough for rigor mortis to set in. Shivering, I gently let go of her wrist and rubbed my hand on my jeans.

From the look of things, her death hadn't been accidental. Her neck was turned too far to the right. Probably broken. On her forehead, an indigo bruise blossomed like an exotic, beautiful flower that had suddenly taken root on her skin. The back of her head looked misshapen, and her hair was thick with clotted blood. Queasy, I looked up at the counter. The corner was right in line with the way she'd fallen, and it had blood on it. I flinched as I pictured her head hitting the marble as she went down. But something . . . or someone . . . had to have struck her from behind because no way could a blow to her temple have caused the back of her skull to break.

The thought that the killer might still be around crossed my mind. It wasn't likely, but no use taking any chances. I edged cautiously back to the door. There was nothing I could do for her. Wherever she was, Lydia didn't need my help — or anybody else's — now. I stepped outside, making sure that I didn't touch anything else, and pulled out my cell phone to call my aunt and the police.

Chapter Four

Kyle Laughlin swept in with his men, looking distinctly out of place among the perfumes and lotions. When he saw me he rolled his eyes.

Thanks a lot, I thought. *I like you too.*

He motioned for his men to fan out. "Make sure nobody's here, don't touch anything — the murderer could have been anywhere in this place." Turning his attention back to me, he asked, "Have you touched anything?"

I frowned. "I work here, I've probably had my hands on everything at one point or another."

Kyle gave me a disgusted look. "This morning," he said, enunciating each word precisely. "I mean have you touched anything *this morning?*"

I raised my eyebrows but pointed to the door. "The handle and probably the door itself, of course. It was locked, by the way. And . . . Lydia. I checked to see if she had a pulse, and I steadied myself on the planter next to the counter when I stood up."

His eyes flickered. "Who was the last person to leave here last night?"

"I was." The minute I said it, I knew it sounded bad. *Good going, Sherlock. Place yourself at the scene of a crime.* All of Aunt Florence's detective shows came flooding back. "I worked late, till about nine o'clock."

One of the men tapped him on the shoulder and Kyle motioned to me that he'd be just a moment. He turned to whisper to the officer, then glanced back at me. "Are you sure of the time?"

"Yes, I'm sure. I looked at the clock before I locked the door to make sure that I'd have time to get to the grocery store."

"And which store did you go to?"

"Shoreline Foods Pavilion."

He jotted a note in his book. "Okay. Are you positive that you locked up when you left?"

I pressed my lips shut and stared at him. What did he think I was? A ditz? "I lived in Seattle, Kyle. I always lock up. And we don't have a security alarm system here, so we always double-check the door."

"Who else has access to the keys for the shop?" He kept one eye on me, one on his notebook.

Something was churning around in that

little brain of his. No doubt some new way to make my life miserable. "Auntie can tell you better than I can. She has the complete list."

"Well, I need to know what time you got to Shoreline Foods, how long you were there, and where you went after that."

I walked over to my station and sat down, watching as the men snapped pictures of Lydia's body and the surrounding area. Maybe I should cut Kyle a little slack. He'd just had a murder dropped in his lap, one that would make the papers for sure. I sighed and glanced around the shop. Something felt out of kilter, but I couldn't quite pinpoint it.

"Okay, give me a minute to collect my thoughts."

Just then, a roar outside announced the arrival of Aunt Florence in her convertible. She'd owned the Mustang for years, and it desperately needed a new muffler, but she insisted "Baby" was in top notch condition and repeatedly ignored the neighbor's pleas for her to quiet the beast.

The medical team was in the process of photographing the body but they paused as Auntie entered the shop, her brilliant mu'umu'u swishing against her legs. My aunt acted nothing less than the island's grandé dame. The officers hesitated as she passed, as if waiting for permission to continue.

She nodded at them, then strode over to Kyle's side.

"Well, if this doesn't tear all," she said, staring at Lydia's body with a pained look on her face.

"Morning, Miss Florence." Kyle shifted so that she could sit down on the bench next to him. "I was just asking Persia who has access to the shop."

Auntie adjusted her mu'umu'u and sat down, still staring at Lydia. "Persia and I both have keys, of course. Tawny has a key, and I gave one to Trevor last week when I asked him to bring down a load of supplies. Other than that — Barbara, next door, in case of emergency." She sucked on her lip for a moment. "Who did this, Kyle?"

"I don't know, Miss Florence. That's what we're trying to find out." He turned back to me. "You were going to tell me where you were last night, after you left the shop."

"I left here at nine o'clock, stopped at Shoreline Foods to pick up some groceries around nine-ten, and pulled into the driveway around forty minutes later." As much as I wanted to give him a swift kick, I refrained. First biting, then kicking . . . maybe Kyle wasn't the only one who hadn't grown up.

He glanced for confirmation at Aunt Florence, who seemed to grasp the situation.

"You can just stop thinking along those lines right now." She puffed up, the stuffed parakeet on her straw hat jiggling precariously. "Persia got home when she said she did. The power went off right at that moment, and I remember thinking we were going to miss *Magnum* if it didn't come back on. *Magnum* runs every night at ten PM on TV-Nation."

Kyle held up his hands. "I'm just trying to establish a time frame, Miss Florence. No disrespect intended. I'd better talk to Trevor and Tawny now."

Aunt Florence glanced over her shoulder at the door. Tawny had just entered and I watched as she glanced around, her eyes lighting on Lydia's cold body. Tawny gasped and reached for the doorframe.

Auntie waggled her finger at Kyle. "You just make sure you're polite to her. She's a good worker. Trevor, too." With that, she glanced back at Lydia's body, which they were now lifting into a body bag. "I hate to think of the hell her poor parents are going to go through." She sighed. "How long will this take? Should I be prepared to close down for several days?"

Kyle scratched his head and squinted. "I think we'll be done by this afternoon, but I'd like to keep tomorrow free, just in case we have any questions that pop up. Meanwhile, if you and Persia could look around the shop and figure out whether anything is missing, I'd be much obliged."

"That's it!" I jumped up. Something had been niggling at the back of my mind and now I knew what it was. Both my aunt and Kyle stared at me like I'd lost my marbles. I pointed to an empty space on the wall next to the door leading to our spa area. "Aphrodite's Mirror . . . it's gone."

"What mirror?"

"Barbara Konstantinos gave me a mirror that I keep here at the shop. It's called Aphrodite's Looking Glass, all handmade from Greece. Yesterday, Lydia got bent out of shape because I wouldn't sell it to her. I thought something was off, but it took awhile for me to figure out what it was."

Aunt Florence gasped. "You're right. I hadn't noticed, but it's gone, all right." She peeked in the till. "I don't think we're short — it's hard to say without pulling it out and counting, but it looks right."

Kyle glanced at me. "You were the last one to lock up, did you count out the till last night?"

I shook my head. "Tawny did."

He called her over and she confirmed that everything looked to be there. The store credit card was still in place, as was the fifty-dollar bill she accepted from a customer the day before. Auntie and I took a thorough look around while Kyle questioned Tawny. Nothing else seemed to be missing.

I leaned close to my aunt. "This is too weird. I know I locked that door."

"Of course you did. So somebody either picked the lock or there's another key floating around. Since I had the locks changed when I first opened the shop, there shouldn't be any more out there."

"Even if I had forgotten last night, it was tight as a drum this morning, and you can't lock the door without a key. A lot of women admired that mirror. A lot of people were also mad at Lydia." I crossed my arms and shivered. "How could she have gotten in here? And why?"

Florence patted my arm. "Don't you fret about Kyle and his questions. I know you two rub each other the wrong way, but he's really a good man underneath it all."

"Um hmm, I'll believe that when I see it," I mumbled, lowering my voice as he wandered over.

"The coroner says that it looks like somebody hit her on the back of the head. The impact knocked her into the marble edge of the counter."

Aunt Florence grimaced. "Did you find the murder weapon?"

"Not yet." He glanced back at the body. "We'll know more after the autopsy. So yes, if you could hold off opening your shop for a day or two, that will give my men the time to go over everything as we learn more about her death. In the meantime, it looks like your staff has an unplanned vacation."

We sat in a corner booth in the BookWich, staring mutely at our coffee. My aunt was never speechless about anything, but when we gathered our things and left the shop, she deflated like a sagging balloon. I wondered what was going through her head.

She absently stirred another spoonful of sugar into her coffee, sipped it, and grimaced. "Too sweet. Persia, I tell you, I haven't felt this worn out since . . . well, since your mother died. I've lost a lot of people in my life, but this is only the second time that I've known someone who was murdered. Tell me what happened."

I squeezed lemon into my tea. "I don't know. I got there, found her on the floor. Pretty gruesome. I've been going over everything I can remember from yesterday, but — here's Barb." I'd left a note for Barbara to meet us in the café.

"What on earth is going on at your shop?" She slid into the booth next to me. "The police are there, and the coroner, too. There's crime scene tape everywhere. Are you okay? I was terrified when I saw your note." She glanced around. "Where's Tawny? Did she get hurt?"

Auntie cleared her throat. "Down, girl. Lower your voice." She looked around. Heddy Latherton was sitting at the counter. "Wonderful, just what we need. The town gossipmonger." She leaned over the counter and whispered, "A customer was killed in our shop during the night."

Barbara gasped. "Oh my God! Who?"

"Hush! Not so loud," Auntie said. "I'll have to field off questions soon enough. I'd like a little time to regroup and think."

Just then, Kyle wandered in. He saw us and gave a little nod, then leaned over the counter to talk to the cashier. She pulled

out a clipboard and jotted down something, then handed him the piece of paper.
As Kyle turned toward the door, a distraught Chinese man raced in. Probably in
his fifties, he wore a rumpled suit and his
face was streaked with tears.

"Who did it? Who killed my daughter?"
The man lunged toward the Chief, grabbing his jacket. "It had to be that punk she
was dating! Who else would want to hurt
my Lydia?" With a sob, he let go as Kyle
gently led him to a chair and motioned to
the waitress for a glass of water.

The BookWich Café erupted into a cacophony of noise and activity. Heddy immediately pounced on Kyle. He pushed
her away with a sharp retort as he tried to
calm down Lydia's father.

Barbara inhaled sharply. "*Lydia Wang*
was murdered in your shop? Oh my God,
that's going to make the news, all right! It
will be on the front page of the *Seattle
Times* and the *Seattle P.I.* by tomorrow
morning."

"Perhaps now would be a prudent time
for us to make our departure." My aunt
tossed a ten on the table and we snuck out
the back entrance, unnoticed in the clamor
surrounding Kyle and Mr. Wang. A little
luck saw us through the parking lot and

around the side of the building to where our cars were parked in front of Venus Envy and the bakery.

Auntie pulled out her keys. "Persia, we should go directly home before anybody catches sight of us. Barbara, any chance you can come over? Whatever we do, let's get a move on. I want to get out of here before that old biddy catches us." My aunt and Heddy Latherton weren't the best of friends.

Barbara nodded. "Let me go tell Dorian. I'll meet you at your place in twenty minutes."

I climbed in my Sebring as Aunt Florence revved up Baby and we took off out of the parking lot, her convertible roaring like a lion on steroids.

I stood by the window, staring out at the inlet. The water was choppy, waves foaming against the shore. A lone dog, someone's chocolate lab, raced along the sand, barking at whatever it could find. The wall of windows in my aunt's house let a world of light and motion into the house, and sometimes during the early twilight, we would sit in the living room, curtains open, and watch the dim silhouette of the waves as they crested and ebbed along the shore.

The events of the morning seemed surreal. Lydia was dead and I had found her. I still wasn't sure how I felt. Death wasn't a stranger to me.

My mother had died of a heart attack when I was four years old. One day, she put me down for my nap and the next thing I knew, the house was swarming with people. Our next-door neighbor wouldn't let me go into the living room. She held me on her lap, and I still remember the sweet, sad look on her face. I was too young to understand what had happened and kept asking where my mother was. When the neighbor told me, "Your mama has gone to heaven," it didn't click. We weren't a religious family.

Three years later, after I came to live with Auntie, we were traveling in England on a winding rural road when the car in front of us skidded into an old pickup. Auntie managed to pull over to the side before we ended up in the pile-up, but four cars plowed into the fray and two of the drivers were thrown through their windshields.

Even though Auntie hurried to keep me from seeing the wreck, I caught a blurry look at one of the victim's faces. His expression was one of a surprise, of realization that — oops — there would be no tomorrow, the ride was over just like that, with no warning. I'd seen the same surprise on Lydia's face.

Aunt Florence carried in a tray holding a delicate bone china teapot and cups. As she placed it on the coffee table, the scent of lemon rose from the pot, which was shaped like a fat black tuxedo cat, the spout being one paw held up in the air. A crunch of tires on gravel announced Barbara's arrival. As I opened the door she dashed through the downpour, carrying a box of freshly baked cookies. For a moment, nobody said anything, then Barbara broke the silence.

"Heddy was looking for you. She popped into the bakery as I was leaving and asked where you were." Barb opened the box and spread out an assortment of peanut butter and chocolate chip cookies on a plate. I inhaled deeply, letting the familiar aromas soothe my frazzled nerves.

"I guess word is out," Florence said. And sure enough, just as she spoke, the phone rang. She sighed and pushed herself out of her chair. "I'll take this call, then I'm switching on the answering machine for the rest of the day."

As Auntie went into the kitchen to answer the phone, I turned to Barb. "What did Heddy want, as if I couldn't guess?"

She grinned. "What else? An 'in' on the latest gossip. So tell me what happened."

I filled her in. "A lot of people didn't like Lydia. What I want to know is why she was killed in our shop? And who managed to get hold of a key?"

Barbara fished in her purse and pulled out her key ring, holding up one with a pink piece of tape on it. "Here's mine — safe and sound. What about Tawny? Trevor?"

"There's a bit of a problem there. Yesterday, Trevor and Lydia had a blowout in the store. It wasn't pretty." The memory of his anguished face flashed in my mind. "They were an item, until she dumped him."

"Do you think he was mad enough to kill her?"

"Trevor? Of course not, but I expect Kyle will be asking me that before long. Just a sec . . ." I leaned over the back of the sofa to peek into the dining room to see if Aunt Florence needed any help. She shook her head, so I turned back to Barb. "I'll have to tell him about the argument, but do I believe Trevor could — or would — hurt Lydia? No, not really. He's a hard worker and a good kid, from what I can tell."

Barb shrugged. "That doesn't mean anything. Trevor could have a secret life you know nothing about. I agree that he seems harmless, but sometimes the most innocuous ones are most dangerous."

I poured the tea and handed her a cup, then added lemon to my own as I bit into one of her peanut butter cookies. Sugar was good for shock, it kept the body moving. "These are wonderful," I said. "Give me the recipe?"

"As long as you don't start competing with the bakery!" She grinned, then sobered. "I hate to say it, but Lydia's death was good for business. All the busybodies stopped in to buy cookies. Kind of gruesome, when you think about it."

The mail truck pulled up while we were waiting for Aunt Florence and I told Barb I'd be back in a moment. I made a mad dash to the mailbox through the rain, almost running in front of Kyle's cruiser as he pulled into the driveway. I jerked my thumb toward the door, then sprinted back to the shelter of the porch.

While waiting for him, I flipped through the envelopes and broke into a cold sweat. One of the letters was addressed to me and

I recognized the handwriting. Cripes! A letter from Elliot, my ex-boyfriend. How had he found me, and what did he want? I'd thought he was still in prison, but the return address was a simple post office box. If he was still behind bars, the prison would have added their "from a correctional institute" stamp.

I thrust the envelope into my pocket as Kyle took the stairs two at a time. Elliot and whatever he was up to would have to wait. As soon as Kyle took off his raincoat and draped it over the porch swing, I knew something was wrong. His stress levels were so high I could smell them. I motioned him into the living room where Barbara murmured a quiet "hello."

Aunt Florence bustled in. "Kyle," she said, nodding. "Have you found out anything yet?" she asked, settling her abundant frame into the overstuffed rocking chair.

"Well, Miss Florence, I came to ask Persia a few more questions." He took a seat in the wing chair by the sofa.

"This better not be what I think it is, Kyle Andrew Laughlin." Auntie pushed herself forward.

He shook his head. "Just routine. Persia, I forgot to ask you who your cashier was at

Shoreline Foods. Do you still have the receipt from last night? That would tell us which checker cashed you out."

Oh jeez, did he really think *I* killed Lydia? I gave him a withering look, then stomped off into the kitchen. This was ridiculous. What motive could I possibly have other than thinking that she was a miserable excuse for a human being? After rooting through the garbage, I yanked out the receipt. It was smeared with old cat food and yogurt, but the date stamp and checkout counter were still clearly visible. I wiped it off and took it back to the living room, shoving it in his face.

"Here. Now you can see that we eat deli meat, salads, and lemon pound cake. The man who waited on me was young, had a spiked Mohawk, and wore three huge earrings in his left ear. Will that narrow it down?"

Kyle gave me a tight smile. "This is fine. We should be able to establish your alibi with this. I'm sorry I interrupted your afternoon," he added, glancing over at my aunt. "I know it's been a troubling day. But I have to ask you a couple more questions. Trevor Wilson was in the shop yesterday, wasn't he?"

Oops, somebody had spilled the beans about the argument.

"Yes, he was," I said. "I was running the shop and he came in to ask about lilacs. Before you ask — yes, he and Lydia mixed it up a little. Lydia treated him like dirt and he lit into her for being such a bitch."

Kyle scowled at his notebook. "Is it true that he told her she'd better watch out or she was going to get hurt?"

Uh oh, somebody had been listening really closely. "Well, he didn't threaten her personally, if that's what you're getting around to." I stopped. Actually, he had threatened her. Twice. First in the front of the store, when he'd raised his hand toward her and said, *"Right now, Persia is the only one who's keeping me from wiping that fucking smile off your face,"* and later in the office, when he'd said to me, *"She makes me so mad, sometimes I just want to . . . to make her hurt as much as she hurt me."*

As much as I dreaded the fallout, I had to tell the truth. I didn't believe for a moment that he was guilty, but if it came out that I had withheld information, things would look bad for both of us.

"Actually, I guess it did sound like he was threatening her," I said, forcing ambiguity into my voice. "But he didn't mean it. Trevor was upset because she'd been

96

spouting off a bunch of garbage at him."

Kyle met my gaze and held it. His eyes were dark, darker than I'd remembered them. "Why don't you tell me exactly what he said?"

I laid out what had happened, hiding nothing, including Lydia's all-too eager delight in trashing Trevor's ego. "She was the queen of mean, tell you that." I glanced over at Aunt Florence, who was frowning. "Auntie, I'm sorry, but I have to tell him what I know. Trev didn't do it — we both know that. I'm sure that he'll be off the hook as soon as they verify his alibi."

She sighed and wiped her eyes, looking tired. "I know, child. You're doing the right thing."

Kyle cleared his throat. "Actually, we've already talked to him. Trevor doesn't have an alibi that checks out after nine o'clock. He went bowling with friends, but left around eight forty-five. He claims to have gotten a call from Lydia, asking him to meet her down on the Lighthouse Spit. When he got there, he said the Spit was empty. We're tracing her calls to see if we can find evidence that she phoned him, but even if we do, he still could have taken her back to your shop and killed her."

Auntie knitted her fingers together.

"Trevor's a good boy. I've known him since he was born. I can't believe that he'd do something like this."

Kyle sighed. "I'm just doing my job. Lydia was murdered in your shop. The door was locked, and requires a key. Lydia was seen having a very public argument with Trevor, her ex-boyfriend, who — for all intents and purposes — threatened her in the earshot of others. He doesn't have an alibi for the time during which she was murdered. What do you expect me to think?"

I slipped over to my aunt's side and gave her a gentle hug. "It's all right. We know Trevor's innocent, we'll help him if they decide to charge him." And heaven help him if Kyle did decide to go after him.

She nodded, resting her head against my shoulder. "I've got a tequila-sized headache right now. I think I'll go get an aspirin." As she wandered into the kitchen, I turned back to Kyle.

"It doesn't look good for Trevor, does it?"

He raised one eyebrow. "You always were a master at understatement." Just then his radio squawked. He moved over to one side to take the call in private while I sat down next to Barbara, who handed me my tea.

As I took a sip, Aunt Florence joined us in our little huddle. "I'd better call my lawyer and tell him to get his hind end over here. The way things are looking they'll have you and Trevor teamed up on this." She shook her head. "I don't get it. Things like this just don't happen in Gull Harbor. And certainly not in my shop, for God's sake."

Kyle clicked his radio off and slipped back into his seat. Something in his face told me he had bad news for us. "Persia, you're off the hook. We found your clerk. Apparently, you insisted that he recheck the register tape because he overcharged you for an item, and you made him go through it three times."

For once, my attention to detail had paid off. "Score one for the squeaky wheel. So everything's okay?"

"For you, yes. But my men found something else." Kyle sobered. "I just ordered my boys to pick up Trevor Wilson. We found the murder weapon."

Aunt Florence, Barbara, and I leaned forward as one. "What?" I asked. A low rumble of thunder raced through the room as the storm picked up speed.

He stood up and jammed his hands in his pockets. "They found a hammer in the back room. Trevor's fingerprints are all over the handle, and it's covered in Lydia Wang's blood."

Chapter Five

I stared at Aunt Florence, a growing knot of dread in my stomach. What the hell? Trevor's hammer? With Lydia's blood on it?

Kyle cleared his throat and headed toward the door. "I've got to get back to the station. If Trevor shows up here, call us. I mean it, Miss Florence." He sounded like he half-expected her to pitch a fit, but she just gave him a faint nod as I escorted him out on the porch.

He peered back over my head toward the living room and lowered his voice. "Persia, I meant what I said. If Trevor Wilson shows up anywhere near here, you call the station. He's dangerous, and I don't want anything to happen to your aunt or you."

He actually sounded sincere. I murmured an assent and shut the door behind him. As I returned to the living room, Auntie was leaning against one of the carved wooden pillars that ran from floor to ceiling, a pained look etched on her face. I led her back to her chair.

She stared at the coffee table for a moment, then leaned forward to pick up a copy of *Vogue* and fanned herself with it. "One moment life's going on as usual, the next, everything's been shot to hell," she said. "I know Kyle has no choice, but I just can't believe he's going to arrest Trevor. Trevor's a good boy, he wouldn't hurt a fly." Her voice trembled with a flutter of doubt.

I wandered over to the window. The rain was pelting the water, rippling the surface with concentric rings that spread out in even circles. All it took was one drop . . . one disturbance, to shake up lives and alter history. A shiver raced up my back and I returned to the warmth of the fire, grabbed the tea tray, and hurried into the kitchen, where I freshened the pot and added more cookies to the plate.

As I returned to the living room, Barbara was saying, "Kyle has to haul him in, Miss Florence. Look at the evidence — he can't ignore it. That's his job. Granted, I don't believe that Trev is guilty, but Kyle's the chief of police. He *has* to go by the book."

"Even though I don't like him, I have to agree with Barbara," I said. "Trevor's his most logical suspect."

Just then, Trubbul leapt up on the sofa

and tried to climb in my lap. I shooed at him, but the orange tabby ignored me and crawled over my hands, settling into a ball on my skirt. Like Delilah, he was getting on in years. Auntie had taken him in from a rescue shelter and — as with all the cats in the household — he was an indoor-only babe. I stroked his fur, breathing quietly as the rumble of his purr lulled some of the tension out of my shoulders.

"Auntie, can you think of anybody else who might have a key to the shop? Did you ever give one to a maintenance man or . . . say, what about Marta? Does she have a key?"

Barbara looked at me like I was crazy. "You're suggesting Marta might have killed Lydia? That's absurd. Marta's too lazy to go around killing anybody, and why would she? What would she have to gain?"

Marta was the cleaning lady for several of the downtown businesses. Aunt Florence, Barbara, and Marianne Stila, who owned Marianne's Closet, hired her to come in and clean for them, and paid her under the table. Marta was seventy if she was a day, took too many breaks, and smoked too much — though not in the shops. Auntie, Barb, and Marianne had threatened to fire her if they smelled a single hint of cigarette smoke.

"Maybe she gave her key to somebody else?" I was clutching at straws.

Auntie shook her head, putting an end to my speculation. "Marta's never had a key to my shop. She comes in twice a week during the early morning. That's why Tawny opens early on Mondays and Thursdays. I told her to keep an eye on Marta because the old girl has been known to take a few five-fingered discounts."

"What?" Barbara straightened up, a curious gleam in her eye. "She steals? I didn't know that. Why didn't you tell me?"

My aunt blushed. "Yes, the old dear steals. I caught her several times before I set Tawny on guard duty. But Marta hasn't got a soul in the world to look after her, and I didn't want to be responsible for her losing work. Really, what she took was minor . . . a bar of soap, a bottle of lotion, and I think once I noticed a bath mitt disappearing into that big old tote bag of hers. She doesn't make a lot of money. So as far as I'm concerned, if she needs a bit of soap, she's welcome to it. I thought I told you about it, but I guess it slipped my mind."

Barbara looked thoughtful. "That could explain our missing inventory. We don't count the number of individual muffins or cookies we make, but now and then it seems like we're a little low on stock compared to what we put away for the night. I thought that maybe Ronette and Colin were getting overenthusiastic and was going to talk to them about it. Maybe I should hold off. What do you think?"

Ronette and Colin, two high school kids, helped out in the bakery on weekends and after school.

"Given Colin's height and age, it wouldn't surprise me to hear that he's been dipping into the doughnuts," I said. "Teenagers eat like they have bottomless stomachs. Auntie's right, though. Marta's on a fixed income and I'll bet she finds it hard to resist a little treat now and then."

"Then I'll just hold off on that lecture," Barb said. "But that leaves me with the question of whether I should I talk to Marta. I don't like the idea of a thief working for me, petty or otherwise."

"Don't be so quick to judge." Aunt Florence sighed and pushed her way to her feet. "Marta has more problems than either of you know about. It's not my place to tell you what she's facing, but trust me — if she steals a cookie or a bar of soap, it's because she needs it, *not* because she doesn't want to pay. Whatever bit of spare money she has is tied up in helping her daughter and her disabled grandson."

"I didn't know that," Barb said. She studied her hands. "I guess I never thought to ask Marta about her life."

Aunt Florence shook her head. "Life can be rough for a lot of folks — young and old alike. Now, if you girls will excuse me, I'm going to go call Winthrop." At Barb's questioning look, she added, "Winchester. My lawyer. Trevor's going to need all the help he can get." With that, she headed into the den, shutting the door behind her.

I stood up. "I think I'll make us some sandwiches. Tea and cookies are fine, but I'm starved. The day's been one shock after another." As we headed into the kitchen, it occurred to me that we really knew very little about the people who touched on the periphery of our lives. For instance, just how much did we really know about Trevor?

The papers were always full of stories that started, "He was such a nice man, nobody ever thought he was capable of such a crime. . . ." Was Trevor one of those people who lived a secret life that nobody knew about? Or was he just a convenient scapegoat? The Wangs were a prominent family in town. They'd want answers and they'd want them fast. I trusted Kyle to go by the book, but would he bother to look outside of it at other possibilities? He'd always had a linear, one-track mind back in junior high.

I pulled out the bread and meat and cheese while Barb got the plates out of the cupboard. As I fixed three roast beef sandwiches, she sliced up a cantaloupe and then we arranged the food on the plates, covering Auntie's with plastic wrap and setting it in the refrigerator until she was ready to eat.

We settled in at the dinette table in companionable silence. I absently looked out the window. It was a gloomy, nasty afternoon that made me glad we were inside. The breakfast nook overlooked the kitchen garden Aunt Florence had planted on the south side of the house. Somebody would have to go out and weed it later. Trevor would be out of commission for awhile; I had my doubts that Kyle would let him out for plant-patrol. Meanwhile, the lilacs needed harvesting, and the other flowers and herbs would be crying out for attention.

Sighing, I wiped my hands on my napkin and grabbed the phone, punching in Sarah's number, hoping she could fill in full-time.

Her answering machine beeped and I left a message asking her to call me back as soon as she had the chance. As I sat back down at the table and spoke to Barb, she jumped, off somewhere in her own little world.

"So, what are your plans for the evening? Do you still want to go out to dinner tonight?"

She shook her head and finished her sandwich. "I left Dorian stuck with all the work, so I don't think tonight is the best night to leave him without a good dinner on the table. He wouldn't complain, but . . . you know. Rain check, okay?"

Secretly relieved — I really wasn't looking forward to the prying eyes that would turn our way once Lydia's murder hit the papers — I walked her to the door. "Not a problem. You know, I'm curious about the missing mirror. It couldn't have just vanished into thin air. Now, I know that Lydia wanted it, but she sure didn't walk out of the shop with it. And if Trevor killed her, what use would he have for it? And why did he leave his hammer in the office instead of dumping it in the water where they wouldn't find it?"

"Those are good questions that deserve good answers. Make sure that you pose them to Kyle. I like the man, but he's not going to look very hard for anybody else if he thinks he's got his murderer. Ever since his wife died, he's changed, and not necessarily for the better."

I gave her a quick look. "I know he was married, and that his wife died, but I don't know much about what happened. Who was she?"

Barbara shrugged. "Her name was Katy. I don't think you ever met her. She moved here a few years after you left. Two years ago, she was driving out on Weirback Road during a bad rainstorm — you know, the winding road that leads up to Klaxon Ridge? And there was this logging truck coming the other way. She skidded, pulled a hard right to try to avoid hitting it, and went over the embankment."

"Oh jeez, what a mess," I said. "Poor Kyle." I felt like an ass. Kyle had reason to be upset with the world. The poor man was still mourning for his wife. I had to quit taking things like that personally. My ego could use a little deflating, that was for sure.

"He took it pretty bad."

The rain had let up and the clouds were pulling away, though they looked like they'd be back in full force a little later on.

A gust of wind whipped past and I shivered, crossing my arms to protect myself from the chill. I stepped back so Barb could pull out. "See you later!"

She honked and waved as she disappeared down the road.

After everything that had happened, I really needed to move, get a breath of fresh air. A glance at the sky told me that I'd probably have time for a walk before the next wave of pendulous clouds made their way to the island, so I ran inside, grabbed my jacket, called the dogs, and we all headed across the street and down the slope leading to the beach.

Coastlines in Washington State were, for the most part, rocky and jagged, with driftwood littering the beach, and pebbles and rocks intermingling with the sand. Even on the islands that dotted Puget Sound, the waves would come cresting in and cause havoc when storms whipped through.

We lived in an area on the island where the beach was smooth sand that changed form with each tide. Tall grasses grew through the sand, sparse and pale, and most of the trees along the shoreline had that windblown look, tilted with branches growing sideways due to the constant gusts buffeting the area.

Gull Harbor averaged forty-five to fifty inches of rain per year, most of it cold. It wasn't unusual for the storms that swept through during the spring and winter to cause landslides, flooding, and general mayhem. Our side of Briarwood Drive sloped up so that the house sat on an incline far enough above the level of the beach for comfort, though Aunt Florence said she'd seen the road wash out several times over the past thirty-odd years.

During the late summer, tourists wandered the island and set up day camps on the beach. Even though it was warm enough to swim by then, few people ventured into the water alone. There was always the danger of a rip current, when the breaks in the sandbars funneled water into long, narrow currents that surged out into the Sound, dragging with them anybody or anything caught in their wake.

Less than a year ago, two teenaged girls got caught by one of the undertows and drowned. Sarah, our other gardener, said that she'd seen their ghosts walking Nakoma Point one night, but so far I hadn't seen anything supernatural on the spit of sand, for which I was eminently grateful.

The sand was compacted from all of the

rain, but I managed to find a log that was relatively dry. The bark had long been stripped away and it had that pale, sandpapered look that came from the motion of water and sand swirling around it during high tide. While the dogs raced happily along the beach, barking at the waves and bugs and whatever else they could find to chase, I stuck my hand in my pocket and felt paper. That's right — Elliot's letter. I pulled it out and looked at it for a long moment. How the heck had he found me?

I cautiously wedged open the flap of the envelope, taking care not to tear the letter. After making sure the dogs were still in sight, I withdrew the folded note. Three pressed violets fell out into my hand. I knew where they'd come from. I'd bought him an African violet plant on his last birthday. Their scent was faded, musty and old. Taking a deep breath, I began to read.

Persia, I can't believe you ran off and left me like that. One mistake and you toss me out like an old shoe and now you've gone into hiding like I'm some common criminal you don't want to be associated with. Well, I've got news for you. I'm free. They shortened my sentence because I turned over evidence, and I've spent the past week tracking you down. I shouldn't bother but I'm feeling generous. I'm willing to give you one more chance.

Don't sweat Benny and Jon — they won't come after you. If they hunt down anybody, it'll be me but since they won't be out for several years, I'm not too worried. If that's why you took off, then I forgive you. I can still smell your hair, feel the whisper of your lips on my own. I'll never forget you, and I don't want to let you go. Come home to me. I'm lost without you. Elliot.

I quietly folded the note and tucked it back in the envelope, making sure the flower petals were safely inside. Well, that certainly wasn't something I'd been expecting to hear. Or wanting to hear. Damn it, why had he bothered to dig me up? He knew I didn't want anything to do with him. I'd told him so when I visited him in jail, after the evidence had come to light that proved he really had swiped the money. In my heart, I was glad he'd gotten caught because I couldn't stand the thought that I'd spent six years with a man who had managed to pull the wool over my eyes while ripping off the accounting firm who had given him his start and treated him like family. Then it came out that the whole company was corrupt and I just wanted away from any ties to the whole mess.

I rested my elbow on my knee and propped my chin on my palm. What should I do? If I ignored the letter, he'd get hold of my phone number and start bombarding me with phone calls. I knew him well enough to know just how persistent he could be. If I responded to the letter, he'd take it as encouragement. Either way, it wasn't a good sign that he'd found me so easily, and I didn't like the desperate, whining tone of his words.

Sighing, I stood and picked up a hefty stick, calling the dogs. They bounded up and I tossed the branch far out on the beach, watching as they panted after it. Auntie had it right. Pets were so much easier than people. No messy interactions, no expectations other than food when they were hungry, a firm hand to pet them, and a lap on which to snuggle.

Open my heart to Elliot again? Not a chance. After the initial shock, I'd discovered that I enjoyed being footloose. When we lived together, I never had a free moment to myself; he was always *there,* always loud even when he hadn't said a word. Now the possibilities opened up like a blossoming flower. Who knew? Maybe tomorrow I'd decide to squirrel myself away from the world. Maybe I'd get the urge to move to Tibet and climb Mount Everest. Maybe next month I'd hop a plane for South America to explore the rain forest.

Or, maybe I'd stay here and take over my aunt's business as the years went by. The point was that I didn't know — and right now, I loved that feeling of unpredictability. I didn't want to my future to be pat and secure. I wanted to be surprised, to let it unfold, to experience all the joys and sorrows waiting for me. I was happy just enjoying the journey — I didn't want to plan out a destination.

As a new spate of rain started up again, I whistled for the dogs to follow me home. Recluse . . . hermit . . . the peace of mind that I'd found in Gull Harbor felt pretty good to me right now, but Elliot's letter threatened to put an end to that. I had to do something. I just didn't have any idea what that *something* might be.

Juniper Girl Bath Salts

It occurred to me not long ago that women need all the extra energy they can get. Everybody's looking for something to recharge and reenergize her. Work, family life, home and hearth, social life, all these factors seem to pile one on top of the other to send the modern woman screaming in frustration. So I developed Juniper Girl Bath Salts — "For the woman on the go, who has too much to do." Health and beauty hints Auntie and I thought might be nice to add to the salts:

- Get enough sleep. This should be your number one priority in maintaining your energy and strength.
- Eat healthy foods as often as you can. Get plenty of fruits, vegetables, and muscle-sustaining protein.
- Drink plenty of toxin-flushing water.
- Limit your caffeine intake — after awhile, too much will slow you down rather than build you up.
- Try to do something nice for yourself

every day, even if it's very small —
take a bubble bath, take a five-minute
meditation break, talk with a sup-
portive friend for a few minutes.
• Exercise — even with our hectic lives,
regular physical exercise will help
maintain and build your ability to
fight stress and illness.

Remind customers that homemade bath
salts can clump, so keep them in a wide
mouth jar, tightly covered so moisture
doesn't get in. If the salts do harden, simply
break off the amount to be used and im-
merse them in one quart boiling water to
dissolve, then add directly to bath water.
There's no change in their effectiveness or
fragrance if they harden.

> 1 cup Epsom salts
> $^2/_3$ cup table salt (plain)
> $^1/_3$ cup baking soda
> 10 drops cedar oil
> 5 drops dark musk oil
> 5 drops violet oil
> 3 drops lemon oil
> Green food coloring (if desired)

In a metal or ceramic bowl, mix the salts
and soda together thoroughly. Add the oils,

one drop at a time, and blend the mixture with hands after adding each oil, breaking up any clumps that may form. During this time, focus on the concepts of rejuvenation, recharging energy, and waking up the senses.

After adding all the oils, add $1/4$ teaspoon green food coloring if desired and again, blend with hands (note to self: wear thin latex gloves for this last step to avoid staining hands. While the bath salts will not stain skin during use, this part of the process can get messy).

Once the bath salts are an even color and scent, store as directed above, and keep out of direct sunlight, which can deteriorate fragrance. Add $1/2$ cup of the bath salts to hot bath water and they will dissolve.

Chapter Six

As I crossed the road to Moss Rose Cottage, my aunt's estate, the dogs padded ahead of me, worn out from their run. I stopped by the trash, hesitating for a moment as I debated whether to dump Elliot's letter in the bin. A little voice inside whispered, *Don't do it, you may need it later if he tries something stupid,* and so, reluctantly, I tucked it back in my pocket, squared my shoulders, and headed toward the house.

Three stories high, Moss Rose Cottage was spectacular, or at least, a spectacle. The front yard was overflowing with flowers, bushes, and trees, and the house itself looked like something out of a fairy tale. Captain Bentley had designed it himself, basing it on pictures of quaint English cottages with thatched roofs and kitchen gardens; however, it was anything but quaint. Built from gray stone and mortar, the house emerged from the tangle of vegetation, a miniature castle in the middle of a forested glen. Tendrils of ivy tenaciously curled across the mossy roof to coil around the chimneys.

Mullioned windows graced the walls. Their trim had recently received an eye-opening coat of white. Below the windows, crimson boxes were cluttered with pansies and primroses. Every time I pulled into the driveway, I felt like I'd entered Faerie Land. The strings of Christmas lights that Auntie used to illuminate the porch and yard during the night went a long ways in furthering that vision, their twinkling lights sparkling like glowing flutter-bugs. Fire-flies couldn't burn any brighter.

Around back, a small lawn with a patio and barbecue buttressed up against a picket fence that divided the yard from the gardens where, among the rose bushes and lilac trees and lavender patches, wildflower glades and bluebell thickets abounded, as well as a sprawling maze created out of hedgerows. Moss roses covered the trellis arching over the path that led to the gardens.

The house was huge, over a hundred years old. Captain Bentley had owned it until his death, at which point it had passed down from one heir to another until Aunt Florence took it off the family's hands. To them it was a white elephant. To Auntie, it was home. And it was also home to me.

She'd been good to her word. The entire

third floor was mine. Five rooms with ceilings that towered upwards of fourteen feet. The walls of my rooms ranged from a tasteful green paisley paper to a rich, golden coppery color that spread across the walls in smooth strokes. Now and then, I heard the Cap'n's footsteps in the hallway, and once I'd seen the doorknob to my study jiggle, but other than that, he left me alone and we existed in solitary contentment in the top of the old mansion.

Cold from my walk, I decided to take a hot bath and hightailed it up the stairs, taking them two at a time. I stripped off my clothes and stretched, luxuriating in the space. I'd felt claustrophobic when I lived with Elliot. His penthouse was cramped and he had a fit if I walked around the condominium naked; he was always worried that somebody would see me. I once asked him just who was going to be flying by the forty-eighth floor besides a few crows, seagulls, and the occasional butterfly, but all he did was mutter something under his breath about my lack of shame.

As I padded across the braided rug into my bathroom, I closed my eyes, listening to the silence. Beneath the veneer of stillness, there lurked the sounds of bird song, and of the cats and dogs running around the house, but gone was Seattle's incessant drone of traffic and the some three million people who lived in the greater metropolitan area. While the city was only a ferry ride across the inlet, it might as well have been a world away.

I turned on the water and poured in a capful of lavender bath gel, filling the old-fashioned claw-footed tub with bubbles. The tub was long enough that I could sink up to my chin, even at my height, and it was separate from the glass-enclosed stand-alone shower.

Auntie had made sure my bedroom was fully furnished, including a sleigh bed, a matching vanity with beveled mirror and bench, and an eight-drawer dresser. The set gleamed, polished lovingly with a rich oil, and was probably worth more than my entire life earnings.

The other three rooms had odd bits of furniture in them, and were slowly evolving into a comfortable home of my own. The one with the coppery paper I had turned into a study; the largest had become my workout room with exercise bike, rowing machine, home gym, yoga mat, and various other goodies to play with; and the coziest, I'd transformed into my own private perfumery.

I slid into the bubble-filled tub and leaned back, not wanting to think about death of any kind, be it murder or natural, until I was clean, relaxed, and warmed through to the bone.

Aunt Florence was making dinner as I emerged from the stairwell. I'd spent the rest of the afternoon experimenting with different fragrances and finally came up with a blend that I thought would sell well. My thoughts turned to food as my stomach rumbled. Auntie was frying up a couple of steaks along with a skillet full of mushrooms and onions. The steamer hummed, filled with broccoli and carrots. I leaned over her shoulder and took a good sniff.

"Oh, that smells good. I think that I found a new line for the shop. I've decided on 'Juniper Girl' instead of 'Mountain Maiden.' "

She gave me an astute look. "I like the name. Who's your market?"

"Hikers, bikers . . . women on the go. The scent's woodsy with an undertone of rose. Strong yet feminine . . . not overtly sexy, but rain-washed and fresh." Along with my talents as a sensory expert, I was now learning how to be an effective marketer. Aunt Florence could turn dog poop into gold if she put her mind to it, and I was determined to learn everything I could from her.

She winked at me and touched her nose. "Sounds good. Start mixing up some samples tomorrow and we'll see how she flies. Although with Trevor out of commission, you're going to have to put more time into the gardens until we find a temporary replacement. Let's aim for an introductory sale in three weeks."

"Speaking of Trevor, have you heard anything more about him this afternoon?" I pulled out the plates and began setting the table.

She flipped the searing meat and sprinkled on Worcestershire sauce and added a dash of port to the pan. A rush of flavor-filled smoke washed through the kitchen. My stomach rumbled.

"I talked to my lawyer and he's going to see me tomorrow, then go talk to Trevor. But there's a hitch in the works. I just got a call from Kyle." She paused to remove the broccoli from the steamer.

"What's up?" I added French bread, butter, and a bottle of steak sauce to the table, then filled two goblets with a rich

Merlot that was one of my favorites.

Florence handed me the platter of steaks and mushrooms. "Trevor seems to have disappeared."

Disappeared? Uh oh. That wasn't going to sit well with the police. Even if Trevor was just scared, it would make him look guilty. And if he *was* guilty, then he was dangerous and on the loose.

"Where'd he go?"

She snorted. "If they knew where he went, I wouldn't be telling you that he's disappeared, now would I? They've set up roadblocks at the ferry and at the bridge. There's no other way off the island. Kyle doesn't think Trevor skipped town yet, because his truck is still parked in his driveway. Persia, I know that I said he's innocent, but my dear, be careful. Even if he didn't kill Lydia, fear has reduced many a man to desperate acts. I don't want anything happening to you."

Carrying the broccoli, she joined me at the table and we ate in silence, amid the tinkle of forks and knives on good china.

After we finished dinner, I let the dogs out to take care of their after-supper business. Dusk had fallen early, with the incoming storm, and I was huddling on the porch, waiting for Beauty, Beast, and Pete to return, when a rustle in the bushes alerted me. I grabbed one of the walking sticks that was leaning against the wall, and cautiously edged over to the south end of the porch, where a set of side stairs led down into the hydrangea garden. As I slowly descended the steps, the rustling stopped and for a moment I thought about going back inside, but then a scent spiraled past me in the wind — the smell of sweat and fear.

I took a deep breath and froze as an unwelcome thought crossed my mind. What if Lydia's killer had been targeting my aunt or me, instead of her? Had she been in the wrong place at the wrong time? What if one of Elliot's friends had tracked me down, deciding to get revenge on him by hurting me? And what if I had just walked into a trap? I turned to race back up the steps but someone leapt out from behind the bushes, slapped a hand over my mouth, and dragged me back against the side of the house.

Leaning into my attacker's weight, I unbalanced him just long enough for me to grab hold of his arm and flip him over my shoulder. I raised my foot, ready to stomp him a good one in the neck, but the satisfying thud as my assailant hit the ground brought him into the light and I jerked sideways, much to the surprise of some smaller muscles in my upper thigh which protested mightily.

"Jeezus!" Leaning over the prostrate figure, I launched into a tirade that would have made Aunt Florence proud.

"Trevor Wilson! What the hell do you think you're doing? I ought to smack you upside the head. You know that I've got years of experience with both Tai Chi and Aikido! I could have killed you."

He winced, pushing himself into a sitting position. "Well, I realize that now," he said, rubbing his head. "Damn, you're good!"

"You got that right," I said, kneeling beside him to make certain that he hadn't broken any bones in his fall. "What are you doing here? I heard you disappeared." I kept my voice low to avoid the attention of any snoops wandering through the neighborhood. Though the houses on this road were spaced quite a ways apart, each having substantial acreage, I didn't want to take a chance. I wouldn't put it past some gossipmonger like Heddy to come craning her neck in hopes of seeing something interesting.

He groaned as I helped him up. Once we were sitting on the side steps, relatively protected from view by a large huckleberry bush in the front yard, I turned to him. "Okay, spill it. What's going on? Why were you hiding in the bushes?"

"I had to talk to you. I didn't kill Lydia. On my word, it wasn't me. I heard they were looking for me and panicked and ran but by then it was too late — the road-blocks were up and the cops were watching the ferry. I don't know what to do." With a mournful shrug, he fell silent again.

I bit my lip, regarding him silently. Trevor was a handsome young man, about twenty-three, with his whole life in front of him. From what I'd gotten to know of him, he was a good-hearted soul and, even if he wasn't the brightest bulb in the socket, he had qualities that more than made up for it. When he said he hadn't killed Lydia, I believed him. Well, ninety-five percent. I never trusted anybody unconditionally, another useful lesson taught to me by my absentee father.

"Here's the thing. You're lucky it was too late to run." When he jerked his head to stare at me, I held up one hand. "No, hear me out. Trev, you have to turn yourself in. If you run, if you make them hunt you down, everybody will assume you're guilty and the cops won't even bother trying to find any other suspects." I paused, debating whether to tell him that the cops found his hammer covered with blood. On one hand, it would be interesting to see his reaction. On the other, if he *was* guilty, I didn't want to be his next target.

He pushed himself to his feet and leaned against the wall, hands jammed in his pockets. "Do you think I'm stupid? I know that! Logically, I know that. But it's so damned scary. Persia, I was angry at Lydia, but I didn't hate her enough to kill her. You believe me, don't you?"

Maybe not enough to kill her, I thought, *but you wanted to hurt her . . . at least that's what you told me.* I kept my mouth shut, though.

"Come on, sit down," I said, feeling trapped between two equally frightening choices. If Trevor refused to turn himself in, and the police found out that I'd talked to him and didn't tell them, I'd be in for a whole lot of grief. On the other hand, Trevor was frightened and relying on me to help him out and if I betrayed him, he'd blame me forever. My gut said he was innocent. My head said, *be a friend, but be careful.*

I tried again. "Listen to me. Aunt Florence called her lawyer. He's the best there is in Gull Harbor and he said he'd take your case. However, if you don't turn yourself in, the court's going to brand you Guilty with a big red G and you know you won't get a fair shake then. Let me call Kyle. If you turn yourself in voluntarily, they'll see it as show of good faith. That can go a long way with a judge."

He scuffed the ground with his foot and I knew he was mulling it over.

"Trev, think how hard it's going to be if you head out on the road. Life as a fugitive won't be easy and murder has no statute of limitations. You'd always be a wanted man." I paused, then shrugged. "There aren't a lot of hiding places on this island. You aren't going to escape."

His voice trembled. "I could end up in the electric chair for this, if they decide I'm guilty." He scuffed his foot on the step and finally said, "If I turn myself in, will you help me? I know that Florence's lawyer is probably the best there is, but I'd feel better knowing that he wasn't the only one on my side. A lot of people hated Lydia, and somebody set me up to take the blame for her death. I'm not taking the fall for anybody."

I held out my hand and he helped me to my feet. "Come on, let's go call Kyle." As we headed toward the door, I added, "I'll do whatever I can to help. I believe you didn't kill her." I just hoped it was the truth.

Wrapped in a thick terrycloth robe, Aunt Florence was coming out of the downstairs bath when Trevor and I walked through the door. Her long silver hair, unbound from the braid in which she usually kept it, hung flowing and wet to the small of her back. She looked at me, then at Trevor, then back at me.

"Good Lord, you two about gave me a heart attack." Her eyes narrowed as she scanned Trevor's face. "Trevor, you are in a heap of trouble. What were you thinking, running off like that? You can't afford any more stupid stunts." She glanced down at her robe. "Persia, call Winthrop and tell him to get his butt in gear. Once he's here, he can notify the police and help Trevor turn himself in. I'll go get dressed."

Before either of us could say a word, she turned and disappeared up the stairs. Trevor slung himself into the rocking chair, a pained look on his face. He knew better than to cross Aunt Florence — we all did. I thumbed through her address book and punched in Winthrop Winchester's number, keeping an eye on Trev so that he didn't bolt. The lawyer's housekeeper answered, and I gave her my name and told her that Florence Vanderbilt needed to speak to him. Within less than five minutes, he was on his way.

I motioned for Trevor to follow me into the kitchen, where I started a pot of coffee and fished out a plate of cookies. As an afterthought, I plopped a thick hamburger patty in the skillet.

"You hungry?" I asked.

He nodded.

"You like mustard, ketchup?" I asked.

"Yeah. No mayo though. What are you doing? Fixing my last supper?" His gaze darted toward the back door. It occurred to me that if he was guilty, he might be thinking about the hammer and where he'd left it. If not, he might just be frightened. Either way, I couldn't let him escape.

"No, just feeding you before reality hits and you faint. You look like you're starving." Trev settled down as I buttered a hamburger bun and popped it into the toaster oven, then placed a thick slice of cheddar over the ground beef once I'd flipped it. By the time I finished cooking the burger, Aunt Florence had returned, wearing a mu'umu'u cut from black tapa cloth and covered with green and purple patterns. Her hair was tidily braided, caught by a green ribbon at the end.

She nodded approvingly at Trevor as he

ate. "Good thinking, Persia. We don't want the boy lightheaded. Did you get hold of Winthrop?"

"He'll be here in a few minutes. He said not to call the police until he gets here." Trev ate at the breakfast nook while I washed up the pan and Aunt Florence tended the pot of coffee. I was just about to hang up the dishtowel when the doorbell rang. The three of us played round robin, staring at the door, and then finally, Aunt Florence made her way over and peeked out the peephole.

"Shoot," she said, hurrying back to us. "It's Kyle. I'll keep him in the living room while you two hide in the den. Don't make any noise. We want Winthrop here before Kyle sets eyes on Trevor."

I grabbed Trevor's hand and pulled him into the den, where I motioned for him to sit down, then cracked the door a sliver to see if I could hear what was going on. Unfortunately, their voices were indistinct and the steady drone of the ceiling fan drowned them out. With a shake of my head I gently eased the door shut, then sat down next to the shivering young man and put my arm around his shoulders.

"It will be all right," I whispered. "Winthrop's a damned good lawyer."

"But what if he can't find the evidence we need to prove I'm innocent? A lot of guys go to jail for crimes they didn't commit. I don't want to spend my life behind bars just because my girlfriend dumped me and I yelled at her."

I shuffled through the top right drawer of Aunt Florence's desk where she kept some of her medications. There, in a bottle that I recognized immediately, was the aromatherapy blend I'd made for her to calm her nerves. I'd designed the scent to soothe anxiety and reduce stress.

I unscrewed the top and motioned for him to give me his hand, then dabbed a few drops on his fingers. "Hold your fingers under your nose," I said. "Breathe slowly and evenly."

Trevor lifted his hand to his face and did as I asked. After a moment, I could see his shoulders loosen just a little, and he slumped back in the chair and closed his eyes, resting his head against the cushion. Just then, there was a tap on the door. Aunt Florence's voice echoed from the other side.

"Winthrop is here, I'm going to let him in now." She ushered in the lawyer, a tall, stocky, beady-eyed man with a Fu Manchu moustache. He wore a dark gray suit and was carrying a briefcase.

After giving me a perfunctory nod, he said, "I'd like to talk to my client alone for a few moments, if you two ladies will excuse yourselves." As we closed the door behind us, I could hear Trevor as he began to answer Winthrop's questions.

Kyle didn't look happy. He shifted his weight as he leaned against one of the pillars on the low wall that ushered the foyer into the living room, but said nothing. Aunt Florence ignored him. I followed suit. Within a few moments, Winthrop Winchester entered the room and spoke in quiet whispers with the chief of police. After Kyle gave him a perfunctory nod, the lawyer disappeared again, then returned with Trevor in tow.

Trevor's gaze flickered over to me. I gave him a stalwart smile, and Aunt Florence patted his shoulder as he passed by. When he was standing in front of Kyle, he straightened his shoulders.

Winthrop cleared his throat. "My client wishes to surrender himself at this time. He is doing so in order to clear his name, not as an admission of guilt." Winthrop listened while Kyle read Trevor his rights, asked if he understood them, and then snapped on the handcuffs. The three men turned and silently passed through the door.

Chapter Seven

I woke to a piercing shriek that turned into a cock-a-doodle-doo as I came to full waking consciousness. As I lay there, trying to shake myself out of my dreams, another round of crowing split the air and I jumped out of bed and yanked open the curtains. Yep, just as I thought. For the first time since I'd moved back to Moss Rose Cottage, Hoffman had decided to hightail it up on the roof and let out a brazen war cry.

Within minutes, I heard a thumping on the stairs as Auntie came rushing into my room. "What's that racket? Not Hoffman?"

I pointed out the window, to where he'd picked a spot to make his stand. "Want me to shoo him down?"

"No! He's not geared toward flight. The stupid bird hardly ever goes outside. Persia, I hate to ask this but could you . . ." One look at Auntie's face was all it took. I pulled on a pair of yoga pants and a tank top and gently opened the window. As I climbed out onto the roof, I held my breath, praying Hoffman wouldn't take it into his head to go zooming off into the wild blue yonder and end up a streak of chicken mush on the sidewalk, but he just looked at me, quizzically turning his head.

The roof near my window was slanted, but not at such an angle that I couldn't navigate it if I was careful, and so I inched my way over to the rooster, gritting as the rain-slicked shingles scraped my hands. "You dumb bird." I kept my voice as pleasant and soft as possible. "Come to mama and we'll make chicken fricassee tonight."

Thank heavens it wasn't raining. Though the roof was wet, I was able to keep my balance and creep right up to his side. Hoffman even helped out, ambling over to stare into my face with his two beady little eyes. I let him get close enough and made a grab with one arm, steadying myself with the other. Bingo! Mission accomplished. Rooster safe and secure. He squawked all the way as I scooted myself back to the window and handed him through to Auntie.

"Here, take him before I decide to make soup." I flashed her a grin to show that I wasn't serious, and she laughed. "How'd he get out?"

She shook her head. "I don't know. He must have slipped out when I woke up around five and decided to step outside for a breath of fresh air. I guess I just didn't notice him. We'll have to be more careful with the doors. The last thing I want is for the cats to get out." She trundled off down the stairs.

After that delightful morning jaunt, I knew I'd never get back to sleep so decided to squeeze in a workout before breakfast. I padded into my home gym. My aunt knew how important fitness was to me, so the day I moved in she handed me a charge card and told me to go crazy at the Fitness Warehouse. I'd taken her at her word and outfitted my home gym with a Bow-Flex machine, stationary bike, treadmill, home Pilates Reformer, exercise mat, yoga mat and blocks, a new stability ball and stretchy bands, and a TV and stereo.

I started out with some basic warm-ups, then decided to work out with my stability ball and stretchy bands. As I reached up, arms over my head, arching my back into a stretch, I fell into the familiar zone that always happened when I set my body in motion. The feeling of movement, of stretching beyond my limitations, energized me and challenged me to go just a little further, to push just a little harder. As soon as I was limber enough, I threw myself into the workout, tuning out everything else until I was done.

By the time I finished, I was ready for breakfast. I jumped in the shower, slid into a flowing beige rayon skirt and a dark brown tank top, and buckled a wide leather belt loosely around my waist, letting it ride on my hips. After slipping on a pair of ankle socks that wouldn't show, I laced up my three-inch-heeled black suede granny boots. Sweeping my hair back into a long ponytail, I quickly curled it into a chignon and fastened it into place with black lacquer chopsticks before descending into the kitchen where Aunt Florence had just finished feeding the Menagerie. She held up a package of bacon and I nodded.

The sun decided to put in an appearance as we fixed breakfast together. It glinted off the water, turning the surface of the Pacific into a gleaming sheet of diamonds dancing on silver. The waves were frothy, but subdued compared to the past few days of stormy weather. I threw open the French doors that led out onto the balcony, letting the cool morning breeze filter in to air out the house.

"I'll fry up the bacon if you make toast and slice strawberries." Aunt Florence yawned. "Hoffman is safely ensconced in his outdoor run, by the way. I think I'll keep him there while we're gone during the day now that summer's coming."

"I wouldn't do that," I said.

"Why?"

"Coyotes. Stray dogs. That run isn't strong enough to withstand a determined attack. I think you should just convert the coal bin into a rooster sanctuary. We don't use it — it was built when the house was and serves no earthly purpose except to encourage the spiders. Have somebody clean it out and renovate it. They can put a sturdy wire door on and bingo — rooster fun."

The coal bin hadn't been built into the basement like in many houses of the era; it was a separate compartment buttressed against the side of the house. If a contractor replaced the doors with wire frame, it would be perfect for housing Hoffman, and if the wire was sturdy enough, would most likely keep him safe.

Auntie nodded, mulling it over. "I hadn't thought of that, but it's a good idea. I don't think we have coyotes here, but you never know. And I do know that those Buffords down the road let their dogs run wild."

I laughed. "So, what's on the agenda today?"

She lined a square skillet with the thick slices of meat. "Well, Kyle said we could reopen Venus Envy whenever we want, now that Trevor's in custody. I have to call the cleaners to take care of that bloodstain on the carpet. And I think we should call Bran Stanton in to cleanse the aura of the shop. He knows what he's doing."

I wasn't going to argue with her there. While not my specialty, the psychic realm was something I firmly believed in and I couldn't imagine opening the shop to customers again without somehow shaking out the energy. Bran Stanton was well known in town for his work with tarot and various other paranormal gadgetry. His twin sister Daphne owned a little bookstore over on Yew Street, where she also sold crystals, candles, and other goodies. We'd had several interesting talks, all good, and I had come to realize that the siblings were both highly intelligent and well educated.

"Good idea. Auntie, do you think Trevor did it?"

She bit her lip. "I just can't believe the boy has it in him to be a killer. But then again, isn't that what everybody says when someone goes over the edge? I don't know, child. I just don't know."

The phone rang and I snagged it up. It

140

was Sarah, finally getting back to me. I quickly sketched out the situation, reassuring her that everything was being done to prove Trevor innocent and that we were standing behind him.

"We'll need you full-time, more if possible. We have to harvest the lilacs and weed the roses and I don't know what else, you'd know better than I do at this point. The problem is that we're going to be short-handed with Trevor out of commission. Today, you'll have to handle the work by yourself. Tomorrow, I'll come home at noon to help. The sooner you can get here, the better, and of course, we'll pay you for any overtime you accrue."

"I've already sheared the flock, so they're ready for summer," she said. "I can spare you a few weeks, but I'll need to get on with my spinning and dyeing in a month. Six weeks at the most, if I'm going to get enough pieces made to sell for the autumn and winter."

Sarah, a forty-two-year-old mother of four boys, raised llamas for their wool, which she spun by hand and dyed. Using the yarn, she wove blankets, hats, and scarves on a loom, and sold them for outrageous prices to the tourists. We carried a few of her items in the shop on consignment and

141

they sold on a steady basis. Sarah also happened to have a green thumb that wouldn't quit.

We made arrangements for the next couple of days and I returned to the table, where I finished my breakfast while filling Auntie in on Sarah's stipulations.

"I thought she might not cozy up to working more hours. Her business is picking up so much that I think we'll lose her in a couple of years — I know her goal is to build into working full-time for herself."

"She's good at what she does." I had one of her llama-wool sweaters and absolutely loved it.

Auntie nodded. "Well, I'll hire somebody to help out if things aren't cleared up in a few days. It won't be easy, but we'll manage." She paused but then left unfinished the thought we were both thinking: What if things weren't cleared up? What if Trevor really did kill Lydia? Dangerous territory, thoughts like that, but I knew that she was thinking them, too.

As soon as we finished eating, we took off for the shop in her car. Baby belched smoke all the way there, and I winced as my aunt hugged the curves with breakneck speed. She drove like a trucker, fast and tight. Her reflexes were spot on, I'd have to give her that, but I was amazed that Kyle let her get away with it. Probably pure intimidation.

Venus Envy looked like it always had, with the exception of the yellow crime tape tagged across the door. Kyle had told Auntie she could take it down and dispose of it. I glanced at her and she cocked her head.

"I suppose we'd better just go for it. We aren't going to open the shop by standing out here gawking," she said as she reached out and ripped away the tape. After stuffing it in the garbage can near the entrance, she inserted her key into the lock, paused to take a deep breath, then opened the door.

The shop bells tinkled as we soberly entered the store. I noticed right away that the cheery Caribbean feel had dissipated and a pallor hung over the room. Even with all the lights on, and the sunlight sparkling through the windows, a gloom seemed to have settled in with Lydia's death.

I gingerly stepped around the blood-soaked carpet. The stain was small, but all too visible and, even more than the sight of Lydia's body, made me queasy. A quiet hush filled the room. I held my breath, shivering. I wasn't really afraid that Lydia's spirit would go winging by, but the smell of death and old blood lingered like stale perfume in some long abandoned boudoir.

"What should we do first?" I asked, setting my purse down on the counter at my station. Something tugged at the back of my brain, a feeling of déjà vu, but I couldn't quite place it.

Florence looked around and I could tell that she was feeling the same thing I was. After a moment she shook her head. "Well, things won't get shipshape with us just standing around here. I'll call the carpet cleaners and get them over here. Then I'll phone Bran Stanton. We can't open to the public until everything's taken care of. Why don't you go in the office and check the messages." As I turned to go, she added, "And I don't want to know if Heddy called, unless she wants to make an appointment for a facial or her nails."

I hesitantly made my way to the office. This was where they'd found Trevor's hammer, I thought as I opened the door and flipped on the lights. Everything seemed as it should be, except for a small series of darkened smudges on one cushion. Blood . . . Lydia's blood. Skirting the chair, I made my way behind the desk and tried to focus on my task at hand. I rewound the answering machine tape and turned it on, pen and pad ready to take notes.

There were five calls asking when the shop was going to be open and three calls from Heddy suggesting we "do lunch" as soon as possible — which meant she was snooping for the dirt. The last call, however, stood out from the others. A muffled voice came on the tape, saying only, "Trevor didn't do it," before abruptly hanging up.

Startled, I stared at the recorder, then quickly rewound the tape and played it again. Yes, I'd heard what I thought I heard. I leapt out of the chair and raced into the main shop. "Auntie! Auntie! Come here, quick!"

Aunt Florence held up one finger. She was on her cell phone. "We need you to perform a purification ritual, Bran. I simply won't feel comfortable opening up until something of the sort has been done. The carpet cleaners are coming today at three. Can you come over this evening? Around six? Wonderful. I appreciate it . . . yes, that works just fine for me. Thank you, and see you then." She flipped the phone shut. "Bran will be over tonight. What is it?

You look like you've seen a ghost." With a nervous laugh, she added, "You didn't, did you?"

"No, thank heavens. That would be all we need. But come with me. There's a message you have to hear." We hustled back into the office, where I replayed the tape for her. We listened to it twice. "What do you think of that?"

She frowned. "No telling whether it's a man or woman, at least not to my ears. What time did it come in?"

I checked the machine. "Eight-thirty. Shortly after Trevor was arrested last night, it looks like. News must travel fast."

Aunt Florence let out a sigh. "It could be anybody — a friend trying to help him, or perhaps somebody who saw something. Whatever the case, we have to give this to Kyle. I'll call him and tell him to get his ass over here. Meanwhile, will you start cleaning the counter and surrounding shelves? We don't want a single blood spatter left. That would be a faux pas I wouldn't want to have to live down. And be sure to wear rubber gloves — I don't want you taking any chances. I'll be out to help in a moment."

I wandered into the utility room where we kept the washer and dryer to wash the face towels and other supplies used for the facials, manicures, and pedicures that we offered in the shop. The cleaning supplies were in the lower cupboard and I rummaged through until I found a good-sized bucket, which I filled with warm water, soap, and enough Clorox to choke a skunk. It made my eyes sting but, like my aunt, I had no intention of leaving any shelf untouched where Lydia had made her last stand. I pulled on the rubber gloves and headed back out to where my aunt was busy clearing off merchandise.

As I scrubbed away, trying to avoid the bloodstain on the floor, my thoughts wandered back to the tape. Trevor couldn't have made it himself. He was in custody by the time the machine picked up the phone call. Who else could have known he'd been arrested? Well, actually, a lot of people probably knew that the police were looking for him. Gull Harbor was, after all, one of those small towns where word traveled fast. Chances were just about everybody knew that he was wanted for Lydia's murder.

It might have been one of Trevor's friends. His alibi put him at the bowling alley until around eight, shortly after which he supposedly got a call from Lydia. However, he couldn't account for the time during which she was murdered. Maybe one of his pals wanted to help out and thought an anonymous tip would do the trick. But why call us? Why not the police?

As I cleaned off the corner of the counter the image of Lydia's bruised temple and the bloody back of her head flashed through my mind. Had she been dead when she fell? Had the blow to her forehead hurt — flesh kissing the sharp marble edge? Shaking a little, I leaned my head against one of the shelves just as the shop bells chimed and, grateful for any distraction from my gruesome task, I stood up to greet whomever it was.

Kyle Laughlin strode in, looking grim. "You found a tape?" he asked.

I wiped my hands on a towel. "Yes, the answering machine tape. It has a message on it about Trevor." He followed me back to the office, where Aunt Florence was poring over an invoice. She set the paper aside and motioned for us to take a seat, then played the tape for Kyle.

He frowned at the machine. "I need to take that in for evidence, Miss Florence. I don't know what this could mean — it's not much help as far as I can tell — but we have to examine anything to do with the case."

She made sure the battery was firmly in place so that the machine wouldn't lose its settings, then unplugged it and handed it to him. "Kyle, you know Trevor didn't do it."

He shrugged. "Regardless of what I think, I can't let my personal opinions interfere with the investigation. This morning we checked out Lydia's phone records — both her land line and her cell phone. There was no record that she called Trevor the night she was murdered. So either he's lying, or somebody else called him, pretending to be Lydia."

"Or she called him from a pay phone. Did you ever think of that?" Aunt Florence squinted.

Kyle shrugged. "Yes, Miss Florence, we thought of that. He has caller ID on his cell phone, and when we went through the received calls, there was one logged in at approximately the time he told us that Lydia called. It came from a pay phone in the Delacorte Plaza, but there's no way to prove it was from her. There's something else. Your golden boy has a record."

"What?" Florence looked shocked. "Trevor's been in trouble? What for?"

Kyle leaned back in his chair, his lips set in a thin line. "Assault. Four years ago

149

when he was nineteen he hit his girlfriend and gave her a black eye. He claims that he went to counseling, that he only did it that one time, but it still counts as a history of abuse. And our records show that Lydia was in the process of swearing out a restraining order on him. She noted on the request that he was stalking her. He says that he was just trying to get a few answers about why she broke up with him. Things don't look good for him right now."

My heart sank as I glanced over at Aunt Florence. Could our instincts be that far off? Had Trevor killed his ex-girlfriend in a fit of jealous rage? It happened all the time. Nice guy turns psycho, kills family or friends. People shocked because he was always the quiet type. The news was filled with stories like these.

My aunt stood up and, for the first time since I'd moved to Gull Harbor, she looked worn out, older than her years. "Well, thank you, Kyle, for coming over. I hope that tape helps."

He nodded. Then, as if he could read how weary she was, he added, "Cheer up, Miss Florence. Maybe new evidence will turn up to clear him. The case is still young." I walked him to the door, mired in the awful feeling that Trevor was facing a bleak future, if any future at all. Just before he left, Kyle turned to me and said, "Persia, we don't see eye to eye, but can I give you a piece of advice?"

"What is it?" I really didn't want to listen to anything he had to say but wasn't feeling up to a battle of wits. I just wanted him to leave so we could finish cleaning and try to get things back to some semblance of normalcy.

He hesitated, then said, "Don't underestimate Trevor just because you think he's nice. Lydia may have been hell on wheels, but she didn't deserve to die like that. Whoever killed her set her up as far as we can tell. It's obviously premeditated. Why else would she have been in your shop after hours?"

"I'd like to know why she was in our shop at all. Trevor's not the brightest boy, but he's not stupid enough to kill somebody in a place that would leave him one of the primary suspects."

Kyle shook his head. "People don't always think clearly when they're upset. Sometimes they do stupid things. Or want to . . . I know. Believe me, I know." Something in his tone of voice told me that Kyle had seen too much of the darker side of the human psyche, given the nature of his job. Gull Harbor might be a small community, but it wasn't immune to the violence that pervaded the country.

I reached out to shake his hand. I might not like him, but I did understand his position, regardless of what he thought. "Thank you, Kyle. I know you're trying to protect us. We'll be careful."

He raised one eyebrow, but clasped my hand firmly. As he left, I locked the door behind him. I returned to my cleaning with a sigh, and after a few minutes, Aunt Florence came out to help me. We sweated away in silence, polishing and scrubbing until every shelf in the place gleamed.

Chapter Eight

While the carpet cleaners went to work on the blood stain, Aunt Florence and I spent an hour at the BookWich, eating thick ham sandwiches and tomato-basil soup. By the time they cleared out, it was going on four-thirty and we were able to finish organizing the shelves before Bran arrived.

Less than forty-eight hours ago, Lydia Wang had stood in our shop, facing the counter, while some psycho bludgeoned her to death. As we worked in silence, every now and then, I thought I heard something, but when I stopped to listen, the noise turned out to be a truck passing by or a sudden gust of wind rattling the doors. By a quarter to six, we were done. The shelves gleamed, the stock was in clean, orderly rows, and the counters sparkled. But a gloom still hung in the air.

"Do you feel that?" I turned to Auntie. "Like something is clouding the shop."

She nodded. "That's why I asked Bran to come in. If anybody can get rid of it, he can. Tawny's refusing to open up in the mornings anymore, unless one of us is here with her."

"That means we'll have to take turns getting down here an hour earlier. She's really spooked, isn't she?" I didn't look forward to being on a restrictive schedule, but there wasn't much we could do about it. Tawny had every right to be creeped out and, as our employee, her safety was our concern.

Auntie picked up the tray containing her cleaning supplies and shrugged. "She's young, she'll get over it. Until then, we'll show up early and make sure she feels safe." She smiled. "I think the girl will bounce back before too long. You can't let fear rule your life, and I hope she'll realize that in time."

I was about to go through my station for a last wipe down when the door opened and Bran Stanton strode though. Bran was . . . how to put it . . . an interesting man. He and his sister Daphne had moved here about five years ago, from what Barb told me. I'd been intrigued when I met them both at a New Year's party to which my aunt dragged me.

Fraternal twins, their resemblances didn't end with looks. They had similar mannerisms, expressions, and finished each other's sentences. I thought they might be a little younger than me, although I wasn't sure. Both brother and sister had a timeless quality, a maturity not usually found until the later years in life. Together, they made an imposing pair. Neither one was married, although Daphne was supposed to be engaged to a professor who was on the teacher-exchange program for a year, over in England.

Bran peeked around the door, then waved before lugging in his briefcase and a tote bag. I caught my breath. Despite our previous encounters, it hadn't registered just how handsome he was. Dark curly hair cascaded past his shoulders and was caught back in a ponytail, and a well-trimmed beard hugged his chin. He favored black jeans, like me, and was wearing a green tank top and, over everything, a black duster kissed the top of his motor-cycle boots. Completing the picture, an Aussie bush hat perched on his head with carefree abandon.

He gently set down his briefcase and tote bag, removed his duster, then swept Aunt Florence up in a bear hug. "Hey, Miss Florence! You look younger every time I see you." He sounded genuinely happy to see her.

"Bran, you're a sweetie, but save your flattery for my niece," Auntie said, but her cheeks were glowing as she motioned me over to her side.

I stepped out from behind the counter and held out my hand. "Nice to see you again."

As his fingers brushed mine, a tingle of shockwaves raced through me and I pulled away abruptly, trying not to blush. He had magic hands, all right.

"Persia, good to see you, too. You look nice today." His eyes flickered over me from head to toe, but with a respectful demeanor; not once did he invade my space. Before I could say a word, he turned to Aunt Florence. "Somebody killed Lydia? I don't know what this world is coming too. Granted, she was asking for trouble. When you treat people like dirt, you have to expect that somebody's going to object. But I can't believe she was murdered like this."

Aunt Florence nodded. "The girl made a lot of enemies. I'm just sorry Trevor got caught up in the maelstrom. He's a good boy and I'll stand beside him until they prove beyond all doubt that he killed her." She sighed. "I'm not looking forward to our reopening tomorrow. The gossip mill will be going full tilt and you know that

Heddy Latherton will show up, looking for dirt."

Bran's dimples crinkled. The deep lines belied how much laughter had passed through his life. "We'll see what we can do about putting a stop to that before it begins." He opened his tote bag and pulled out a short bundle of tightly tied sage — a smudge stick — and a Tibetan singing bowl. Venus Envy carried smudge sticks, as well as small singing bowls, although Bran's was larger and more ornate than the ones we kept in stock.

Aunt Florence set out a few purple and white taper candles. "Do you need anything else?" she asked.

Bran studied the counter for a moment, and I had the feeling he was listening to something that neither Auntie nor I could hear. After a moment, he shook his head. "No, I've got everything. Why don't you two come back in about an hour? I work best alone."

Disappointed, I realized we weren't going to be allowed to watch. I leaned on the counter. "You mean we have to leave? I thought we'd get to see you in action." Nope, wasn't just saying that because he was a handsome man. Not me. I could rationalize a better reason than that. After

157

all, I had friends in Seattle who worked with psychic energy, but had never had the opportunity to participate and I'd always wanted to observe.

He laid one hand over my own, and I felt weak in the knees. "Lydia died violently. That kind of death can leave a stubborn mark on the energy of a place. Even if she passed through the veil quickly, the act itself embeds what I call a psychic engram onto the area."

I looked at him quizzically. "Engram?"

"Think of it this way: The memory of the act becomes imprinted in the space in which it took place. That's what often happens when people talk about hauntings. The spirit doesn't necessarily hang around, but sometimes the energy of the death itself does. I need to focus in order to clear the shop and, frankly, I can't do that with you around. You'd distract me." He beamed at me, throwing me off guard.

"I suppose I could be insulted by that, but I'm not."

He winked, then abruptly turned back to double-check his supplies. Oh yeah, he was charming all right.

"Come on, Auntie," I said. "Let's go talk to Barb."

We headed over to the bakery. Dorian

was in the back while Barb minded the counter. She brightened when she saw us.

"I am so glad you're here," she said, immediately filling a plate with doughnuts and hot buns. "Today has been the day from hell. You wouldn't believe the rush we've had."

We settled in at a table and she joined us, bringing the iced tea pitcher with her. "What's going on?" my aunt asked.

"What do you think? Lydia's death. Since you were closed this morning, everybody and their brother popped in here to ask what I knew about Trevor being arrested. People seem to think that since Persia and I are such good friends, I'm harboring secret information. I can't seem to convince them otherwise."

I picked up a chocolate éclair and bit into it. The creamy filling flooded my mouth in one big wave and I swallowed, then licked my fingers. "Well, I wish I did know something more. I might be able to help Trevor if I did."

My thoughts wandered back to the message on the answering machine. Kyle had promised to do his best, but he had been skeptical whether they could make out any more than we had.

Barbara leaned back in her chair. "Well,

I wish to hell whoever killed Lydia hadn't run off with that mirror. It was one of a kind. Trevor certainly wouldn't have had any use for it."

"True," I said. The missing mirror bothered me, too. I knew it related to Lydia's murder, but I couldn't figure out how or why. Kyle didn't seem to think it mattered, but I had a gut feeling that the murder and theft were linked and if we solved one, we'd solve the other.

Ever since Barb had given me the mirror, I'd noticed something odd about it. Aphrodite's Mirror reflected hidden assets — as if reaching into the soul and pulling all of a woman's charms to the forefront; a beauty the majority of women never recognized as being their birthright. Almost as if the looking glass could reveal a glimpse of all the qualities they wanted to project to the world . . . confidence, sexiness, poise.

All attributes that Lydia possessed, except for personality. The fact that she'd wanted it so much told me that maybe it revealed a hidden spark in her, too — something that she'd never been able to dredge to the surface. There had to be a link between the theft and Lydia's murder.

"What are you thinking about? You seem a million miles away." My aunt polished off her doughnut and finished her coffee.

I told her. "It's ludicrous to think that Trevor would take the mirror after he murdered her. He had no motive. Men weren't attracted to the mirror."

"I know, but we have to give Kyle something to go on if we expect him to act. And he may be right — the connection may be incidental. That's a hard lesson I've learned over the years; never jump to conclusions because you may well be wrong." She sighed. "I wonder how much longer Bran is going to be? I'd like to get everything ready to open up again tomorrow. It's going to be awkward at first. You and Tawny need to prepare for a rush of curiosity seekers."

Great. Just what we needed — people who buttered their bread on misfortune. "You can bet your ass Heddy Latherton will be in," I said.

Auntie grimaced. "Don't remind me. That woman has done more harm in this town with her mouth than a kissing bug with mono."

Barbara glanced at the clock. "Almost seven." She stood and yawned. "I hate to break this up, but we've got to close up shop. You're welcome to stick around, but I need to give Dorian and Ari a hand."

We gathered our purses as Bran stuck his head in the door. "You can come back now, ladies," he said, giving Barbara a little wave.

"Okay then," she said, her hands full of empty trays that were on their way to the dishwasher.

Even from the outside, Venus Envy looked better — there was a welcoming feel to the door and the moment I entered the shop I could feel the difference. The energy had shifted. The shop's aura sparkled as brightly as the counters. I caught a whiff of burning sage, a comforting scent that soothed my frazzled nerves. I'd gotten in the habit of burning it regularly back in Seattle and now realized just how much I missed the woodsy aroma. As I glanced around the shop I realized that whatever energy had been knocked out of kilter by Lydia's murder was back in alignment. The air felt clean again, the gloom swept away by some cosmic broom leaving light and clarity in its wake. If Lydia's spirit had lingered after her death, there was no sign of her now.

Aunt Florence took a deep breath and let it out slowly. "This is so much better. Thank you, Bran."

He gave her a kiss on the cheek. "Not to

worry, Miss Florence. You shouldn't have any problems now." He paused, looking a little uncomfortable.

"What is it?" Auntie asked.

"There is one more thing . . . I didn't know whether to bring it up or not."

"Go on," I said, curious.

He slid his hands in his pockets. "All right, then. While I was smudging the shop with the sage I had a sense . . . I suppose you'd call it a flash. I think there's a man who holds the key to a lot of Lydia's secrets, but he's hidden from my view."

"You don't know who it is?" I asked, curious. Intuition was something I understood.

"No, I don't. And I don't have the faintest idea where you can find him. I wasn't going to mention it because the information seems so nebulous, but then thought maybe I should." He stopped, looking slightly embarrassed.

Auntie and I glanced at each other. Well, we had called him in for his expertise, and he was offering what he could.

I squinted, trying to think. *A hidden man who holds many secrets . . .* That could be just about anybody. That was one reason I tended to steer clear of dabbling in spiritual matters; things were seldom cut and dry and — as one friend had told me long ago — spirits could lie just as much as people. Now plants, plants were honest. Their essences contained specific energies, attributes, and qualities, and I got along just fine with them. People — they were another matter. But Bran wasn't pushing himself into the spotlight and he seemed to understand how vague he was being.

"Hmm. You can't pick up anything else?" Auntie said.

Bran shrugged. "I'll see what I can do." He paused, closed his eyes, then after a moment shook his head. "Nothing. Well, that sucks. I wish I could help more, but at least your shop's clear."

He was right on track there. He'd done a wonderful job of cleansing the shop, and was trying to help in his own way.

Aunt Florence patted his arm. "My dear, your advice is appreciated. At some point, we'll know what you're talking about. How much do I owe you?" She opened her purse but he waved her off.

"Forget it. You always know you can call me if you need me. Just steer a few people my way during the summer. Besides, I like doing this. It makes me feel like I've given back to the universe a little for what I've received, you know?" He slipped into his duster, plopped his hat on his head, and gathered his things. On his way to the door, he turned around and said, "Persia, are you doing anything this coming weekend?"

I caught my breath. Granted, I wasn't in the market for a relationship, but that didn't mean I planned on staying celibate. Bran was gorgeous and seemed a likable fellow. In fact, I got the feeling he ran deep behind that fancy-free façade. I tossed him a slow smile. "What did you have in mind?"

He returned my smile and upped the ante a wink. "I thought we might check out Gardner's Gym. They have a rock climbing wall, and I heard that you wanted to give it a try. If I'm not mistaken, you're keen on hiking and mountain climbing, right?"

I glanced over at my aunt, who was trying to hide her amusement. Only two people knew how interested I was in trying out that wall — Barbara and Aunt Florence. Auntie must be the leak. I rolled my eyes at the smile lilting over her lips and turned back to Bran. "I'd love to go. Sunday good for you? Maybe sometime in the afternoon?"

He tipped his hat. "I'll pick you up at

your place around three," he said, then slipped out the door into the deepening dusk.

"Auntie!" I whirled around but Aunt Florence grabbed her purse and pointedly ignored me as she jingled her keys and headed for the door.

"Let's go. The Menagerie will be starved and we'll catch it for sure when we get home."

I stood my ground, hands on my hips. "You told Bran about me, didn't you?" Somehow, she must have picked up the fact that I thought he was cute.

She gave me a gentle smile and slipped her arm through my elbow. "Persia, you probably don't realize this, but you have the same eyes that your mother did — dark and soulful, so deep that a person could fall into them and never come out. I miss Virginia, but you carry her genes, and her passion, and her strength of will. Good God, you remind me so much of her."

I'd seen pictures of my mother. We could have been twins.

"I miss her, I think. I don't remember much about her, you know, except for her perfume. She wore Shalimar." I closed my eyes, conjuring up the all-too few images that remained from my tender years.

"When she used to get ready to go out at night, she'd sit at her dressing table and put on her makeup, and I thought she was the most beautiful woman in the world." A vague memory of my father shouting at her filtered through the image, but I blocked it away. I had so little left of her, I didn't want it tainted with his anger.

Auntie seemed to sense what I was thinking. "Your father was a cold man. I'm sure he never meant for her to follow him across the world, and I'm sure he didn't want to hurt her. But he was a player, and your mother was blind when it came to love. One of her faults."

"I wish I'd had longer to know her," I said as Auntie locked the door.

"And I wish I could have given you more of her. I'm afraid that I wasn't able to teach you some of the lessons she would have. Virginia was a loving woman, open and vulnerable, yet strong and set in her ways. One gift she would have given you, one you're going to need, is how to open up, to let someone through that gate you bar so tightly."

As we headed toward the car, I tried to shrug off her comment. I didn't want to open up my gates and let the world in. "What do you mean? I lived with Elliot for six years."

She stopped under the streetlight, pulling her voluminous jacket tighter. The light shrouded her like a warm halo in the deepening evening. "Persia, tell me this. Did you really ever love him? Truly? You never talked about him like you did. No," she said as I began to protest. "Don't think I'm criticizing you or that I think you should have stayed with him, because he turned out to be pond scum. But in your heart, didn't you know it would be over if he ever got to the point where he asked you to say 'I do'?"

I frowned, scuffing the ground. Maybe Auntie was right. Had I chosen Elliot because I thought he was safe, because I couldn't envision him as husband-material? I'd never once complained about the lack of proposals, never once felt jilted or slighted when he cancelled plans to work late, though now I questioned just what that "work" had consisted of.

Not sure what to say, I sidestepped the question. "So, tell me about Bran. Does he help his sister run her bookstore?" I asked, climbing into the passenger seat and making sure my seatbelt was tightly fastened. Auntie had a way of making me hang onto that belt for dear life.

She gunned the engine and laughed.

"Oh no, my dear. During the summer he runs a tourist boat and teaches scuba diving and swimming. During winter, he teaches classes on woodland survival skills and rock climbing at the community college's adult education center. He's a real outdoor nut."

My heart began to race faster. My aunt had me pegged, collared, and stuck in a box. "Scuba diving? Survival skills? Maybe I'll have to sign up for one of his classes," I said and grinned. Hey, so what if I already knew my way around a snorkel and I could build a fire without a match? Refresher courses never hurt anybody.

Auntie made popcorn so we could have something to munch on while we watched the *New Detectives.* I checked for phone messages, wondering if we'd have a repeat at home of the message we'd received at the shop, but the only person who had called while we were out was Jared.

I glanced at the clock. Too late to call him back tonight, so I jotted a note in my Day-Timer to get in touch with him tomorrow. Just as I finished the phone rang and, startled, I dropped my pen.

Kyle's voice rang out from the other end. "Persia, that you?"

"Yep, it's me all right. What's up?" My gaze wandered over to the television as Auntie flipped it on and settled in her rocking chair.

"I just thought I'd let you know what we've found out about that message."

My attention instantly turned tail. "You found out something? What?" My heart leapt. Was Trevor about to receive a stroke of good luck? But the news wasn't as exciting as I'd hoped.

Kyle cleared his throat. "Hold your horses, it's not that helpful. We checked your caller ID and found out that the call was made from the pay phones in the aquarium at the Delacorte Plaza. Oddly enough, it's the same bank of pay phones where the call to Trevor originated from, the one that was supposed to be from Lydia. We're asking around, trying to find out if the attendants might have noticed anybody making a call around that time, but chances are pretty slim."

I sighed. "Well, finding out where it came from is a start, I guess."

He must have heard the disappointment in my voice because he said, "Hey, your friend has a good lawyer, thanks to your aunt. He'll get a fair trial. We'll keep looking. I know you and Miss Florence set great store by this kid, so I'm willing to take a look at anything you might have, as long as we have some substance to go on and not just wild shots in the dark."

"Say, Jared called tonight. Do you happen to know what he wanted?"

Kyle's voice instantly chilled. "You know better than to ask me. We don't run in the same circles."

Since I'd moved back to Gull Harbor, Jared and I'd picked up where we left off — only as friends. He'd come out of the closet and I realized that he only dated me to cover up his interest in boys, but our friendship had stood the test of time. Kyle and his cousin were still on the outs, but I kept hoping they'd make up. Apparently, I'd been hoping in vain.

"Yeah, right. Stupid of me to ask."

He cleared his throat. "Persia — about Jared," he said, slowly as if he was debating on whether to go on.

"Yes?"

A pause. "Nothing, never mind. I haven't heard from him in awhile."

I hung up slowly. Well, at least this time we'd managed to remain civil. Maybe there was hope yet. I told my aunt what they'd found out. She looked as crestfallen as I felt.

"We have to keep our hopes up," she said. "I simply refuse to let them railroad Trevor. Kyle thinks he's being open-minded, but the truth is, he going to rush this through. I know it — I just know it. I talked to Wanda Jansworth today — she's Winthrop's receptionist. She told me that the Wangs are already putting pressure on Kyle. They have a lot of clout in this town, and Kyle is in an elected position. We can't give up because I don't for a minute believe that the law's on Trevor's side."

Unfortunately, I had a sinking feeling she was spot on. Kyle was being as nice as he could, but I knew he thought Trevor was guilty, and I had no doubt that he'd push for a trial as soon as possible. Winthrop could probably get an extension, but it was impossible to avoid the fact that Trevor was in a lot of trouble, without much hope in sight.

Chapter Nine

In the morning before we left for the shop, I put in a call to Jared. His first class was at seven AM so I figured he'd be back in his office by the time I phoned, and I was right.

"What's up?" I asked when he answered the phone.

In the intervening years before I moved back to Gull Harbor, Jared got a degree in computer science, went to work for Microsoft for a few years, then quit to move back to Gull Harbor and teach computer science in the community college. He did some consulting on the side and made a tidy income. He'd offered to help us buy a new computer system for the shop, but Auntie was stalling. It meant just that much more work learning how to use it.

"Kyle called me last night, told me all about Lydia, and asked me to keep an eye on you."

That surprised me. Kyle's distaste for his cousin was obvious. Jared had confided in me that they were still on the outs. "What?

But you two never talk."

Jared cleared his throat. "Well, darling, he's worried about you and your aunt and he knows you'll listen to me where you might not listen to him. He asked me to tell him if you said anything strange or odd about the case."

Hmm. Sounded like Kyle was fishing for information that he might suspect Auntie and I were hiding. Maybe, but then again, maybe not. His concern for our safety seemed genuine. I sighed and ignored the thought that he was using Jared to get info out of me. No use in stirring the pot, and I might be wrong. What puzzled me was his trust in Jared's confidence. "What makes him think that you'd tell him anything I confided to you?"

"I asked him that," Jared said. "He said that he knew I wouldn't want anything to happen to you, so I'd better let him know what was going on."

Well, that answered that. Kyle *was* worried about us, but why? He already had Trevor in custody. Maybe he knew something that we didn't. If so, I knew we'd never pry it out of him. We weren't exactly friends, and even Auntie wouldn't be able to squeeze him on official business. I changed the subject, launching into a discussion about my upcoming self-defense class. Jared had volunteered to play the part of the attacker; he wore padding to give my students someone to practice on. A good sport about it, he was as thrilled as I was when one of the timid students opened up and really let fly.

After breakfast, Auntie and I took off for the shop. The weather hadn't made up its mind yet about what it wanted to do. Patches of sky were peeking between clouds that threatened to make good on their promise of more rain, but it looked like the sun would have a brief foray before they took over. I inhaled deeply. The scent of water permeated the air; we'd be drenched before night. Spring in western Washington — water, water, and more water.

Tawny was waiting next to the bakery. Good to her word, she had refused to open up alone. I unlocked the door and propped it open to clear out the last lingering hints of burnt sage, while my aunt disappeared into the office. Tawny looked around, a nervous glint in her eye.

"So, like, you cleaned up the blood and everything?" Her eyes were fixated on the carpet where Lydia's body had sprawled.

"Yes, Tawny. Don't worry. The carpet

and all the shelves have been cleaned, and Aunt Florence asked Bran Stanton to come in and perform a purification ritual. Everything's all right." Even as I said it, I knew it wasn't true. Everything was far from all right. Lydia had been murdered in our shop and, as nasty as she was, she didn't deserve that. When Tawny still didn't budge, I asked, "Were you friends with her?"

She gave me a startled look. "Friends? As if. I knew her in school and all, but we didn't run with the same crowd. By junior high, half the class hated her and she got worse as the years went on. I mean, it's awful that somebody killed her, but if you want to know the truth, a lot of people had reason to. She was downright vicious to anybody who wasn't part of her own little clique."

Hmmm . . . it seemed as if bitches were born, not made. "Anybody in particular that she tormented?"

Tawny popped her gum and laughed. "Yeah . . . let's see . . . Corky — he was president of the chess club back then, and Lydia talked two of her jock friends into pantsing him in front of the whole school. Nobody knew he was a cross-dresser until then. And Shawna. Lydia stole her boyfriend the day before the prom just because Shawna bought the dress Lydia wanted. Who else? Edgar — Lydia used to cheat off his homework."

I could tell that Tawny was starting to get warmed up and settled myself down to listen.

"Don't forget Brandy. Lydia turned her in for possession of pot and got her suspended and thrown in juvie for a few days, which put an end to the chance she had for a Vandyke Scholarship that would have paid her tuition for four years of college. The scholarship went to one of Lydia's friends instead. Funny thing is, Brandy never smoked pot so how the stuff got in her purse is a mystery."

"What about Trev? Tawny, did Trevor have any run-ins with Lydia back then?" Whether or not that would have any impact on the case, I didn't know, but it seemed like a good thing to ask.

"Oh yeah. Trevor had a thing for her even back then, but she ignored him until about a year ago. She didn't bother him, though — not like the other kids. He was cute and I guess she was keeping him in the wings for one of those in-between-serious-boyfriend times. Who else? Tina, the fat girl of the class. Lydia made her absolutely miserable, even though Tina was talented and funny. Lydia used to call her some awful names. Oh — and Debbie. Lydia really had a chip on her shoulder about Debbie for some reason. Should I go on? There are more."

I shook my head. Her list sounded like roll call from a body-count movie and reminded me of what high school in Gull Harbor had been like. Cliques rule, everybody else drools. And Lydia reigned supreme over all. Nightmare on Prom Street.

"Sounds like she terrorized your class." I readied my station and leaned back in my chair.

Tawny perched on the counter, swinging her legs. "I guess. My friends and I, we didn't pay much attention. We just tried to avoid getting caught near her. We used to joke about it. Who was going to be her Victim of the Day and all. I never made it onto her list, but a lot of people hated her, Persia. Even some of the teachers. And yet, ya know, she ended up homecoming queen and she was voted 'most likely to succeed' for the senior yearbook."

She stretched and wandered over to the counter, where she began folding a stack of star-and-moon print scarves while I digested what she'd said. Even when I'd been in junior high, the cliques had been just as bad; but since I'd started taking martial arts in seventh grade, I'd escaped all that. Nobody messed with members of the Tai Kwan Do club, not even the jocks. By the time I graduated early and left home at sixteen, I'd acquired a certain mystique — I didn't have many friends my own age, but I had even fewer enemies.

I shook myself out of my memories and was about to start in on the samples for the Juniper Girl line when the door opened and Heddy Latherton swept through. Great. Just great. I wanted to get some work done today, but Auntie had warned me we'd be deluged by curiosity-mongers. Could I make a quick escape? I glanced at the office door and calculated my speed against Heddy's determination. Nope, I'd lose, hands down. She was headed straight for me, a greedy glint in her eye. The woman was hungry for news. I squelched my instinct to run, bracing myself against her onslaught.

In her mid-fifties, Heddy had been divorced and remarried three times. Third time must have been the charm, because she hit the jackpot with old man Latherton. Chester had been seventy-eight when they married a year ago, my aunt told me, and within two months, he was in his grave. Heart attack, no doubt brought on by actually having to live with his new bride. Heddy had lost a husband, but gained a fortune.

"Persia Vanderbilt! Aren't you looking pretty today — how are you? Is your aunt here? I had to come in and tell you just how much I worried about you two when I found out what happened! What a shame that such a thing would happen in your shop, would you ever believe it? And Lydia, our local beauty queen at that — now who could possibly believe that Trevor would be angry enough to kill her? Of course, you never can tell. They always say it's the quiet ones you have to watch out for."

As she ran out of steam, I pounced on the brief silence. "Thank you for your concern. We're standing behind Trevor in this, and we're positive that the evidence will prove that he's innocent."

It came out sounding stiff, but I had to say something. I just wished I felt as sure as I sounded, but regardless of my own doubts, I had to squelch the rumor mill before it got out of hand. As I listened to her run on at the mouth, a thought began to crystallize that Heddy and her insatiable nosiness might be of some use in our investigation. I doubted that Kyle had bothered to ask her anything; hearsay and rumors weren't evidence.

"Why don't you have a seat and chat with me for a moment?" I said, trying to figure out the best approach. Blunt wouldn't work, Heddy liked to feel as if she were doing her listeners a big favor by parceling out information. I let her drone on for a few moments, then let out a loud sigh.

Her eyes flickered. "Is something wrong, dear?" Yep, a pounce, just like I'd hoped.

"It's just that, oh, it just seems awfully cruel. As you said, who could have hated her that much?" I let my voice drift for a moment. "I mean, wasn't she awfully young to have enemies?"

Heddy gave me a keen look, then glanced around to make sure we weren't being overheard. She leaned in. "That's why I think Trevor did it. He had the biggest motive. My dear, I understand that you and your aunt want to stand up for him, but we have to face facts. Jealousy is a powerful motivator, and brings even the strongest men to their knees. Why my very own Chester —"

Bingo! I jumped on the opening before she could run off on a tangent. "Jealousy?

Well, I know she broke up with him recently but . . ."

A coy smile curled around her lips and
then she winked. "Oh, my dear, it wasn't
the breakup that hurt his ego so much. It
was the other man! Some men simply
cannot stand being supplanted."

Other man? Lydia had already found
somebody else? If that was true, then
maybe Trevor *had* gone off the deep end. I
mulled over the thought for a moment, then
said, "So she was seeing someone else? I'd
heard rumors but . . ." Again, the bait. And
again, she rose like a fish to the worm.

"Well, yes. That's why they broke up,
you know. Lydia told Trevor that she'd
found somebody new. Melinda was talking
to Allison, who told her all about it, and of
course, Melinda told me —"

Whoa, slow down! I cleared my throat.
"Melinda? Allison?"

Heddy was in full thrall now, revved to
go. "Melinda is my youngest niece. Allison,
a friend of hers, was one of Lydia's best
friends. Apparently Lydia found a new
boyfriend and told everybody that Trevor
wasn't worth her time; that her new beau
was far more exciting."

As she paused, I had a distinct tingling sen-
sation in my neck. This was important, even

if I didn't know how or why. "Does anybody know who her new boyfriend is? Was?"

"No," Heddy said, almost sadly. "She wouldn't say. Melissa said Allison gave her the distinct impression that the man might be . . . well . . . on the wrong side of the law or something. But Allison said that she didn't know who it was, although she thought he might have something to do with the contest."

I sat back, pondering what she'd divulged. Another boyfriend, possibly a tad bit shady. Could shady equal dangerous? And then I remembered Colleen's insinuation the other day. *At least I didn't screw the judges in order to win.* Had Lydia slept with the judges in order to get her crown? Could her boyfriend actually be one of the judges? I filed away the thought and gave Heddy a bright smile to ward off further questions.

"Well, that's all very enlightening. What a business, don't you think? Now, did you come in for a facial today, or are you looking for something in particular?"

"Oh, one of your aunt's facials, my dear. They're the best in town."

I escorted her to the counter to make an appointment with Tawny and returned to my station, my thoughts a million miles away from my work. I put away the oils, too distracted to pay attention to what I was doing. I'd mix up some generic rose bath salts. They required little more than measuring and stirring and it meant I could try to sort out what was rapidly becoming a complicated situation.

An hour later I slipped into the office to talk to my aunt, but she was on the phone. I grabbed a notepad and scribbled, "I'm headed to the Delacorte Plaza" and held it up for her to see. She nodded and waved. As I stopped to pick up my purse, I felt the same déjà vu that I had the other day, but damned if I could figure out what it was about. With a shrug, I told Tawny that I'd be out for awhile. As I headed toward the door, Barbara came through it.

"You want to go with me?" I asked after telling her where I was going.

"Sure, just stop in with me so I can tell Dorian. Ari's on top of things today, so I can take off without feeling guilty."

Ari was Dorian's nephew who had recently come to the United States. His uncle hired him and put him to work, and Ari had proved to be a stable and competent righthand young man. The two men just waved when I told them I was kidnap-

184

ping Barb for an hour or so.

I pulled out from my parking space and navigated through downtown Gull Harbor. The air pulsed as shoppers hurried along the sidewalks, trying to avoid the chill in the air by ducking into the various bookstores, cafés, antique stores, yarn and sewing shops, and all the other fun haunts that made up the unique flavor of the town.

Gull Harbor was laid out on a grid, with most of the streets running in a crosshatch pattern. Island Drive ran through the center, crossed by numerous major intersections. Moss Rose Cottage was on the northeast side of town, while Delacorte Plaza sat in the southwest, away from Puget Sound. I turned right onto Morocco Avenue. Traffic was light, though in a month it would be thick with tourists. During the summer months, all the locals took the back roads, avoiding the heavy traffic, and left the main thoroughfares to the sightseers.

Gull Harbor was visitor-friendly. Parking was plentiful, streets were wide and clean, the sidewalks were dotted with benches, flower boxes everywhere were filled with ivy and morning glory, and well-groomed shade trees provided respite from the summer sun and a place to hang

Christmas lights during the winter.

The shop windows were inviting, with few of those hole-in-the-wall dives that made people shiver and cross to the other side of the street. Like all towns, Gull Harbor had a seedy side, but it was found on the outskirts. Over along Oak and Pine and Elmwood the taverns flourished and even a rumored brothel ran under the auspicious eyes of Clarice Wilcox, the local madam. But all in all, crime was under control, and the Gull Harbor that the tourists saw was pristine and beautiful, albeit rainy.

Delacorte Plaza was situated at the corner of Fortune and Gates Avenues, and took up a good block. Essentially a giant shopping mall, the complex housed everything from the Gap to a six-theater movie cinema. The complex also housed a four-thousand-square-foot interactive aquarium at its center. While I preferred shopping in smaller boutiques, I'd been to the DP, as the locals called it, on more than one occasion and always found myself lured into the aquarium, entranced by the beauty of the fish and the sea creatures in the giant backlit tanks.

I pulled into a parking space and turned to Barbara. "Kyle said that both the phone message on our tape and the one that

186

Lydia supposedly made to Trevor originated from the payphone bank in the aquarium, so I guess we should go in and have a look."

Barb nodded. "Let's make a stop on the way. I want an Orange Julius."

The shopping crowd was sparse and we were able to get our drinks without waiting. Within ten minutes we were standing with our backs to a tank containing a variety of jellyfish, staring at a bank of pay phones. Kyle hadn't said just which one it was, but I guessed that it didn't make any difference — it wasn't like I was here to take fingerprints or anything.

Barb glanced over her shoulder at the jellies and shuddered. "They make me nervous. Dorian and I went to Australia a few years ago and I narrowly missed getting stung by a box jelly. One of the sea wasps. We were out on the shore by ourselves, and if Dorian hadn't spotted it and stopped me, I probably would have died."

"You never told me you've been to Australia. What else have we missed dishing about?" I asked, wandering over to read the information on the plaque next to the tank. *Chironex fleckeri*, better known as the sea wasp, had an impressive defense mechanism. Since the creature was rather delicate, its defense acted as a pretty good offense, too.

Actually quite beautiful, it looked like a wispy, bell-shaped lampshade with long flowing streamers. One of the creatures could kill an adult human within minutes, and some of the larger jellies had enough venom to take down a dozen or more people. The poison caused respiratory failure, circulatory collapse, and a nasty shock to the heart unless antivenin was delivered right away. Delightful. I planned on surfing Australia someday. Before I went, I'd be sure to come study these babies a little more closely so I knew what to look out for.

I glanced back at Barbara. "We won't be dipping our hands in the tank, that's for sure. I'm surprised they allow such dangerous creatures here."

She shrugged. "No more dangerous than having a rattler or a fer-de-lance in a reptile house, I guess. The tanks are well sealed and there's no real chance anybody could get in there unless they break the glass. I'd imagine it would take a sledgehammer, because the glass looks tempered to withstand a lot of pressure. But all the same, they give me the creeps." She sucked on her straw. "Well, now that we're here, what do we do?"

Good question. What were we looking for? I realized as I looked around that I had no clue as to what I expected to find. I walked over to the bank of pay phones and eyed them critically. One had an out-of-order sign on it and the date was from last week, so it was obviously out of the running. The other three were all prime suspects. I noticed a woman pushing a cleaning cart toward the back of the aquarium.

"Excuse me!"

She turned. "Yeah? What do you want?"

As I walked over to her, I cringed, but managed to keep my composure. She was a short, rail-thin woman who had to be a rabid chain smoker. Her teeth were yellowed and the wrinkles around her mouth were deep set and premature. The scent of smoke rose from her hair in a stale cloud, gagging me. Clearing my throat, I said, "I'm wondering if I might talk to whoever works the evening shift? Specifically, last Monday night."

She gave me a one-shouldered shrug. "That would be Andy. You one of his bimbos? You look a little old for him."

A little old? I did *not* look my age and I knew it. I shoved aside the comment, focusing on why we were here. "No, I'm not. I'm . . . I'm helping the Winchester Law

189

Firm. We're investigating a murder. I want to talk to whoever was on duty that night."

With her hands on her hips, she snorted. "Won't do you no good. Andy already told the cops everything he saw — which wasn't much, considering he was in the break room when he should have been out here on duty. If you're looking to talk to him, you might as well call him at home because the boss let him go this morning. Lazy little slob." A trickle of spittle flew out of her mouth.

I ignored her churlishness. "Thank you. Do you happen to know where he lives?" Just as I'd figured, she wasn't up on the notion of confidentiality. She sighed and poked around in the desk. Apparently they hadn't bothered to hire someone to fill in for good old Andy yet. After a moment, she came up with a notebook and wrote down a number and an address on a Post-It note for me.

"Here you go. Say, if there's any reward involved, do I get a share of it for making sure you can get in touch with him? My name's Zelda Donovan, by the way. That's D-o-n-o-v-a-n."

I took a deep breath, then immediately wished I hadn't. Not only did she reek of smoke, but of rum as well. I wasn't sure how she managed to keep her job coming to work like that, but it was a pretty good bet that she'd be following dear ol' Andy out the door pretty soon, unless she was related to the owner.

"I'm sorry, we can't discuss matters like that when the case is still open." It seemed a logical answer and she accepted it, nodding like she was in the loop. I thanked her again and Barbara and I hurried out of the aquarium.

I glanced at the paper in my hand. Andy Andrews. Oh boy. With that name, he was probably teased unmercifully during school.

"He lives . . . hmm . . . he lives right across the street. Let's go."

As we were headed out of the aquarium, I saw a rack of brochures on the wall and snagged one. *Stanton Scuba & Snorkeling Services.* So Bran really did run a diving business. I tucked it away in my purse, thinking that maybe I could use a good brushing up on my underwater skills.

The address that Zelda had given us led us directly across the street to a five-story apartment building that looked like it had seen better days. Old and weatherworn, the building appeared to house some of the poorer residents of town. The walls were faded gray stone, and the double doors leading into the building creaked when we pushed through into the lobby. We passed a long row of mailboxes on either side, until we came to the elevator at the end of the hall.

I glanced at the slip of paper again. "He lives in apartment 522A. You want to take the stairs?"

Barbara looked at me like I was nuts. "Why should I take the stairs when transportation awaits?" She pointed to the elevator and, with a grin, I shrugged and hit the button. We stepped into the empty, noisy unit and pushed the button for the fifth floor. The elevator coughed and chugged. For a moment I was worried that it was going to break down with us inside, but then it gave a loud clunk and the doors opened.

"That thing sounds worse than Zelda's lungs did," I said, stepping out into the hallway. Barbara followed me. We were standing in a long hall that was covered in worn sage green shag carpeting. The walls were the color of the filling in Mint Oreos, and windows at opposite ends of the hall overlooked Delacorte Plaza on one side, and on the other, a park of some sort behind the apartment building. There were a few paintings, mostly motel art, scattered along the cracking walls which looked like they hadn't been given a paint job in several years at least. The air was chilly and I shivered, glad that I wasn't living here.

Apartment 522A was at end of the hall. I stood at the door with Barbara behind me, wondering just what I was going to say. Finding no doorbell, I knocked firmly on the door. No answer. I knocked again. Nothing. With a sigh, I turned to Barbara.

"Nada. He's probably out looking for work. I'm going to leave a message and my number." I hunted in my purse for a notepad and pen, scribbled my name and number along with a request that he call me when he got the chance, then slid the paper under the door.

"I guess that's all I can do about him for now. Let's get the hell out of here, this place gives me the creeps."

Barb nodded and we raced out of the building. I glanced back and thought I saw someone watching us from one of the windows, but it was probably my imagination and I shook it off as we headed for my car.

Chapter Ten

I dropped Barb back at the bakery, stopped at Wendy's for a burger and shake, and headed home. It was eleven-thirty and I'd promised Sarah that I'd be there by noon to help out. As I pulled into the driveway the clouds were waging war with the sunlight, but rain was still a few hours away. I hurried into the house, pulled on a pair of black jeans and a forest green tee, then headed out to the gardens.

Moss Rose Cottage sat at the front of the thirty acres. In the backyard a fence divided the gardens from the lawn. I passed through the trellis onto the trail that led past the gazebo, to the acreage where we grew our flowers. As I headed toward the lilac grove, I could hear Sarah cursing. I rounded the curve in the path and saw that she was on her knees, stabbing at the dirt. A blackberry had taken root beneath one of the trees. Her voice rose as she struggled to dislodge it.

"Out, damned root! Out!"

Blackberry roots delved deep, plunging

far below the soil to take hold and spread out, cropping up yards away as new shoots. "Hey, Sarah, having some trouble with MacBlackberry? I hope you haven't seen the ghost of those morning glories we weeded out last month."

She jerked around, blushing. "Hey there, Persia. These things are so stubborn. Honestly, they're such tenacious plants."

"Well, let me help. I'm yours for the afternoon." I slid on a pair of leather gloves and fell in beside her.

She stretched, leaning back. Sarah had a farmwoman's body — sturdy, not too tall, not too short, child-bearing hips. She was tanned from the constant wind and sun but her eyes twinkled bright blue, and she had an infectious good humor that seemed to affect everyone who came into contact with her.

With a glance in my direction, she said, "Can you dig over there while I take this side? I don't think it's created suckers yet, but by the size of this thing, it won't be long. Once it takes hold, it will be almost impossible to eradicate without using an herbicide."

We worked steadily until we came to the root. The blackberry was firmly entrenched, but we managed to yank most of it out and dug a few more trowels of dirt for good measure, hoping to get all the root hairs. Once we were finished, we sat back and stared at the gaping hole.

"People could take lessons from them," she said. "Blackberries never give up. They go after what they want and they usually get it." She wiped her forehead, leaving a streak of dirt behind. "Kind of like my llamas. Those critters are a trial in patience, I'll tell you that. But I guess they're worth it."

At first, I had thought Sarah was some spacey new-age hippie wannabe, but I'd soon discovered that she was practical, grounded, yet deeply spiritual in a way that defied categorization. Her work was a prayer, and everything she did was done with deliberation and a sense of sacred duty.

"Persia, can I ask you a question?" She pushed herself off the ground and produced a couple of buckets from the little motorized cart my aunt had bought for the gardeners to save wear and tear on the back muscles while carting their gear around.

"Sure, what is it?" I accepted one of the buckets and a pair of shears as she set up the stepladders by one of the trees. We ascended and began clipping the flower stems from one of the lilac trees. The flowerets were at the perfect stage for drying for sachets and potpourri, and we'd have to work fast over the next few days in order to preserve the blooms at the optimum stage.

"What's going on with Trevor? You don't really think he killed that girl, do you? I work with him every day and I can tell you, he's not a murderer." She set down her clippers and leaned against her ladder, frowning.

I sucked on my lip. "You know, Sarah, I don't think he did, either. Neither does Aunt Florence and that's why she hired her lawyer to look out for Trev. But the truth is that evidence points to him being guilty and isn't easy to overlook. The chief's just doing his job." I paused, and it occurred to me that Sarah had said a mouthful when she'd said they worked together every day. Maybe she knew something we didn't. Maybe he'd mentioned something to her that could be helpful. "Have the police questioned you yet?"

She shook her head. "No, nobody's said anything to me about it except you and your aunt. And my boys are devastated. Trevor sometimes comes over and helps out around my house. I give him a little extra cash, and the boys think he's *super cool*."

I stared at the tree limb that stretched out in front of me. The tree — or bush, as lilacs were properly called — stood a good eight feet tall. My aunt had asked Trev and Sarah to keep the bottoms of the shrubs clear of foliage, and the grove looked like so many purple puffs. Heavy, drooping flowers scented the air with an intoxicating wash of perfume. Almost overpowered, I found myself getting swept under by the fragrance. With a shake of my head I snapped out of it and selected another stem to clip, dropping it gently in the bucket.

"Sarah, did Trevor ever talk about Lydia to you? Did he ever say anything about his relationship with her?"

Sarah scrunched up her nose. "You know, now that I think about it, he did. A little over a month ago, before they broke up. He said she was the most gorgeous girl he'd ever laid eyes on and that he couldn't believe she was actually going out with him. He seemed totally obsessed by the fact that she'd agreed to date him, so much so that I was a little worried. It seemed like she didn't matter as a person." She leaned against the ladder, squinting as a ray of sunshine broke through the overcast skies and illuminated the grove.

"What do you mean?"

"Well, it's hard to say. Almost . . . like she was a symbol of something to him. Maybe success? Anyway, I tried to warn him to be careful, that looks can be deceiving, but he wouldn't listen."

I wasn't surprised. It was clear to me that Trevor had conveniently overlooked the girl's personality, like so many young men in the thrall of their hormones. He'd seen her as a prize, and whether the prize was bitter or tainted wasn't relevant — all that mattered was that he won.

"What did he say when you warned him?" My guess was that he'd shrugged her off politely and ignored her advice.

She hoisted herself up another rung on the ladder. "That was the strangest thing. He said that he didn't have to worry. He said that he was sure she loved him, even if she wasn't good about showing it. I mentioned the trip to New York, because she'd won the contest and I knew she was supposed to leave soon, but he said 'Don't worry, I've got it under control.' "

"What did he mean by that?" A tingle in the back of my neck told me that whatever

Trev had planned had backfired, but I shrugged it away. Right now, any information we could use would be helpful.

Sarah screwed up her face. "That's what's so odd, and out of character."

Uh oh. "Odd? Odd as in how?"

She sighed, shaking her head. "Persia, he told me that she wasn't going to go. He was absolutely convinced that he could persuade her to stay, that they were meant to be together. I pressured him a little. He finally said, 'Well, if she was going to get married and have a baby, that would stop her from going, wouldn't it?' Then he took off for the house and that was the last time the subject came up. A week later Lydia dumped him and he clammed up. Now she's dead. Do you think I ought to tell the police what I just told you?"

I groaned. Kyle would want to know, that was for sure. As far as I was concerned, it was just one more nail in Trevor's coffin. The stupid kid! What if he'd tried to persuade her to have a baby? Or what if he sabotaged his birth control? But surely she'd been on the pill? She'd been too smart of a girl to leave her protection up to the man.

Whatever went down between them, Lydia had walked out on him. Even I was

200

beginning to believe that her rejection had hurt his ego so bad that he sought revenge, and that wasn't a good thing. If I didn't believe him, how could Kyle? I didn't want to think badly of Trevor, but the way things were headed, he'd be in that cell a long, long time.

"What should I do?" Sarah asked again.

I sighed. She had to tell Kyle, but this could sink Trevor for good and, as it was, the poor kid was already treading water.

"I don't know, Sarah. I just don't know. Let me talk to Winthrop and my aunt." I went back to my lilacs, wishing fervently that I'd kept my mouth shut and not asked so many questions.

When I wandered back to the house around five, I found my aunt on the floor, her briefcase dumped out in front of her, with Buttercup wandering over the stacks of paperwork. Buttercup was a classic silver tabby with beautiful emerald eyes whose personality fit that of her namesake from *The Powerpuff Girls* — in other words: hiss first and ask questions later. Auntie was already in a mood and I dreaded adding to it, but I'd decided that Sarah had to tell Kyle what she knew.

"What's going on? It looks like a whirlwind hit your briefcase."

She glanced up at me, her face a study in "I-am-peeved." "The judge will be arraigning Trevor on Monday for Lydia's murder. Winthrop is trying to stall for more time but Kyle's pushing hard. I think that Charles Wang is getting to him. I'm looking for my address book so I can call a few of my friends and ask them to put the pressure on Chas to back off a little."

As worried as I was about Trevor, I couldn't help but feel sorry for the Wang family. I knelt down beside her and laid one hand on her arm. "Auntie," I said softly, "you can't blame him. His daughter's been murdered. She may have been a first-class bitch to everybody else but the fact remains that she's dead, and she was his little girl. Do you really think you'd do any different?"

A pained expression crossed her face as she tossed the file back on the stack and rubbed the bridge of her temples. "Child, sometimes I wish you weren't so fair-minded, but you're right."

I helped her pick up all the files and carried everything to the table where she could sort it all out. "Auntie, they've got a lot of evidence. Kyle is doing what he has to. And now Sarah has to talk to him." As quickly as I could, I told her what Sarah had told me.

She groaned. "That stupid, stupid boy. Oh, how did he ever get himself involved in this mess? Kyle will use this as an excuse to bulldoze the case along, but you're right. As much as I hate to admit it, we can't keep something like that under wraps." She forced a smile and gave me a tired shake of the head.

I gave her a kiss on the cheek. "I'm going to run and get the mail while you organize your papers and tuck them back in your briefcase."

I ran on out and yanked open the mailbox, glancing at the sky. The sight of the clouds crowding in off the inlet stopped me in my tracks. Picture perfect against the dusky fading patches of blue, they billowed, cruising slowly toward shore. Streaked with long fingers of tangerine that splashed against the sky from a muted sunset, the sky had reached that juncture that signified the perfect hush before night, the moment when birdsong echoed through the air as dusk faded into twilight.

And then, in the space of an instant, what there was left of the sunlight disappeared. Dusk hit full force, bringing with it the chill that always accompanies the Pacific Northwest forests during the night. A peculiar scent of moss and mildew, blended with the smell of moving water, spelled home to western Washingtonians, and it was a smell like nowhere else in the world.

I shivered and pulled open the mailbox, reaching in to grab the handful of letters. As I walked back to the house, one of the envelopes caught my eye. It was addressed to me but by name only, and had no stamp. Someone had shoved it into the mailbox during the day.

As I lightly tripped up the stairs, I opened the letter and withdrew a single page. On it, in letters cut out from a magazine and pasted to the paper, was the message: *"Trevor is innocent. Please help him."*

I stared at the page. What the hell? Was it the same person who had left that message on our machine? I raced inside and, holding the page by the edges to avoid destroying any further evidence, I showed my aunt. "Somebody really believes he's innocent," I said.

Aunt Florence peeked around my shoulder. "Good heavens! Well, I wish whoever's doing this had the guts to step forward. I wonder if they know anything about the murder? Maybe they're afraid?"

She had a point. Of all the reasons to remain anonymous, fear seemed the likeliest motivator. Perhaps the person had seen something that night — maybe witnessed the murder itself? If so, it was feasible that they might be afraid that the killer would come after them if they stepped forward.

"You might be on to something, Auntie." I picked up the phone. "I guess I'd better call Kyle."

"No dear, just put the letter back in the envelope and tuck it in a paper bag. I've got my aqua aerobics class tonight, so I'll stop at the station and talk to Kyle on my way. I'll tell him to talk to Sarah, too." My aunt had been taking water aerobics for a year now and had stabilized her blood pressure, increased her mobility, and lessened the pain that her arthritis caused her.

"That sounds like a plan. I think I'll hit the pillows early tonight. I'm tired and just want a long bath and a good night's sleep."

While Aunt Florence took off to her bedroom to get her suit, I nipped into the pantry and slid the envelope in a lunch sack. I left it on the table and headed for my room, passing my aunt as she was coming down the stairs. "The bag's on the table. Lock the door on the way out, would you? I'm going to be upstairs most of the evening."

"Before you run off, I just remembered — you got a phone call earlier. Someone called for you shortly after noon. I left a message."

I peeked at the board. Andy Andrews had called, and he left his number. "Oh, good! I was hoping he'd call."

"A date?" Ever optimistic, my aunt wanted me to find the right man, even though she knew perfectly well that I wasn't interested in settling down.

"No, not a date. Information that might help Trevor, I hope. Andy was on duty at the aquarium when our mysterious caller left that message for us on the answering machine at the shop."

I picked up the phone. My aunt sat down at the table, waiting to see what I could find out. As I punched in the number, I held my breath, but the phone rang five times before an answering machine picked up.

"I'm outta here. Leave a message, dude. You know the drill."

Oh boy, skateboard city here. I left my name and number again, and hung up. "Looks like we're playing phone tag. I doubt if he knows anything, but maybe I can think of something the police didn't ask."

Aunt Florence waved and headed out to the Gull Harbor Aquatic Center. The residents had fondly nicknamed the center GHAC, pronounced "gak" for short. I glanced at the clock. Too early for bed but I was beat. I decided to watch TV and wandered into the living room, where I found Delilah and Buttercup curled up asleep together in the middle of the sofa. I knelt down and scooped them up in my arms, buried my face in their fur, and playfully chased them out of the room. A trail of startled "purps" and meows drifted in their wake.

"Ha! That will teach you two to interrupt my sleep!"

The remote was sitting on the end table and I grabbed it and fell into the rocking chair, propping my feet on the matching embroidered footstool. With a wide yawn, I flipped on the TV and began to channel surf. There wasn't much on, and I finally settled for watching a special on Discovery about a group of climbers who got stuck up on Everest. Halfway through, I rested my head against the back of the chair and closed my eyes, drifting into that indefinable state between waking and sleeping.

I'd been dozing about ten minutes when the doorbell rang. Who on earth could that be? Barbara always called before she came over. Stifling another yawn, I pushed myself out of the chair and headed toward the door, flipped on the porch light, and took a look through the peephole.

Oh shit! Elliot! What the hell was he doing here?

"What on earth are you doing here?" I said as I yanked the door open.

The stupid grin on his face grew wider. "Persia, I've come to take you home with me! I wrote you a letter but you didn't call. Didn't call at all. It's time for you to come back to Seattle. I haven't got the penthouse anymore, though. The feds confic— consti— confisticated it so you'll have to get a job and an apartment for the both of us."

Joy of joys, he was drunker than a duck in a gin mill, as my Aunt Florence always said. Could he really be so dense as to believe that I'd go back to him? Or was he just on the ego trip of the century? Either way, I had no intention of letting him in the house. I grabbed a sweater off of one of the hooks by the door and slipped into it, then propelled him over to the porch swing. He dropped into it with a queasy look. With luck, he wouldn't upchuck all over the porch.

I leaned against the railing, facing him. "Elliot, I don't know what you expected, but you're not going to find it. I told you not to contact me and I mean it." I folded my arms across my chest.

He gave me a dreamy smile and leaned against the back of the glider. "Did you know your porch moves? Back and forth and back and . . . what was the question? I'm just so glad to see you!"

As he tried to hoist himself to his feet, I lightly jumped back a step. I knew that look. It was his "I-want-a-hug" look and I wasn't about to make nice-nice. "Do you even bother to listen to me? Now, I'm going to drive you to a motel because there's no way you should be behind the wheel tonight, and then tomorrow morning, you're going to leave town and never bother me again." I glanced at his car. It looked intact. I just prayed that he hadn't hit anybody or anything on the way here. "Give me your keys. I'll catch a taxi home."

"Persia, my sweet Persian Rose. I missed you, you know. Even though you were a pain in the butt, I missed you while I was in ja . . . ya . . . ja-yul." He'd reached the point where he was exaggerating syllables in order to remain halfway coherent. Time to get him out of here.

"Stay here!" I pushed him back into the swing — he'd take awhile to get out of it again — and hauled ass into the house where I grabbed my purse and keys, then locked the door behind me. "Come on buster, down the steps." I tugged on his sleeve and he stumbled to the stairs and promptly tripped and spilled headfirst down to the sidewalk.

"Elliot! Oh my God! Are you hurt?" I raced down behind him, praying that he hadn't broken his neck. All we'd need would be a lawsuit from my estranged boyfriend. But, as often happens with drunks, Elliot had gone limp and was fine except for what looked like a scraped nose. He'd been so relaxed I doubted if he'd remember how he got it. I got him up and over to his car, where he puked beside the passenger door while I winced and looked away.

"You done there, cowboy?" Why, oh why had he decided to come looking for me? Was he brain-dead?

He mumbled something, having lapsed into the stage preceding blackout, and I shoved him in the seat and buckled his seat belt. He grabbed my hand and tried to force it down to his pants but I smacked him lightly on the face and he let go, so out of it that I had my doubts that he even knew what he was doing.

"Persia, Persia . . . you're the only one for me. She didn't mean anything, really . . ."

I froze. "What? Who are you talking about?"

He hiccupped and a thin stream of spittle flew out to land on his jacket. "Leah . . . she didn't mean anything. I jus' needed a good lay an you were mad at me —" His voice drifted off and he began to snore.

I stood there a moment, staring at him. Leah? Leah had been our next-door neighbor, a young woman who was short, perky in all the right areas, and who had about as many wits as she did extra pounds. She was as filling as fat-free cookies: all sugar and no substance. Apparently, Elliot had developed a sweet tooth during our time together, and decided I was a little too bitter to satisfy his cravings.

I slammed the passenger door and climbed in the driver's seat. Elliot snored all the way to the Bay-Berry Hotel, a seedy little dive near the docks. After checking in under his name, and paying the bill with three twenties I found in his wallet, I managed to wake him up long enough to get him inside. I scribbled a note, instructing him to never set foot on our property again and to cease all contact with me in any way, shape, or form, then propped it up on the nightstand along with his wallet and keys. I thought about doing something stupid and childish, like writing "Jerk" all over his face, but it seemed more trouble than it was worth.

On second thought, maybe it would teach him a lesson. I dug through my purse and found a Sharpie permanent marker that I used to write labels at the shop and ripped open his shirt, popping the buttons as I did so. He mumbled, but didn't wake up. Good.

In bold, bright red letters, I wrote: "HI THERE! I'M ELLIOT AND I'M A JERK! FOR YOUR OWN GOOD, DON'T DATE ME!"

Grinning, I popped the cap back on the marker and headed for the door. I was done with this fish and he could fry for all I cared. I hied myself over to the diner across the street, where I called a taxi and went home.

Chapter Eleven

I warned Auntie about Elliot while we were eating breakfast. "He's really hitting the bottle now — harder than I've ever seen him, and I don't think jail did him any good. He's degenerated a lot. If he calls, take a message but don't encourage him. I just hope I don't have to get a restraining order." I wiped my mouth on the napkin.

Auntie let out a long sigh. "I hope not, too. I'll try to keep him at bay if he starts calling you."

"I still can't believe he showed up here. I thought he'd gotten it through that thick skull of his that I don't want anything to do with him."

She reached over and patted my hand, then stuck another biscuit in it. "Eat up, you've barely touched your food." As I obediently nibbled on the bread, she added, "Some people just can't accept rejection. He sounds like he's not too swift — and if I remember him right from the times we met — he's not too keen on being pushed aside, either."

That was certainly true. Elliot was so self-centered that he couldn't stand it when anybody else was in the spotlight. "Well, whoop-de-do. He's going to have to get used to the idea that he's no longer a part of my life. And now, I'd better get on down to the shop. I've got an idea." When I laid out my plan for her, she groaned.

"Just keep me out of it. You know how I feel about that woman," Auntie said as I swallowed the last bite, grabbed my purse, and hit the door.

As soon as I got to the shop, I braced myself, looked up Heddy's phone number, and gave her a call. She sounded surprised, but pleased to hear my voice. I had the suspicion that Heddy didn't have too many fan clubs and maybe had fewer friends than she let on.

"I have a really big favor to ask you," I said, knowing full well that she'd respond better if I begged. "I know you're a busy woman, Heddy, but you're the only one I can think of who might be able to help me."

A spark of curiosity rippled through her words. "You know I'm always eager to help out, Persia. Is this about young Trevor?" She lowered her voice, shifting into conspiracy mode.

"Yes, actually. We're helping to pull together his defense, and I was hoping that you might be able to set up a meeting for me with your niece Melinda? And, if possible, her friend — the one you mentioned? I believe her name was Allison?"

That did the trick. Heddy couldn't resist being part of the inner circle and promised to do what she could. I spent the next hour helping Tawny stock shelves, then went over some inventory forms that Aunt Florence had asked me to look through. At eleven, the phone rang.

"Persia, line three. It's Mrs. Latherton," Tawny said.

I picked up the phone. "Persia speaking," I said, tapping my pencil against the desktop.

Heddy's breathless voice came on the line. "Persia? Melinda and Allison can see you at noon — they'll meet you at the BookWich. I hope you don't mind, but I told them you'd buy lunch. That got their attention."

"Not a problem. Thank you so much — I owe you one." I shuddered as I replaced the receiver. Owing Heddy Latherton a favor was not at the top of my wish list, but both she and I knew that she'd collect on it, so why not get it out in the open? I glanced at

215

the clock. Forty-five minutes. I could clear out of a lot of backlogged paperwork in that time and free up my aunt from having to deal with it. Lydia's death had thrown a glitch into our schedule. We needed to balance the books for last week and Auntie hadn't had time to go over everything.

On my way to the meeting, I stopped in at the bakery. Barbara was up to her elbows in dough. I peeked into the kitchen and quickly filled her in on everything, including my lovely experience with Elliot.

She rubbed her nose on her shoulder. "You ever thought of a hit man? I'm sure we could find somebody willing to oblige." With a grin, she added, "If I were you, I'd run him out of town on a rail. That man is trouble, and if his buddies get out — the ones he put away — you know they're going to come looking for him and anybody he cares about. Don't you dare get back together with him."

"I have no intention of getting involved with Elliot again," I said. "I just wish I knew how he got my address. I'm going to throttle whoever it was that spilled the beans." I glanced up at their clock. "I'd better get moving. I'm meeting the girls for lunch in five minutes."

She waved a floury hand at me. "Have

216

fun, and let me know what they say. And what happens with Elliot. I mean it. Call me!"

I blew her a kiss, then headed to the BookWich, wondering what, if anything, I could learn from Lydia's friends. Maybe I'd luck out and they wouldn't be as abrasive as she'd been. I wasn't holding my breath.

When I walked into the café, I immediately zeroed in on the girls, who were waiting near the door. Both young women affected the same haughty look that Lydia had sported, though Allison carried it off a lot better than Melinda. I introduced myself and led them to a table, scoping them out as I slid into my chair. By the time the waitress handed us menus, I had them pegged.

Melinda opened her menu, studying it closely. She took after her aunt, desperately wanting to be a major player in the social strata. She'd never make it, though. While she had enough money to polish the rough edges, she lacked that *je ne sais quoi,* that cutting-edge persona that often passed for class among Gull Harbor's nouveau riche.

New money and old money were two different animals. Old-moneyed gentry wore their class quietly. They might have servants but would treat them with aloof dignity. They might have money but would never flaunt it like a matador in a bull ring. They might blackball you from their clubs, but would never be so gauche as to tell you that to your face. They'd charm you out the door, and you'd walk away with dignity.

But among the nouveau riche in Gull Harbor, there were two distinct societies. The first were the techies who were rich because of their jobs, not because they aspired to be rich. They shopped at Trader Joe's and Whole Foods Market and, since most were liberals, contributed to every Green cause you could name. With environmentally friendly mansions overlooking the ocean, they were primarily focused on their work. Class structure meant little when it came to bank balances. Looks were no help in identifying them. That twenty-two-year-old skateboarder who frequented the neighborhood skate park might be a barista at Starbucks or pulling down six figures at Sand Bar Software.

Then there were the nouveau riche that included Lydia and Allison's strata. With money from family businesses that managed to grow over fifty to seventy years, they formed cliques to which only the most beautiful trendsetters were allowed access, and woe be to those who let their style slip even once in public. Shame and ridicule were powerful weapons among this wealthy subset, frequently used to keep the members in line. They weren't invited to mingle with old money, generally, but they had their own country clubs and lounges and they never, ever slummed.

And Melinda and her aunt Heddy desperately wanted to be accepted by the snot-nosed group of upstarts, but neither would ever make it further than the outer court. They simply didn't have the necessary cachet.

"Is that a Donna Karan?" I pointed to Melinda's dress. "It's pretty."

Allison broke in, with a fractured laugh. "Oh, no, that's a knock-off. It's actually a dress my cousin bought me for my birthday, but it's too big for me and besides, I'm totally loyal to Versace and won't wear anything else this season. So I gave it to Melly." She smiled at Melinda, showing just a little too much teeth. Oh yeah, she was keeping Melinda in line. One of those friends that some women kept around to make themselves look better.

Melinda blushed and fiddled with her nails. I had already noticed the scuffed toes on her shoes. That alone was fashion faux pas enough to keep her out of Allison's little club. But her long straight hair shimmered gold under the light, and when she smiled, she lit up the room. Quite different from her aunt in that respect.

I studied her a little more. Behind that desperate need to please I had the feeling there was a good brain, but little self-esteem. I sighed. Yet another young woman cowed by the unattainable goal of perfection. It occurred to me that perhaps Melinda wasn't altogether happy with the role she was trying to play. Perhaps her desperation to fit in was borne out of an attempt to pacify family rather than her own desires.

"Well, I think it's pretty, regardless of whether it's a knock-off. And that's really what counts. Something hideous isn't going to be appealing just because you slap a designer label on it." I flashed Melinda a wide smile.

Allison broke into a throaty laugh. "True . . . true," she said. "But the lack of a label doesn't make for appeal, either. In some quarters, hideous might just be considered gorgeous. Look at the goth kids. After all, beauty is in the eye of the beholder, isn't it?" With a soft pout, she gave me a quick wink.

I arched one eyebrow. "Touché." So Allison was smart as well as beautiful. She looked like she'd just stepped out of a planning meeting for a debutante ball. Southern charm with northern reserve.

The waitress hurried over to our table again. The girls ordered plain salads with dry toast on the side, diet Cokes to wash them down. Melinda looked longingly at the menu as she handed it back to the waitress.

I scanned the menu quickly. "I'll have a cheddar, Swiss, and roast beef on sourdough with all the trimmings, and black tea with lemon, please."

Melinda gave me a little "o" of surprise, but said nothing. Allison raised one eyebrow. "Skip breakfast?" she asked.

"No, I like food," I said. "And I've got a fast metabolism."

She murmured something that I didn't quite catch. Not worth pursuing. What Allison Montgomery thought of my eating habits had absolutely nothing to do with why I'd asked them to lunch. I took a deep breath. Time to wade in and hope for the best.

"As you know, our gardener, Trevor Wilson, has been accused of murdering Lydia. We don't think he did it." Before they could say a word, I held my hand. "I know, I know — he had motive. But frankly, I don't believe he's capable of killing anybody."

An undercurrent rippled between them and Allison asked, "What do you want from us?"

I gave her the once-over. "I know Lydia was seeing somebody else, so don't try to cover it up. A man that may — or may not — be dangerous. I'm thinking that we shouldn't overlook the possibility that he might be her killer."

Melinda shrugged. "Well, if she was seeing someone else, and I'm not saying she was, maybe she didn't want anybody to know about it. Her reputation had to remain spotless in order to win that contest."

Bingo. Just as I thought — Mystery Man was somebody who could have hurt Lydia's reputation. Melinda, like her aunt, seemed to have trouble with the art of keeping secrets. In fact, I'd bet that she'd never be able to hide anything from anybody.

"You're right," I said. "And if she was dating somebody who could have tarnished it, maybe he was also capable of murder."

Allison shifted in her seat, picking at a breadstick. "Lydia wouldn't want anybody to know —"

Time to wake them up a little. "Listen girls, Lydia's *dead*. Dead as in *forever.* Dead as in *stone-cold-on-the-slab,-won't-ever-see-her-next-birthday* dead. She's not coming back. And a young man is accused of snuffing out her life and I don't think he did it. You went to school with Trevor. Whether or not you like him is moot. The question I'm asking you is this: Can you honestly sit there, look me in the face, and tell me you believe that Trevor murdered Lydia?"

Allison closed her eyes briefly, and for one moment I saw a distraught young woman instead of a polished mannequin. She snapped the breadstick in half and tossed it on her plate. "No, I guess I can't."

She knew something, all right. "Who was Lydia dating, Allison? You were her best friend, from what I hear. She would have told you, of all people."

"Dating wasn't exactly the word I'd give it," she muttered, and Melinda gave her a startled look. Allison shrugged it off. "Melly, they're going to find out sooner or later. I might as well tell them what I know before things get ugly." She didn't look happy about the idea but with a little more prodding, I could probably get her to cave.

"Good idea. Somehow I doubt if you

want the chief of police to show up on your doorstep. This way, nobody else has to know you were the one who divulged the information." One thing I'd learned from all the cop shows I watched with my aunt was that the fear of the rumor mill often outweighed the fear of spilling the beans.

Melinda toyed with her salad, moving the lettuce around with her fork but not eating. She was eyeing my sandwich with a look that reminded me of a vulture. Poor thing was probably starved. I fought back the desire to push aside her plate and order her a real meal.

"You might as well tell her, Ali," she said. "You know more about him than I do. I only know what you told me."

I leaned across the table and gazed into Allison's eyes. "If you want to help find the person who murdered your friend, you'll tell me what you know."

Allison sighed. "I don't know his name — really, I don't." She dug through her purse and tossed a packet of matches on the table in front of me. "All I know is that he works at this club."

I picked up the matches. The flap had a blue dragon etched on a white background and the logo below it read: The Blue Dragon. The address was from a seedier part of Seattle. I tried to envision the neighborhood — I'd spent a lot of time driving through it on my way to the outskirts of the city when I was working temporary jobs. Then, something in the back of my mind clicked.

The Blue Dragon — a recessed hole in the wall that I'd passed on my way to Xander Dreams Potpourri Company, where I'd churned out hundreds of buckets of a dried, heavily scented mishmash waiting to be shoved into plastic bags and fobbed off as the real thing. Shortly after taking that job, I got hired by the Alternative Life Center and turned in my resignation. Working at Xander's hadn't been my proudest moment, but it had paid the rent for a few months.

"I remember this place. I never went in, but there were always a few well-dressed thugs standing around outside. She was dating somebody who works there?"

Allison nodded. "Uh huh. She wouldn't talk about him much, though. And I think . . ." Allison paused and her eyes flickered up to meet mine.

"Yes?"

Melinda cleared her throat. "We might as well tell her the rest." She turned to me. "Three weeks ago, Lydia told us she had

225

broken up with Trevor. She said he was a wimp and could only hurt her career."

"They'd been going together for quite awhile, hadn't they? Since before I moved back, and that was in December. I seem to remember Trevor mentioning Lydia shortly before Christmas."

"They started dating in September. Lydia won the contest in February." Melinda toyed with her salad. "Trevor really believed she loved him. I think she was duping him all along."

"I don't think she was," Allison broke in. "But she didn't respect him — she liked ambition, and Trevor was happy with a simple life."

"Why would she go out with somebody she didn't respect?" I asked.

Melinda stared at me like I was blind. "Have you seen the man? He's gorgeous. And let's face it, eye candy is a whole lot better than nothing until the real thing comes along. Lydia was in a dry spell, as far as her love life was concerned."

"But then she won the contest," I prodded.

Allison nodded. "She was supposed to go to New York next month — the last week of June. The week after Easter, we were trying on new clothes and Lydia

226

pulled off her blouse and she had this big bruise on her upper arm. I asked her what had happened and she said that she tripped and fell against the corner of her dresser. But the bruise wasn't an accident — it looked like fingerprints to me. Like somebody had grabbed her by the arm and pinched her really hard."

"We asked her if Trevor did it. She said 'no,' and that's when she told us that she was breaking up with him." Melinda bit into another breadstick. "Things really got out of hand between them after that."

So Lydia had been abused. Had Trevor been the culprit? Or her mystery man? If Trev had been the one, I had my doubts as to whether she'd have kept quiet about it. Obviously, she didn't want anybody to know who hurt her. But why had she broken up with Trevor? Could she be in love with somebody who beat her? I shuddered.

"Do you know if she ever loved Trevor?" I asked. "He seems to think that they had a future together. I wonder if maybe he proposed to her?"

Another unspoken look passed between them, then Allison took a deep breath and let it out slowly. "You know a lot more than I thought you did. Trevor did propose. Told her he wanted to marry her and have a baby. That was oh . . . a month or so ago?" She looked at Melinda for confirmation.

Melinda nodded. "Yeah, about then. About a week before the bruises showed up."

"Lydia told us that she didn't love him, that it wasn't a good idea but she hadn't said no yet," Allison continued. "Then she made a trip up to Seattle and when she returned, she told Trevor to beat it. That's the last she ever mentioned getting married. It was right after that when we saw the marks on her arm."

"So he loved her and she . . . wasn't ready for a nice guy."

"Oh, it's more than that," Melinda said. "Her family would never have accepted him. Trevor comes from a poor family. The Wangs are rich and they didn't see him as good husband material. They also didn't want her marrying outside their ethnicity. Family honor or something like that."

That, I already knew. Some loyalties ran deep and Lydia would never have dared to disappoint her parents that way, dragon lady or not. "What do you think happened over in Seattle?"

Allison shrugged. "I have no idea what happened to her. She wouldn't say and I'm not going to speculate."

I could tell that Allison's patience was wearing thin, and Melinda seemed lost in her own thoughts. One last question. "This other man . . . suppose he knew something that kept her in his power? Maybe he scared her enough to push Trevor away? What could he give her that Trevor couldn't?"

Allison pushed back her chair. "Well, that's a no-brainer."

"What's the answer, then?"

With a gaze as steady as a rock, she said, "I think this other guy was her dealer. I think she got her speed from him."

I fell back against my seat. "Speed? Lydia was using?"

Allison snorted. "Using? How do you think she kept so thin? She was hopped up most of the time. I doubt that Trevor knew. He wouldn't have put up with it. Although it was against the contest rules, I think Radiance Cosmetics looked the other way. In fact, I'll bet almost all the girls were on something — diet drugs, mainly. If anything about it hit the papers though, Radiance would have booted Lydia out the door — they have their reputation to protect. Do not pass Go, do not collect your prize package."

I gave her a long look as she picked up her purse and motioned for Melinda to follow her out the door.

"Thank you both," I said. "If you re-member anything else, let me know. You've given me a lot to think about."

I poured myself another cup of tea and added lemon. So Lydia had been a speed freak. No wonder she was so tightly wired. There was a lot more to her than met the eye. And maybe, just maybe, her mystery boyfriend-slash-dealer held the answer to who murdered her. Or maybe, her mystery man had a reason to want her dead.

Chapter Twelve

On my way over to talk to Kyle, the thoughts whirled through my mind. What if Lydia's boyfriend really was a drug dealer and she'd ratted him out? Or he thought she had? Or he'd gotten worried that she would? And what if he thought she might tell Trevor about him? Maybe he'd kill two birds with one stone — shut her up and frame somebody else who had a reason to be jealous.

But that didn't solve the question of why she'd been killed in our shop, or how the murderer had gained access and lured her inside, or why Aphrodite's Mirror was missing.

I almost managed to run a red light in front of the police station but saw it just in time to stomp on the brakes. Fortunately, nobody was in back of me, and I managed to clear my head enough to focus on parking.

Kyle was behind his desk when I knocked on his door. He motioned me in. "What can I do for you?" he asked, taking off his wire-rimmed glasses. As he leaned back in his chair, he looked comfortable, more than I'd ever seen him. His desk was clean and tidy. Neat stacks of paperwork lined one box, and another held a handful of letters and memos.

Feeling a sudden goodwill toward my prickly nemesis, I said, "You were born to be a policeman, weren't you? I can tell that you love your job."

Startled, he gave me a tentative smile. "Well, I can't fault you there. You're right — I was born to be a cop. It's what I do best. Now what can I do for you? You find out anything important?"

"I think so." I filled him in on what the girls had told me and showed him the matchbook. "Somebody needs to go over there and check on this guy. What if he killed Lydia?"

Kyle frowned. "All very interesting, but just how am I supposed to do that? And it still wouldn't explain why he picked your aunt's shop for the scene of the crime. Or how he got in. Do you have anything more to go on?"

"Apparently Lydia was bruised up on a return trip from seeing him. He sounds like a rough character."

He waved me into a chair. "There could

be lots of explanations for her bruises. Trevor, for one. Don't forget that he was arrested for assault once before. Or she could have fallen into or hit a door. Or her father might have slapped her — I gather Charles Wang isn't above disciplining his children with the rod, even the ones who are over eighteen."

Damn, I'd forgotten about Trev's record. And I hadn't known that Mr. Wang was abusive, though it fit in with what Allison had told me about him not wanting Lydia to marry outside their ethnicity. Which brought up an entirely new thought.

"If Charles Wang hits his kids, maybe he killed Lydia?"

Kyle shook his head. "We checked. He's been known to bust their butts, but never anything much worse than that. He was home the night Lydia was murdered and can prove it. Nope, he's clean."

"Okay. So what about the drug allegations? Can you have Lydia's body exhumed? If there were drugs in her system, that might give more credence to the theory that this guy is responsible."

Kyle blocked me at the pass on that one, too. "Yeah, the lab results tested positive for speed, but there's not much we can do. Her levels were fairly high, but not enough to OD on. You're right, though. It looks like she was a chronic user. But it's too late to exhume the body for further testing. The Wangs had her cremated yesterday. There's nothing left of Lydia now but an urn full of ashes."

He stared at the top of his desk. "I'd like to help you. I really would, but I can't afford to send a man over to Seattle to check on everybody who works in or patronizes this club. What if the guy is just a customer? What then? Waste days on a wild-goose chase? I don't have the budget."

"But what if this dude's involved?" I slammed my hands down on his desk and leaned across to stare him in the face. Didn't he understand the consequences? "Trevor's life could be at stake here, Kyle."

"Listen, I know you're looking for every possible angle to help out the kid, and I don't blame you." He tossed the matches back across the desk. "I'm sorry, Persia, but I have to have more to go on than that."

Disappointed, I picked up the packet and shoved it in my purse. "You aren't even going to consider the possibility?"

"I didn't say that." He sighed. "Look, you bring me something solid, like a name, and I'll do what I can." Before I could say another word, he held up his hand. "Whatever you bring to me has to be something that I can act on. Something substantial. I recommend that you talk to Trevor's lawyer. He might want to hire a P.I. to go take a look. Then maybe I can do something. But with the evidence that we have against Trevor, there's no real justification I can make to slow down the trial."

I sighed. "All right, I'll talk to Winthrop about it." I took a deep breath. "Now, on a totally different subject, what do I need to do in order to take out a restraining order?"

He leaned forward, eyes narrowing. "Somebody bothering you?"

"Yeah, my ex-boyfriend showed up drunk out of his mind last night." I laid out the bare bones of the situation. "I don't want Elliot hanging around, especially if his friends are anywhere near to getting out of prison. Big bad, you know. Not conducive to good health."

A strange look crossed his face and he motioned me to sit down, then picked up the phone and said something to his secretary that I couldn't catch. After a few minutes, she popped into the office, handed him a packet of papers, and then disappeared again. He shoved them across the desk to me.

"Here are the forms requesting an order

for protection, but I don't think you have enough for the judge to approve one. If this guy repeatedly shows up — especially if he makes any threats — then you fill these out and turn them in. Until then, keep your eyes open, and document any contact you have with him. I'll make a note that you formally requested my advice on this subject today so we'll have a file started in case things turn ugly."

I thanked him, and started to excuse myself but he stopped me before I reached the door. "Persia, be careful. You don't need this guy stalking you."

I gave him a thin smile. "You can say that again."

He arched one eyebrow. "And, if by chance you take it upon yourself to go nosing around the Blue Dragon — and don't pretend you aren't thinking about it — watch yourself. You might be able to overpower an attacker, but a bullet can still put a hole in you."

As I left the building, I wasn't sure what to think. I'd been expecting outright hostility. His advice and counsel had thrown me for a loop. Maybe Kyle was coming around after all. I shrugged as I climbed into my car. Next step: talk to the lawyer.

I caught Winthrop just before he was

headed out to the jail to meet with another client. After filling him in on what I'd found out, he nodded. "This could be very helpful. Hold on while I make a call."

As he picked up the phone, I sank into one of the arm chairs that faced his desk. Just the kind of office I'd expected. Leather chairs, big oak desk, built-in barrister bookshelves with heavy glass doors. Diplomas and degrees framed on the paneled walls. I looked around for the requisite family picture that usually adorned desks and saw one of an older woman and three young adults. Probably his wife and kids.

After he hung up, he gave me a calculating look. "I just asked an associate about the Blue Dragon. It seems that Lydia's friend associates with a nefarious crowd. This club may have ties to the Chinese Mafia. At the very least, it seems to be a front for a couple of the better-known drug dealers and possibly a transit station for the illegal immigration of women for the sex-slave industry. Nobody's ever been able to prove it, though, so the cops have left it alone."

Drugs? Sex slaves? Chinese Mafia? I'd pegged Lydia for a troublemaker, but I couldn't imagine she'd get herself mixed up in something like that. "What do you

237

think? Should we check it out?"

Winthrop leaned his elbows on his desk, resting his chin on the points of his fingertips. "This could be delicate. Clubs like that are dicey. The bouncers can smell a private dick a mile away, same with a cop. If I hired somebody to go up there, he'd get the runaround. I've dealt with enough disreputable elements to know when I'm on the tail of a rat. Or a pack of them."

I eyed him closely. Nope, he didn't look like he was trying to get out of doing a little legwork. In fact, he looked concerned. "What's wrong? What have you got in mind?"

His brilliant blue eyes sparkled. Even though he was a good thirty years older than me, for a brief second I caught a glimpse of how handsome he must have been when young.

"I'm thinking that I really believe Trevor Wilson when he says he didn't do it. Somebody deliberately framed that boy, but the question is: Why? Maybe we're barking up the wrong tree, though. Did Trevor have any enemies? Could this be revenge against him, not Lydia?"

"I don't know," I said, trying to remember anything Trev might have said over the past few weeks. "If so, I suppose killing her at Venus Envy was done to implicate Trevor?"

Winthrop shrugged. "Right on target, my dear. Either way, a good thief with a set of picklocks could probably have opened that door."

I shook my head. "No dice. Auntie has one hell of a deadbolt on there. It wouldn't budge for picklocks or credit cards."

"We'll figure out how they got in later. My point is that the murderer could have swiped the hammer from the back of Trevor's truck during the afternoon, used it to kill Lydia in a place he's known to frequent, then left it behind for the police to find. You have to admit, Trevor would have to be terribly stupid to implicate himself like that. We both know that, although he's no genius, the young man has his wits about him."

"What about his fingerprints? They were on the hammer."

"Smudged, but yes, they were. So was Lydia's blood. But it wouldn't be too hard for a killer looking to frame Trevor to use gloves, now would it?"

I thunked myself on the forehead. Gloves? Why hadn't I thought of that?

"Okay," I said, squinting as I tried to piece things together. "Say that somebody decided to frame Trevor — it doesn't matter whether the main goal was Lydia's death or not. The real murderer would have to have known something about him. And who better than a rival boyfriend? Someone who might be holding a nasty grudge?"

"Or someone who might have been afraid he'd end up in jail for drugs if Lydia opened her mouth to Trevor," Winthrop added.

"So, if the club bigwigs can spot a P.I., what's our alternative?" I knew what he was going to say so I saved him the trouble. "Maybe I should go check it out."

Winthrop smiled. Yep, I knew it. Spider and fly, and he had spun a nice little web around me. "My dear, I think that's the best idea we've got at the moment. You're more likely to cage information out of them, as . . . well endowed as you are. Don't give me any feminist rhetoric and don't pretend to be shocked," he said before I could protest. "You and I both know that a pretty woman will attract men into talking a lot faster than an old geezer like me. The question isn't whether it's most efficient for you to go, but whether it's *safe* for you to go."

I leaned back in my chair and gave him

an easy smile. "I've got you covered there. I can bring down a grown man and make him cry."

He gave me an inquisitive look.

"I've been studying the martial arts for years. I also climb mountains, though I wouldn't try Everest . . . yet, and I snorkel, scuba, swim, and most importantly — can run like hell if the need arises."

Throwing back his head, Winthrop let out a belly laugh. "Persia, your aunt said you were a ripsnorter, and she was right! Okay, say you go to the Blue Dragon. What are you going to look for?"

Good question. I hadn't thought about it when I went to see Kyle, but now I could understand his reluctance to send a man up there. "I'm not sure. Got any suggestions?"

Winthrop rubbed his hands together and gave me a sneaky grin. "Oh my dear, yes I do. I do, indeed."

As I hurried back into the shop, I glanced around. By now, it was going on late afternoon and Venus Envy was practically empty. I'd either missed the rush or we were having a slow day. Aunt Florence was pricing inventory. She waved at me and I headed over to fill her in on what I'd learned. She hesitated when I mentioned the idea of going to the Blue Dragon myself.

"Persia, child, I know you can hold your own, but are you sure you want to go alone? Maybe you should take Barbara with you?"

Barbara? I laughed. "Auntie, she'd stick out like a sore thumb. I can pass. I'm good at blending in, but Barbara . . . No, I don't think so."

Just then the shop door opened and Bran Stanton walked in. I blushed as Aunt Florence winked and jostled me with her elbow. "Stop it," I whispered. "He'll see you."

She motioned Bran over to the counter. "What can we do for you today?"

He took off his hat and kissed her cheek. "Miss Florence, how are you?" He turned to me. "I thought I'd make sure we're still on for Sunday," he said in a smooth voice. My stomach flipped again, and I found myself looking forward to more than our date.

"Better be. I don't like being stood up, you know. Can we make it two o'clock, though? I have a self-defense class to teach that night."

"Two o'clock is fine." He grinned. "And any man would have to be nuts to stand you up."

I was suddenly aware that both my aunt and Tawny were watching us with amusement. Clearing my throat, I let the banter drop. "So, is there anything else we can take care of for you?"

He shook his head. "Not unless you've got a seven-inch quartz crystal for sale. Last night, some yahoo I invited over decided to play light-saber with one of my best spikes and the damned idiot dropped it and broke it. Made me so mad, but it was my fault for not stopping him."

I groaned; those crystals didn't come cheap. "No, we don't have anything like that here. Try Malley's Gem Shop out on Oceana Drive. I'm sorry, though."

"Thanks, that's where I got several of my crystals. I suppose I should drive out there today. The next time I try to be nice to some lout who just broke up with his girl-friend, I'll take him to a bar and not invite him over for a drink." Bran shook his head, grinning like a chastised schoolboy.

Aunt Florence spoke up. "You're just too sweet for your own good. But then, you always were. Persia, why don't you escort Bran to his car while Tawny and I start arranging a new display table?"

As I walked Bran out to his car, the wind picked up and I stopped, lifting my head to catch the breeze on my face. I motioned for him to remain quiet as I listened to the currents of air as the brisk gusts race through me.

"There's more trouble coming," I said. "I can smell it on the wind. This isn't over yet. Some thread linked to Lydia's death is still playing itself out."

Bran leaned against his truck — a sleek black Honda CRV. "What is it? Can you tell?"

I tried to glean more information but the impending storm overwhelmed me; the hairs on my arms stood straight. Lightning was on the way, and thunder, and waves that would crash against the shore, eating the sand. "No," I said slowly. "I can't catch hold of it, but something's about to happen."

Bran pulled out his keys. "You know where to reach me if you need me. I've got to go batten down my boat. A bad storm could do some serious damage." He waggled his fingers and climbed into his car.

As he sped away, I looked up at the sky. The clouds were building, layer upon layer of gray, and the weather had warmed, turning muggy. Rain would come in an hour — the edges of moisture tickled my skin. And it would bring with it whatever was making me want to run home, climb into bed, and hide my head under the covers.

A gale-force gust slammed past and I jumped as a crash from across the street splintered the air. An old oak standing in the corner lot — which had been turned into a garden sanctuary for shoppers — plunged to the ground, taking the power lines with it. Auntie, Tawny, Barbara, and several other shopkeepers rushed outside to find out why the electricity had suddenly cut off. A shiver danced up my spine. Something was afoot all right, and it was riding the edges of the storm.

Barbara shouted a choice curse or two and headed back inside the bakery — she had an oven full of baking bread and no backup generator. I slipped past Auntie and Tawny, and began closing up shop. The power was down for the count and it would take the city awhile to get it back up, that much was apparent by looking at the mess across the street. I just hoped the sparking wires wouldn't cause any fires, but the high pitched keen of sirens told me that the fire department was on the way to keep watch.

Aunt Florence and Tawny bustled in and together, we closed up as quickly as possible.

"Auntie, why don't you go home and I'll finish up here? There isn't much left to do, and you can make sure all our emergency supplies are ready. That oak may not be the only tree toppled by this storm." The winds were whipping like crazy outside the shop now. We were in for a real bruiser.

"Good idea, Imp. You be careful on the way home, and don't take too long — I don't like the looks of that sky. Leave everything that doesn't matter and lock up the deposit envelope in the safe. Don't bother stopping at the bank."

She gathered up her purse, grabbed a handful of candles, and headed for the door. Tawny followed shortly after. I'd just finished locking up the receipts and deposit envelope and was about to leave when Kyle Laughlin pulled up in his prowl car. He tapped on the window, and I unlocked the door for him.

The shop was beginning to cool down. Without the heater working, I could already feel the sharp tang from the salt air that was spraying through the town. I lit a second candle.

"Hey, Chief. What's up?"

He frowned. "Your aunt employs Marta, doesn't she? As your cleaning lady?"

"Here at the shop, yes." I shrugged. "But

we hire her as an independent contractor, so she's not officially considered an employee. She comes in a couple times a week. Why?"

With an imperceptible nod, he said, "Marta's dead. We got a call from the woman who lived across the hallway from her — old Mrs. Fairweather. She heard some a scream and called nine-one-one. When we got there we found Marta, dead."

Dead? I stared at him. "What happened? Was it her heart? She was under a lot of strain. I know she was having money problems."

Kyle let out a loud sigh. "No, not her heart. She was murdered this afternoon. Hit over the head from behind."

"Hit over the head?"

"From behind. First, Lydia's found in your shop, dead. Then the woman who cleans your shop is murdered. I don't know if there's a link, but something strange is going on here. It's too bad Mrs. Fairweather is blind, or she might have been able to tell us more."

"Mrs. Fairweather can't see, but Marta could," I said slowly, a thought occurring to me. "Maybe Marta saw something? She cleans several shops in this block, you know. Maybe she was around the area when Lydia was killed and saw the murder? Maybe the killer found out, so he came back and took care of her before she could tell the police."

Kyle held up his hand. "That's a big stretch. Although, it would fit in with the call you got on that tape from the Delacorte Plaza."

"Why?"

"Because Marta lived across the street in those apartments, and she didn't have a phone. She had to go across the street to the Plaza whenever she wanted to make a call. Perhaps Marta was our mysterious caller." He shifted, sitting on my counter. "So, in other news, I hear through the grapevine you're going out with Bran Stanton?"

I glanced at him. News sure traveled fast in this burg. "Yeah, we're going out on Sunday. Why?"

He raised one eyebrow and leaned forward, taking care not to topple the burning candle. "Persia Vanderbilt, you mean to tell me that you'd actually go for some guy who believes in crap like that? I always thought you were some sort of genius or something back in junior high. You went away to college at what . . . sixteen? And yet you believe in all this woo-woo stuff?"

Regardless of what my beliefs were, I didn't like his tone. I treated the world of the paranormal just like any other belief system. I didn't have to partake in something to offer a show of respect.

Hands on my hips, I said, "Whether you believe in prophecies, omens, or the tooth fairy doesn't mean jack-shit. Bran is a nice man and he helps a lot of people. Our shop feels ten times better after he cleared the energy."

Kyle snorted. "A guy like Stanton could read *Mary Had a Little Lamb* backwards, shake a whirlybird pinwheel three times, and you'd fall for him, wouldn't you?" He picked up his hat, shaking his head. "But hey, if you're gullible enough be taken in by Stanton's smoke and mirrors, be my guest."

That did it! Nobody called me gullible and got away with it. I stepped around the counter and jabbed him on the chest. "I don't care if you're the chief of police or a sideshow freak. Show a little respect for me and maybe then I'll show a little back."

He slowly stood up so that we were almost eye to eye. A few inches taller than me, I had a feeling he wanted every inch of the advantage he thought his height gave him.

A hostile look clouded his face and, for the first time, I was a little afraid of him, but I held my ground. Never turn your back on a lion. "How about this little scenario? What if Bran Stanton wants to get in good with you because your aunt has a lot of money and he knows you'll inherit someday? I trust him about as much as I trust Ed McMulheny's rottweiler, which is why I made Ed get the dog neutered and keep it on a short leash. I should do the same with Stanton."

"You think he's asking me out because of my aunt's money? Kyle, you better get your head out of your ass before you get hemorrhoids. Stay off his back. And mine."

We stared at one another, in a standoff neither one of us was willing to break. He suddenly grabbed my arm, yanked me to him, and planted a kiss on my lips. Furious, I backhanded him a good one across the cheek, the sound of my slap ringing through the room as he grimaced.

Kyle dropped my arm like he'd been burnt and stepped away. "Damn you," he whispered. "Why did you come back to Gull Harbor?" As if aware of what he was saying, he stopped abruptly and turned his head. I stared at the counter, not sure what had just happened. After a moment, the cool, reserved chief of police had returned.

"That shouldn't have happened. I am so sorry. Please, accept my apology." He waited and I knew that he was hoping I'd let him off the hook rather than filing a sexual harassment charge, which I'd be within my rights to do.

Not wanting to tread any further into what had become an unfathomable bog, I swallowed. "Don't ever let it happen again."

Obviously relieved, he exhaled. "I'd better go check on what my men have found out. I'll drop by later tonight to ask your aunt some questions about Marta. I'd appreciate it if you'd tell her what happened so it won't come as a shock when I show up. I don't know how close they were."

I forced a smile to my lips. Nothing like glossing over problems by making nice-nice. "Fine, I'll be glad to help." I pointed out the window. The storm was in full force right now and I wasn't looking forward to the drive home. "I'd better get on the road now."

He silently followed me out of the store and waited until I'd locked up and was safely in my car. As I pulled out of the parking lot, the memory of his lips on my own flooded back. His kiss had left me angry and confused, and yet . . . and yet . . . yet nothing! Nobody manhandled me and got away with it.

My thoughts were a jumble as I drove home through the crashing thunder that had swallowed up the town. The water in the sound swelled in tumultuous whitecaps as I wound along Beachcomber's Drive, the roar of the storm so loud that it sounded as if it were going to envelop Gull Harbor with one giant wave.

Chapter Thirteen

I pulled over at a turnout in the road, dug through my purse for my cell phone, and punched in Barbara's number. Her voice came crackling over the line.

"Hey Barb, has Kyle talked to you yet?"

"No, why should he?"

"Marta's dead."

A heavy silence rang over the line and then, her voice tinged with both disbelief and shock, she asked, "What happened?"

"I'm on my way home. Can Dorian spare you for awhile? I've got to tell Aunt Florence before Kyle shows up to ask her some questions about Marta. I'll explain everything then. I'll stop on the way to pick up some takeout."

Barbara agreed to meet me in fifteen minutes. I pulled into the drive-thru at Yoshie's Southern Fried Chicken & Sushi Bar, where the power was still on, and ordered a twelve-piece bucket of crispy chicken and a Happy Variety Platter of sushi. By the time I arrived home, Barbara was easing into the driveway. She climbed out of the car, holding a large pink box which could mean only one thing. Cake. Salivating like a Pavlovian puppy, I hoisted my bags and we headed up the porch steps together, saying little more than hello. I could tell that my news about Marta had shaken her. I wasn't looking forward to spilling the beans that it had been murder.

Auntie was waiting for me, looking worried. "I was about to call you. That storm is shaping up into a nasty squall." She glanced over at Barbara. "Aha, a stranger bearing gifts."

The table was set, candles were lit around the room, and Auntie had opened the curtains so we could watch the storm rage across Puget Sound. The wind whipped the trees into a frenzy as the clouds reflected an eerie silver light, punctuated by occasional bursts of lightning. Seattle traffic, especially on the 520 floating bridge, was probably a mess. That is, if they hadn't closed the bridge yet. When a sustained wind of forty-five miles per hour had been recorded for over fifteen minutes, officials shut down the bridge to all traffic. Gusts were already rattling our windows here, and once again, I felt a sense of relief that I'd moved back to Gull Harbor.

Barbara helped me arrange the chicken and sushi on platters, while my aunt fixed a quick salad. I dug through the cupboard and pulled out the olive oil and balsamic vinegar and placed them on the table, and we were ready to eat.

"What brings you out on a night like this?" my aunt asked Barbara.

Barb gave me a hesitant look.

Oh hell, I'd been hoping to wait until after dinner. I wasn't good with things like this. "I asked her to come over. I've got something to tell both of you." I set my fork down and pushed my plate back. "Kyle stopped by today, before I left."

Aunt Florence gave me a quick look. "What's wrong? Is it something about Trevor? I was going to go see the boy today, but now I'll have to wait until tomorrow."

I shook my head. "No, Trevor's fine . . . but there's been . . ." I hesitated, not sure whether my aunt and Marta had been close friends.

Aunt Florence sighed. "Well, for heaven's sake, out with it, child."

Taking a deep breath, I said, "Marta's dead. They found her in her apartment. She's been murdered. Kyle will be over in awhile; he needs to ask you some questions about her."

255

My aunt's jaw dropped open, while Barbara let out a little "Oh!" and covered her mouth.

"Murdered? You told me she had died, but you didn't say she was murdered," Barb said, aghast. "How horrible!"

Aunt Florence just closed her eyes briefly, a pained expression crossing her face. "Poor old dear. I don't know what Gull Harbor's coming to. Two murders in one week —" She paused. "Kyle thinks it's related to Lydia's murder, doesn't he?"

"Yeah, I think he does. Marta was hit over the head from behind, just like Lydia. She lived in the apartments across from the Delacorte Plaza, and that's where the phone call on that message tape originated. Now Kyle is thinking maybe Marta was the one who made the call."

Barbara bit her lip. "As in, she saw something?" She stared at the chicken for a moment, then shook her head. "I think I just lost my appetite."

I put my hand on her arm. "Eat. There's nothing we can do for Marta now."

Barb nodded. She stared at the plate and, after a long sigh, finally selected a piece of chicken and three sushi rolls. As she passed the platter to me, I glanced over at my aunt. She looked dejected, but was taking it better than I'd hoped.

"I was worried about how you were going to handle this," I said.

Auntie patted me on the hand. "My dear, I've lived through a lot of deaths, and many of them were far more painful. The older you are, the more you get used to hearing the news that somebody you knew died. It's one of those little things they never warn you about when you're young."

She picked up her chicken. "You know, girls," she continued, "if Marta was killed because she saw something, Kyle should let Trevor off the hook because there's no way he could have hurt her."

"I think this will help Trev's case," I said, "but then again, we can't forget that the evidence is stacked against him, what with him having no alibi, and the bloody hammer, and Sarah's report of what he said to her about Lydia. However, this should make Kyle think twice about rushing it through. There are too many loose threads, too many questions. And I intend to find out a few of the answers."

My aunt regarded me solemnly. "I assume you're talking about the Blue Dragon? I wish you wouldn't go, Persia. It's too dangerous, especially now that Marta's been killed."

"Blue Dragon? What are you talking about?" Barbara perked up, looking at me closely. "What are you planning that has your aunt so worried?"

I frowned. "I've learned that Lydia had a boyfriend on the side who's rumored to work at the Blue Dragon, a club in Seattle. I talked to Winthrop about it and he did some digging." I told her what we'd found out.

She frowned. "I see why Miss Florence doesn't want you going up there by yourself. It sounds dangerous. Tell you what, I'll come along. That way, you won't be alone." Her eyes glittered with a look I was beginning to recognize. Uh oh. Once Barbara made up her mind about something, she was unshakable.

"Barb, you don't know what you're getting into. I can blend into places like that. I don't think you could. You're too . . . too . . ."

She gave me a dark stare. "Say it, I dare you."

I tried to repress a smirk but broke out laughing. "Oh Barb, you just wouldn't fit. You'd stand out like a Tiffany lamp in a dungeon. Okay?"

Aunt Florence laughed gently, but then the laughter turned to tears and she rested her elbows on the table, leaning her forehead against her hands. "Poor Marta . . . poor Lydia. Who did this? I know Trevor didn't have any part of it. I know it!"

I crossed behind her chair, rubbing her shoulders as I tried to think of something to say. She raised her head and gave me a pale smile. "Persia, please take Barbara with you tomorrow night. I don't want to chance losing you!"

I blushed, feeling a flicker of guilt. Aunt Florence didn't deserve the grief I was causing her. I leaned down and kissed her on the top of the head. "All right, Barbara can go. I promise that we'll be careful." She let out a long breath as I returned to my chicken.

We'd barely finished dinner when the doorbell rang. Aunt Florence answered and, as expected, it was Kyle. He took off his raincoat and left it on the porch to dry out, then turned to Aunt Florence.

"Did Persia tell you why I'm here?"

She motioned him into the living room. "She told us about Marta. Would you like some tea or coffee? You look like a drowned rat."

He flashed her a brief smile, but it disappeared quickly. "I'd love a cup of tea, if it isn't any trouble."

I hied myself into the kitchen to fetch

the teapot and more of Barb's cake while he settled himself on the sofa. I carried the tray into the living room, where we all settled around the fireplace.

"Cream? Lemon?"

"Lemon, please." He turned to Barbara. "I'm glad you're here, Mrs. Konstantinos. I need to ask you all a few questions." He accepted the cup I handed him and shivered as the hot liquid met his lips. I slipped over and added a couple logs to the fire.

Kyle took out his notebook. "As you know, Marta Mendoza was killed in her apartment this afternoon. The blow broke her neck and fractured her skull. It looks like she put up a fight, but the door wasn't forced, so we think she knew her assailant. Mrs. Fairweather reported a scream coming from the apartment, but that's all she knows."

Barbara raised her hand. "Mrs. Fairweather? Who's that?"

He glanced over at her. "A neighbor. Blind woman."

"Did you find the murder weapon?" I asked.

A combination of embarrassment and hesitation flickered over his face as he stared into my eyes. "No, we haven't. Marta lived across from the Delacorte

Plaza and she didn't have a phone in her apartment, so I'm thinking she made her phone calls from the Plaza. Which is, of course, the same place where the call to your shop originated."

Auntie broke in. "Did you find any fingerprints off that note that was in our mailbox?"

"No." He shook his head. "We dusted it but found nothing except Persia's prints where she opened it. Nor did I find any matching paper in Marta's apartment, but that really doesn't prove anything. I'm inclined to believe that she knew something about Lydia's murder, something that made her unwilling to come forward to the police."

"Why would she keep it a secret? Trevor never did anything to hurt her." Barbara looked confused. "Marta could be a dingbat, but she wasn't cruel. If she could get Trevor off the hook, wouldn't she have tried harder than making an anonymous phone call or sending a note like that?"

"I don't know the answer to that, but we did find something interesting," Kyle said. "Yesterday she made a five-thousand-dollar deposit to her checking account. We found the receipt."

"Five thousand dollars?" Aunt Florence

sat up. "Where did she get that kind of money? Marta was always starved for cash."

Kyle nodded. "You're right. When we checked the bank, they said she deposited the funds in one-hundred-dollar bills, which is fishy enough by itself. I also found a blank deposit slip on her dinette table when we searched her apartment, with tomorrow's date written on it, but no amount filled in. Was she expecting a paycheck from either of you?"

Auntie shook her head. "No, I pay her a hundred fifty dollars every two weeks. She spends about two hours a day at my store. Payday isn't until a week from this coming Monday. What about you, Barbara?"

Barbara shrugged. "We pay her the same rate, and on the same day that you do. When we first hired her, she asked us to coordinate payday with her other jobs, so she wouldn't have to make so many trips to the bank." She stared at the floor. "It's hard to believe that she's dead."

Florence patted her hand somberly. "Marta wasn't terribly bright. It's easy for me to believe she got herself into a situation over her head. I remember having a conversation with her a year or so ago. She told me that years ago she'd deliberately gotten herself knocked up so she could drop out of high school. She knew that her parents would insist she get married — they were Catholic."

I kept my mouth shut, but silently thanked Auntie for raising me to be independent and to think for myself.

"Yeah," Kyle said. "And look where it got her. Working past retirement, alone and trying to help support her kids long after they should be supporting themselves."

Florence shrugged. "It's not Marta's fault she's alone. Her husband died while working a construction job. I think he fell off a building."

With a sigh, Kyle said, "I know she didn't have it easy. She lost one son to the streets. She only hears from him when he's begging for a handout, and then there's her daughter. The girl means well but she's not very stable."

My aunt glanced at Kyle for a long moment before speaking. "Yes, Delia can't cope very well with the problems life has thrown her and Marta tries to help out. What with her grandson and his disabilities — well, it's just been one hard turn after another."

"So I understand," Kyle said. "And it takes a lot of money to pay for his care.

Brentwood Manor isn't cheap."

I stood up and took the teapot into the kitchen to freshen it. Thoroughly depressed, I made a fresh batch of tea, added more cake to the plate, and returned to the living room. Kyle jumped up and took the tray, setting it on the coffee table for me. I must have looked surprised because he winked as if to say, "Want to make something of it?"

Returning to his seat, he tapped his notebook with his pencil. "Miss Florence, Mrs. Konstantinos, did Marta ever talk to you about any troubles she might be having? Anybody who might be mad at her?"

Barbara and my aunt glanced at one another. Auntie spoke up first. "Marta kept most of her troubles to herself."

Kyle jotted down the information, then turned to Barbara. "And you?"

Barb squinted, trying to think. "You know, I seem to recall her saying something yesterday morning that struck me as odd. She was talking to Ronette, who works the early morning shift. What was it . . . let me think for a moment."

The chief set his notebook on the table and bit into a slice of cake. "This is wonderful," he said to me. "Did you make it?"

I snorted. "If I had, you'd be using a

264

sledgehammer instead of a fork. It's from Barb's shop."

He laughed and Auntie joined in as Barbara snapped her fingers.

"I remember now. Yesterday, Marta was chatting with Ronette while I was arranging stock in the display cases. Usually Marta's always asking us if we know of other people looking for cleaning ladies. Well, Ronette mentioned that a friend of her mother's is looking for a full-time housekeeper. The pay is good, nice benefits . . . no children — an ideal job for Marta."

Kyle quickly began jotting down notes. "Go on."

Barbara frowned. "I don't remember her exact words, but Marta thanked her, then said something to the effect of, 'I'll take her name and number, but if things turn out right, I may be able to retire sooner than I thought.' I remember wondering if she won the lottery. Come to think of it, I don't think she even wrote down the name of the woman looking for help."

Auntie finished her tea and set her cup down on a coaster. "That *is* odd. Marta would normally jump at a chance like that."

I ticked off facts. The blank deposit

check. Lack of interest in a job that might have helped ease the stress in her life. A belief that she might be able to actually retire. A word was beginning to form in the back of my mind. One that had a nasty little feel to it — that might cast a new light on Marta and make her petty thievery out to be more than just a poor old woman trying to get by.

"Did you know Marta was a thief?" I blurted out. Auntie gasped as Barbara blushed and stared at the ceiling.

Kyle frowned. "A thief? How so?"

"Go on, Auntie. Tell him what you told us. It won't hurt her now, and it might shed some light onto her murder."

Aunt Florence gave me a quick glare, but quietly told Kyle about the petty thefts. Barbara added in her observations.

When they both finished, I leaned forward. "Auntie, I'm not trying to smear her character, but think about it. What if she found out something that she might think was worth money? Maybe someone threatened to turn her in for stealing and she countered with some secrets of her own? Or maybe . . . just maybe . . . she saw something and decided to make a few bucks by promising to keep quiet about it?"

"Blackmail?" Kyle's eyes lit up. "That

thought had crossed my mind. Blackmail is serious business and usually leads to somebody getting hurt. If Marta was attempting extortion, she might just have opened the door for her own demise."

My aunt jumped up, her hands on her hips. "How dare you say that, Kyle Laughlin? She was a poor old woman looking for a way to get by." She abruptly fell silent and stared out the window. The storm had taken full hold, shaking the trees.

I slid over next to Aunt Florence and pulled her back down on the sofa, next to me. "Auntie, if we're on the right track, this information might lead to her killer. And maybe help Trevor. If Marta saw Lydia being murdered and now she's dead, then that means that the murderer is still running around loose. That it's not Trevor."

Barbara murmured agreement.

Auntie wrung her hands. "I suppose you're right," she said. "Marta wasn't terribly bright. She might have seen what she thought was an opportunity to take care of her daughter and grandson."

"Then I suppose the next step is to figure out who her friends are," Kyle said. "If you can make up a list of anybody you knew, people she hung out with, I'd appreciate it. We've talked to her daughter, but the woman is totally distraught. After all, her mother's just been murdered. We're talking to her neighbors to see if anything comes up."

He folded his notebook shut and tucked it away in his pocket. "If you think of anything — no matter how trivial it sounds — call me."

"Winthrop and I've decided that I should hang out at the Blue Dragon tomorrow night. Maybe there's something going around the grapevine there." I escorted him to the door, stepping out on the porch with him.

"Do you think that's a good idea?" He picked up his raincoat, which was still damp, and shrugged into it.

"We talked it over. He thinks that a P.I. would just attract attention." I shivered as the wind bit into my skin, raising goose bumps along my arms.

"And you won't attract attention?"

I gave him a slow smile. "That's the idea, actually."

With a frown, he said, "Well, if you have to go, I can't stop you, but for God's sake, be careful."

"Hey, if you aren't willing to send out an

officer to investigate, then somebody else has to pick up the slack. You told me to go to Winthrop, and I did." There, I'd caught him. How could he complain if he wasn't willing to do the job himself?

Kyle started to say something, then closed his mouth. He glanced out at the yard. "Gale blowing in tonight. Hope the boats in the marina are tied down safe." He glanced back at me and bit his lip. "Persia," he said softly. "About this afternoon . . ."

I shook my head. "Don't worry. It's forgotten. I'm not mad."

He sighed, as if I'd said something wrong. "I don't care if you're mad or not. I was kind of hoping . . ."

Hoping. Hoping what? Now it was my turn to frown. "Kyle, if you want to say something, just come out and say it." I shivered, pulling my shawl tight around my shoulders. The wind was raging at a steady forty to fifty miles per hour.

He stared at me for a moment, holding my gaze, then roughly shook his head. "Never mind. Just never mind. If you, or your aunt or friend remember anything else that might be important, give me a call."

As he sprinted toward his cruiser, there was a loud crack and one of the trees across the street toppled, bringing down the power lines. Yeah, the old oak wasn't going to be the only victim of this storm.

The lights in the neighborhood flickered and died, and Kyle let out a blue streak of swearing as he climbed back out of his car and radioed for a city crew to come take care of the damage. He made no move to return to the porch, and so I slipped back inside to inform Barbara that she wasn't going anywhere for awhile.

Aunt Florence was in the process of lighting more candles. The fireplace already had a nice blaze going in it, and the room glowed with warmth. She peeked out the front window.

"I hope nothing catches on fire out there because of those downed lines," she said. "That wind is whipping up something fierce."

"Don't worry about it. Rain's coming down in buckets. Everything's too drenched to burn. Do you want me to start the generator?"

My aunt shook her head. "We've already had our dinner. The upper floors will be cold, but we have enough blankets to manage. If the power's not on by morning, I'll start it up then. The freezer will be fine for the night and there's not much to lose in the refrigerator. Barbara, you're not going to be able to get past those wires for awhile."

Barb pulled out her cell phone. "I'd better call Dorian. Hopefully, they'll get the road cleared within a couple of hours." She punched in her number while Auntie and I, armed with a couple of flashlights, headed into the kitchen in order to feed the Menagerie. After we set out all the bowls and refilled the water dishes, my aunt excused herself.

"I'm tired and I'm going to go to bed. Persia, can you show Barbara to the guest room? Good night and sweet dreams, children." She kissed me on the forehead.

Barbara and I watched her slowly ascend the stairs. The events of the past week were weighing heavily on her shoulders.

I turned back to Barb. "She looks so tired. Thank you for coming over tonight. I think having you here helped. My aunt thinks the world of you." I took another look out the front window. Several city vehicles were present, all with flashing yellow lights, and it looked like a truck from the Port Samanish PUD was just pulling in. "They're starting work on that mess. Once the roads are clear, you'll be able to leave if you want."

Barb curled up in the overstuffed rocking chair. "So, you and Kyle seemed to have something going on. What was that look that passed between you two earlier? When he grabbed the tray from you?"

I settled onto the sofa, folding my legs into the lotus position. "Barb, the weirdest thing happened today. We were in the shop and got into an argument and he grabbed me and kissed me."

Barb's hand flew to her mouth. "He what?"

"He kissed me. Took me by surprise, and frankly, he's lucky I only slapped him instead of cold-cocked him. I was so pissed. Nobody grabs me like that and gets away with it."

She shut her jaw, which had fallen open. "Uh, I hope he apologized?"

I nodded. "Yeah, he did, but I'm betting only because he was afraid I'd report him for inappropriate behavior. Then he asked why I came back to Gull Harbor, but in that angry rhetorical way." I blushed. Until now, the incident had just seemed odd. But telling Barb what happened made it feel too intimate, almost embarrassing.

"What did you say?" Barb pulled down one of the afghans draped over the back of the rocker and spread it over her legs. The heat from the fireplace was fierce up close, but a few yards away the chill of the house took over. I was beginning to regret not firing up the generator.

I slowly shook my head. "What could I say? I was pissed off. Anyway, I know his wife's dead and I'm sorry, but I just don't want him following me around again like he did in school. Kyle can be a nice guy, but he's not my type."

Barb leaned her head back, staring at me. "You'd be surprised, Persia. Don't write him off yet. Maybe he's not your type, for all I know you don't even have a type, but don't close and lock the door."

I sighed, exhausted. The day had been far too long. "Uh huh. Whatever."

With a slow smile, Barbara said, "Kyle never got over you, Persia. Not even when he married Katy. It's something you're going to have to face head-on one of these days."

"Maybe, but today's not that day." I knew she was right, but I didn't want to think about it, didn't want to deal with any more baggage than I'd accumulated with Elliot. I'd come home, hoping for a clean slate, a new start, but Kyle was promising to be an obstacle to that goal. I leaned closer to the fire, searching for answers in the flames. None were forthcoming.

273

From the Pages of Persia's Journal

Narcissus Dreaming Oil

So many women are unhappy and lonely — even when they're in relationships — that I decided to create a blend to intoxicate the senses, to sweep women into a time when beauty was a gift from the Divine. Aphrodite, Venus, Freya, Hathor, Erzulie, Shakti . . . each a goddess of love, desire, and beauty. Each captured the hearts of their worshippers and inspired art, poetry, music, magic, and passion. I believe we can draw upon their inspiration to ignite our own inner goddess and to discover the power of our own beauty, within and without. Because until we love ourselves, how can we expect anybody else to love us?

As always, I should include a checklist of time-tested hints for women who want to bring a spark back into their bedroom:

- Make sure you have clean, comfortable sheets and bedding on your bed. Buy something that you like instead of something utilitarian.
- Keep the TV out of the bedroom.

- Don't be afraid to experiment with toys or books on the subject of sexuality.
- Soak in a long bubble bath, eat good foods, buy clothes that make you feel sexy.
- Treat yourself as you want to be treated.
- Establish "date night" with your partner to make sure you get some time together every week.
- If you have children, hire a babysitter once every two weeks and spend a long evening with your partner, child free, without worrying if anybody is going to come barging in the door.
- Discuss your needs with your partner outside of the bedroom.
- Learn to dance — even if only in private — because dancing is sexy.
- Regular exercise increases libido.
- Use scented oils and fragrances to enhance the mood, like *Narcissus Dreaming oil.*

To blend the oil, gather a dark bottle and stopper, and an eyedropper, as well as the following ingredients:

> *$1/4$ ounce almond or apricot kernel oil*
> *40 drops narcissus oil*

21 drops dark musk oil
21 drops amber oil
14 drops rose oil
8 drops orange oil

OPTIONAL:
Garnet and rose quartz chips
(you can use chips off a
gemstone chip necklace)
1 shredded, dried rose petal

Using the eyedropper, add each fragrance oil to the almond oil. Gently swirl the bottle to blend the scent. After adding the orange oil, cap and shake gently. At this time, add the shredded rose petal and/or the gemstone chips to the bottle for added energy, if desired.

My crystal research indicates that rose quartz crystals are excellent for inspiring peace, happiness, and love. Garnets empower sexuality, passion, and inner strength. The rose petals will intensify the scent and add a decorative touch. As always, remind customers to avoid eating or drinking the oil, to keep it in a cool, dark place, and to keep out of reach of children and animals.

Chapter Fourteen

My eyes shot open and I bolted into a sitting position as a flood of light washed over me, startling me out of my sleep. Who the hell was in my bedroom? I leapt out of bed and looked around, but then realized that I'd left the light switch on and that the power had come back on. Woohoo! We had electricity again. I glanced at the alarm clock. I'd always used a battery operated one just in case of emergency. Two in the morning. Barbara had left around eleven PM, easing her car out along the freshly cleared road.

I flipped off the lights and crawled back in bed, but something furry was holding down the covers when I tried to slide my feet back under them. I squinted through the darkness to peer at the bottom of the bed. Delilah, sound asleep. Gently, I reached out to stroke the slumbering cat's fur.

"You really do like me, don't you, you little bugger?" She wiggled her ears, shifted, and continued to snore as I maneuvered around her. With the wind rattling the windows, I closed my eyes and fell asleep to the sound of pounding rain.

After a brief but intense stint on my exercise bike that left me a sweaty pile of Jell-O, I soaped up under a hot shower and then slipped on my usual tight black jeans, a black turtleneck, and a pair of high-heeled ankle boots that zipped up the sides. Aunt Florence had breakfast ready when I dashed into the kitchen and planted a kiss on her cheek.

I snitched a piece of bacon from the plate as I carried it over to the table and popped it in my mouth. "Yum, smoky."

"You wait for me, missy." Auntie added a dish of scrambled eggs to the table, along with toast and a bowl of lightly sweetened peaches and cream. "I want some of that bacon and you always *hog* it." She grinned.

Snorting at her pun, I brought over the pot of Earl Gray and filled our cups, then sat down and piled a man-sized breakfast on my plate. Aunt Florence was looking over the paper. She let out a little "Oh."

"What is it?" I poured two glasses of milk and handed her one.

"Radiance Cosmetics certainly hasn't

wasted any time." She cleared her throat and began to read the article to me.

Radiance Cosmetics announced this morning that its new spokesmodel will be Colleen Murkins, of Gull Harbor, Washington. Ms. Murkins was the first runner-up in the Radiance Cosmetics Beauty Contest, losing by only a few points to Lydia Wang, also of Gull Harbor. Julia Skyler, Vice President in charge of public relations for the company, commented that, "Everyone at Radiance Cosmetics has been deeply shocked by the death of Ms. Wang and we extend our sympathies to her family and friends." Ms. Wang was murdered this week. According to the rules of the contest, Ms. Murkins will assume the crown and begin her duties on May 15th, after the contracts have been finalized. In unrelated news, Radiance Cosmetics has announced yet another delay in the unveiling of its new China Veils line of cosmetics.

Aunt Florence pushed the paper aside and picked up her fork. "I understand their need for expediency, but Lydia's barely cold in the grave. That's business for you, though. If I were in their shoes, I suppose I might do the same." She munched on her bacon as she stared out the window. "The storm left a real mess out in the gardens today. Sarah will never manage it by herself." She sighed. "It's time I faced up to reality. I'm going to call Day Labor and hire some temporary help, just until Trevor's back with us."

I nodded. "That makes sense, even though it's hard to face that he might not come back for a long time unless we can find a way to help him out. While Marta's death opens up several intriguing possibilities, we still can't prove that he's innocent, nor that there's any link between the two deaths."

The phone rang, interrupting me mid-bite. Tawny was on the other end. "I've scheduled an early appointment for you, Persia."

"You're already at work?" I asked, repressing a grin. "What happened to 'I'm not going in the store alone'?"

She sounded a little sheepish as she stammered out, "Oh, well, see . . . I got here early and was hanging out in the bakery when Mrs. Konstantinos offered to come with me while I checked to make sure everything was okay. Anyway, I scheduled an appointment for you with Juanita Lopez. She wants a custom-blended scent. She'll be here at ten-thirty."

"I'll be there." I dropped the receiver back in the cradle. "That was Tawny. I've got an appointment this morning. Guess things are back to normal. At least, as much as they can be." Since Lydia's death, most of our customers had been more interested in gossip than goodies, and our sales had declined while our foot traffic increased.

Auntie pushed back her chair and began clearing the table. "As soon as I arrange for some help for Sarah, I'll head out. What time do you and Barbara need to leave for Seattle?"

"Let's see." I glanced at the clock. "If we take the ferry at four, we'll be there with time to spare. So we'll need to be at the dock by three at the latest." Sometimes the line of cars waiting for the ferry was backed up for half an hour.

"Are you taking into account the possibility of missing one and having to take the next?" Aunt Florence raised one eyebrow.

"That won't matter. We don't need to be at the club until around nine." The party at most nightclubs didn't get started until close to midnight, and we wouldn't have to fight traffic too much. The ferry docked right down at the port of Seattle's landing and our drive to the Blue Dragon would take an hour or so depending on city traffic.

"Are you going to stay the night? When does the last ferry return to Gull Harbor from Seattle?"

I hadn't thought about that. "I don't know, but I'll call you if we need to stay in the city." I picked up the last of the dishes and handed them to her, then retrieved the sponge and dishcloth and washed the table. "Actually, while I'm over there, I should drop in at the Radiance Cosmetics Boutique."

Aunt Florence glanced at the clock. "Then you'd better leave earlier, to make sure you get there before they close. Say two at the latest. Go on now, and talk to Barbara. I'll be there by noon. Tawny can handle the shop by herself for a few hours, so don't wait for me if I'm late."

The storm had died down sometime during the wee hours of the morning, and the sky was a pale blue gleaming through puffy remnants of clouds. Within another month the island would be in full swing with families and tourists, but we were still on the tail end of the rainy season and I had the feeling there would be another good blow or two before the weather opened up. I paused by my Sebring, inhaling a lungful of the air that had been charged by the storm. There was something inherently crisp about salty breezes that made me feel alive.

The sound of a screeching car interrupted my thoughts and I spun around, just in time to hear someone shouting, "Persia! Persia! Wait up!"

Oh God, no! Elliot jumped out of the car, looking more rumpled than ever. When he hadn't contacted me the day before, I'd thought that maybe he'd gone home. That maybe my message scrawled across his chest had finally gotten through, but no such luck.

"What the *hell* are you doing back here? I told you to get lost. I mean it! Beat it, scram, hit the road, Jack. I don't want you around here so take the hint and leave me alone." I marched over to his car. He'd narrowly missed taking out one of the rose bushes that lined the driveway. Stupid bastard. What had I ever seen in him?

"What the hell did you mean by this?" He pulled open his shirt. His chest was red where it was obvious that he'd been scrubbing, but my body graffiti was still crystal

283

clear. Or should I say, crimson red.

Exasperated, I said, "I thought maybe you'd get the message. Elliot, just go. Get out of here and get out of my life."

His anger turned to confusion. "But I thought we could talk. You can't mean it, Persia. We can't be over. I'm out of jail now. Things can go on just the same as before." He stared at me with that stupid blank look reserved for kittens, puppies, and other young waifs. It just looked creepy on grown men.

"Are you insane? I don't want anything to do with your thieving, lying ass. You're a cheat and you're a thief and you're in my way! Get back in your car, turn the hell around, and hit the road because you're not staying here another minute." I started forward, one deliberate step at a time, and he backed up, all too aware of what I could do to him. Elliot was far from athletic.

He paused by his car door. "Don't throw away the best thing you've ever had, Persia. But I'm willing to be big about it, to take you back if you apologize. You won't get any better, not being the cold, ballbreaking bitch you are."

"Do you really think it's wise to say that kind of crap to me?" I jumped toward him and he scrambled into the driver's seat and threw the car into reverse.

"You aren't going to get rid of me that easy!" he shouted as he wheeled out of the drive and screeched down the road.

As I watched him go, I had the uneasy feeling that he meant his parting shot. As Kyle had instructed, I noted down the time and everything that I could remember from the conversation. Damn, what a way to start the day.

I sped along Beachcomber's Drive, carefully skirting the downed branches that littered the road. A few of the side streets had been hard hit. Here and there, utility crews still worked on the power lines, scurrying to get them back up and running. A lot of the houses along the road were still dark, and plenty of wood smoke spiraled into the air.

As I turned onto Island Drive, I saw that the power was back on for everybody in the downtown area. The oak had been cleared out of the way. I parked in front of Venus Envy and strode into the bakery. Barbara was slipping a tray of crullers into the display case. I pointed to the maple bars, holding up two fingers.

"Elliot showed up at the house this morning. I need two of those, stat!"

She laughed. "Oh great, what did his jerkiness want?"

"To rail against what a bitch I am, what else?" I muttered. "Anyway, so when can you leave today? I was thinking if we headed over to Seattle early enough, we could check out the Radiance Cosmetics Boutique. I think there's one downtown in Pioneer Square."

Barbara grimaced. "Dorian wasn't all that thrilled when I told him I was going to a nightclub with you, but he finally relented. I'm tied up until noon, though. Will that be okay?"

I nodded. "Noon is fine. We'll have time to dress, catch the ferry, and hit Seattle by three o'clock. Do you know what you're going to wear?"

She snorted. "I have a little outfit that I think will knock your socks off."

I was banking on a pair of tight black jeans, a Lycra halter top, a pair of spikes, and my leather jacket for myself. I just hoped Barb wasn't planning on a retro job. I vaguely remembered seeing her dressed for a date when I was twelve. She had stopped to say hi and had been dressed in a tight Spandex miniskirt and a glitter headband.

"As soon as you can get away, come over and get me." I snagged up my maple bars, tossed two dollars on the counter, and returned to Venus Envy, where Tawny was trying to cope with a distraught customer. I deposited my pastries and purse at my station and hurried over to help.

The customer had a bitter, pinched look on her face and Tawny looked about ready to blow a gasket. She took a deep breath and let it out slowly. "Mrs. Winters has a complaint. She found . . ." She paused, then winced as she said, "She found dried blood on her bottle of bath salts."

Oh, good Lord! I gingerly took the bag that the red-faced woman handed me and peeked inside. Lemon Verbena salts. They'd been on the shelf next to where Lydia had been killed. I slid the bottle out of the bag and sure enough, the back and bottom edge were speckled with blood. Aunt Florence and I had fallen down on the job. Wincing, I forced a smile and cleared my throat.

"I am so sorry. I have no idea how this happened. I can assure you that we cleaned up everything here after . . ." I stopped. There was nothing I could say that would make it any better, and most likely, I'd just make it worse. "Would you like a refund or an exchange?"

She let out a loud sigh to let me know how exasperated she was. "Well, I've never had problems here before. I suppose an exchange."

Quickly, I sized up the situation. She wanted to be compensated for her shock and a simple tit-for-tat wasn't going to cut it. "Tawny, please get Mrs. Winters two Lemon Verbena bath salts from the back, along with a matching bottle of body lotion. Then go over that shelf with a magnifying glass."

Tawny nodded and I escorted the woman over to one of the benches lining the wall and poured her a mug of orange-zest tea. She gave me a guarded smile and said, "You know, I love this shop and I was so surprised yesterday when I got home and found the blood."

"It should never have happened," I said. "And I apologize again. I don't know why we didn't notice it before you left the store with your purchase."

She gave me a broad smile. We'd been forgiven. "Well, I was in here yesterday, right when the oak tree came crashing down. With the power out and so much confusion, it probably escaped Tawny's notice. No harm done. Well, I won't keep you, dear. I'll be fine."

I stood up and gave her a gracious nod. "If there's anything else I can do for you, just let me know."

As I passed Tawny on her way out of the back, I whispered, "Make certain that all the other bottles are clean. In fact, if you find any with blood or other questionable material on them, take them in the back and put them in a basket with a note. Auntie and I were sure we found everything but you never know — we were both in shock at the time."

By the time I'd settled in at my station and wolfed down the maple bars, my 10:30 appointment had arrived. Juanita Lopez was one of our regulars. She came in like clockwork every week for a facial, and she must have owned every product we had on the shelves. Sometimes I wondered where she stored them all.

Juanita was short and plump, with a gleaming black braid that hung down her back to the small of her waist. She had clear skin and incredibly warm eyes, and was altogether charming, if a little lacking in self-esteem. This morning, however, something seemed off kilter.

I motioned her to sit on the bench opposite my table. "Hey lady, how you doing?"

She shrugged instead of giving me her usual dizzyingly brilliant smile. "I need one of your potions, Persia. A strong one."

I glanced up. Her voice was guarded and

I tried to read her eyes. "Tell me about it."

Juanita stared at her hands for a moment. The nails were short, her hands worn rough through years of hard work. They had character, those hands, as much as the woman herself.

"I think my husband is having an affair. I want something to remind him that I'm the one who's stuck by him all these years. Something that makes me smell beautiful and young." I started to speak but she stopped me. "No, don't say it. You always tell me I'm beautiful but I don't believe it. I can't. Not with this figure, not with these wrinkles on my face. I know I'm beginning to show my age, but I can't afford Botox or a plastic surgeon."

A sinking feeling surging in the pit of my stomach, I understood what she was asking from me. A love potion. Something to make her look and feel radiant again. I knew I could create something that would help shift her mood. And, if she felt differently about herself, others would probably react differently to her, but it wouldn't be a magic potion to change her husband's mind if he had found comfort elsewhere. As gently as I could, I explained this to her.

She shook her head. "I know you aren't

really a *bruja,* I know you can't work miracles. But you can have a way with herbs and plants and perfumes, Persia. I've seen it in you. Your clerk could sit here and blend up a fragrance using the same recipe you created, and it wouldn't smell the same. You put passion into your work, and I need that."

Her voice was raw, her nerves frayed. Tension rolled off her like waves of heat on a summer afternoon. Well, hell. She really believed I could help, and maybe that alone would be enough. Maybe whatever I created would inspire enough self-confidence in her that she'd go home and confront her husband, or show him what he'd be missing if he left.

"All right," I said. "Let's get started."

I asked her to wash her hands and, while she was gone, I leafed through one of the reference works I kept on a shelf behind my station. Herbs and fragrances had personalities, energies inherent to their nature, according to modern witches. Having worked with plants a good share of my life, I believed them.

Skimming through the index, I came to a listing of traits. *Herbs to Inspire Love and Passion.* Let's see. Orange and rose, and — of course — amber and musk. I was already building the scent in my mind. Narcissus would act as the base — a fragrance as intense as its name. Oh yeah, we'd make her husband sit up and take notice, and if this turned out as delicious as I thought it was going to smell, I might have to make some for Barbara. Get Dorian sparking again. By the time Juanita had returned, I'd jotted down a page of notes.

Starting with a base of almond oil, I added the foundation note of narcissus to cement the perfume. Then, a few drops of musk, a hint of amber, and a highlight of rose, swirling gently after each addition to blend but not bruise the scent. I added a top note of orange, then a few chips of garnet and rose quartz and a shredded rose petal. As I closed my eyes and brought the bottle to my nose, I thought I was going to faint. Heady and intoxicating, the scent made me want to roll in it. I dabbed a few drops of the oil onto Juanita's wrists and told her to walk around the store for a moment. While she was gone, I went over to our bulk herb section and filled a sachet with lemon balm, damiana, angelica, dill weed, and some powdered dragon's blood resin. I tied it up with a pretty bow as Juanita returned.

"What do you think?" I asked.

She sniffed her wrists and her face crinkled into a smile. "I love it! It's perfect. If that doesn't catch his notice, nothing will. Thank you so much!"

"Don't thank me for something that hasn't happened yet. I'm just glad you like the scent and I hope everything works out. Here." I handed her the sachet. "These herbs are supposed to promote devotion and love. I don't know if it will do any good, but it smells nice and you can tuck it in your lingerie drawer."

Juanita clutched the little velveteen pouch, her eyes misting over. "Thank you, Persia. I appreciate what you've done."

Unable to handle her joy — if her husband *was* cheating I couldn't understand why she'd want him back — I pulled out my invoice pad and asked, "Do you want this in a cologne base, or just as the oil itself?"

"The oil is fine," she said. "I prefer it to cologne."

I wrote up the order and handed her the invoice. "The sachet is on me. Good luck, and I hope . . ." What could I say? I hope your husband quits cheating on you? I hope you're mistaken? But she just gave me a quick nod and took the receipt up to the counter to pay. As I watched her walk away, I had the feeling that it was already too late. No perfume — magical or otherwise — would help her if her husband had found somebody else. Had I given her false hope? Perhaps, I argued with myself, but at least I'd been up front about it. With a sigh, I tucked away my oils and glanced at the clock. Quarter to eleven.

I really didn't feel like working. Storms always made me restless. My moods shifted with the wind, and right now they were hungry for the open road, for something — anything — to take out the tension that had been building ever since I'd found Lydia's body. At least tomorrow was my date with Bran. Climbing the rock wall in the gym would help, but even that paled in comparison to what I really wanted — a good hard hike under the open sky, smelling the dirt and the grass and the ocean, feeling the wind rush through my hair.

I glanced around the shop, looking for something to occupy my thoughts, when the phone rang and Tawny motioned to me. It was Andy Andrews.

"Andy? I'm Persia Vanderbilt and I'm working with Winthrop Winchester on the Wang case. Thanks for calling back. I was wondering if I could drop over and ask you a couple questions?"

He cleared his throat. "You a cop?"

"No, I'm not —"

" 'K. Say, how old are you? You don't sound very old to me."

I rolled my eyes and stared at the ceiling. Andy was beginning to sound pretty young to me, too, but then I'd been forewarned by his answering machine. "I'm under fifty, okay? Now, may I come over?"

What sounded suspiciously like a beer burp deafened me. "Sure dude, come on over then."

Already regretting my trip into Beavis-and-Butthead land, I grabbed my shawl, told Tawny I'd be back in about forty-five minutes, and hit the road.

Chapter Fifteen

Andy must have been waiting near the door. I'd barely knocked when it flew open and he looked me up and down. His eyes lingering on my breasts, he beckoned me in with a lazy smile.

Oh jeez, don't even think it, I thought. *Nope, not in a million years.*

"So, you're Persia. Nice to meet you. *Very* nice." His gaze traveled up my body to my face where, seeing my expression, he coughed and forced a "ha-ha-just-joking" smile. This boy was hard up, and his clothes looked it.

Classic grunge, but with a faded look that was for real, not chic. Ground-in grass stains on the legs told me he was really too poor to afford anything better. His pants clung precariously from his hips, three sizes too big, showing off the top of his faded underpants. A camouflage tee shirt stretched tautly across his loosely muscled chest, and he wore a baseball cap turned backwards over long, dirty blond hair well on the road to dreadlocks. His sneakers weren't tied, the tongue protruded, standing at attention. Yeah, he was with it, all right.

"Andrew Andrews," he introduced himself, grimacing. I repressed an urge to smile. Parents could be cruel, very cruel. He thrust out his hand before I had a chance to extend my own and I gingerly took it.

I sucked in a quick breath and exhaled just as fast when the scent of stale beer and pot assaulted my nose. "I appreciate you taking the time to talk to me. I know you talked to the police, but I want to double-check on what you told them. It's really important. Are you sure you don't remember anything about that night? Anybody unusual?"

A look of disappointment played at his lips and he flopped down on one of the sofas and planted his feet on the coffee table, leaving me standing.

"I already talked to the cops," he said. "I don't remember nothing. Maybe there was somebody there. Maybe not. I dunno."

Couldn't get much vaguer than that. "Well, did you know Marta Mendoza? She lived in this building —"

Bingo! That got a rise. "Marta? Yeah, I know her. Why?"

I had the feeling he didn't know she was dead. "She was murdered yesterday. In her apartment."

He blanched, the first real sign I'd seen that he was capable of being interested in anything outside of himself. "Marta? Dead? Who'd want to kill her? She's just a nice old lady." He leaned forward and clasped his hands together, staring at the coffee table. "She reminds me of my grandma."

I shrugged. "Cops don't know. What I'd like to find out is whether you remember Marta being at the aquarium that night? Did she come in to use the phone?" Maybe, just maybe, I could jangle his pot-addled memory.

Andy squinted. "Not that I know of. She usually showed up early in the evening, if at all, but she wasn't there that night."

Now we were getting somewhere. "But she could have come in while you weren't looking?"

He shook his head. "Nah. That I'm pretty sure about. Marta only came in when she saw me there because I gave her quarters out of the till to use the phone. It's like, fifty cents now, y'know? I'd tear up ticket receipts to match the amount so the management didn't know. Marta was always broke. I did what I could to help." He gave me a sullen look. "You going to report me?"

I flashed him a slow smile. Even slackers had their good sides. "No, Andy, I won't report you. I just wanted to know if you'd seen her. Again, thank you for your time." As I headed out of the apartment, I turned back. "Do you know what apartment she lived in?"

He nodded. "412B. Say, you sure you don't want to hang out? We could have a beer. Maybe fool around a little?" He stared pointedly at my crotch. "You're one hot-looking chick."

Not even worth the energy to smack him. I snorted. "Thank you for the scintillating offer, but I think I'll pass." I took off for the stairs.

The fourth floor of the building looked much like the fifth. It occurred to me that if Mrs. Fairweather was on the opposite side of the hall, I might be able to drop in on her, but that thought went out the window when I noticed that Marta's door was open. I peeked inside and came face to face with Kyle.

"What are you doing here?" he asked. "Oh no, don't tell me you're going to bother old Mrs. Fairweather? She's blind and can't see you coming. I forbid it, Persia."

Nonplussed by how quickly he read my intentions, I snapped, "You can't forbid me from talking to anybody I want to, but the fact of the matter is that I stopped in to see Andy Andrews."

He let out a quick snicker, unable to keep a straight face. "Good old Andy, huh? He's quite a prize. Smart kid, low ambition. Too lazy to even be a slacker. You thinking of dating him after you get done with Stanton?"

"Wipe that smirk off your face, Chief, or I'll do it for you." I glanced around the room. "So, this is Marta's apartment. Mind if I take a look?"

He frowned but nodded me in, closing the door behind me. "We finished here this morning. I was just picking up some things we left before we release the apartment to her daughter."

The apartment was a haven to memory. Old linen tea towels covered the neatly polished surfaces of cheap furniture. Carefully knitted afghans were casually draped over a thrift-store sofa and rocking chair. As I gazed at one wall, which must have contained fifty framed photos, it occurred to me that I'd thought of her as the cleaning lady, but Marta was a human being, with a private life, and her job had reflected only one aspect of that life.

The photographs were old, some of them with an antiquated look. An old black-and-white picture appeared to have been taken in a small Mexican village and was of an older man and woman. The woman, dressed in a woven poncho over what looked like a flowered dress, looked very much like Marta and could have been her mother. But judging from the setting and look of the photo, I had the feeling the pair were probably her grandparents. Another was a picture of a lovely young woman and a baby.

I glanced over at Kyle. "Marta's daughter and grandson?"

He jammed his hands in his pockets, staring at the photograph. "Yeah. Poor kid. I think we'll start up a charity fund at the station for his care. Marta's daughter isn't a slacker, she's just so unprepared for what life threw at her."

Yet another side of Kyle I didn't know existed. I reached out and patted his arm. "You're a good-hearted man, know that?"

He looked down at me and shook his head. "I just can't figure you out, Persia. Why are you here? You don't strike me as a curiosity hound."

I shrugged. "I don't really know. I just felt like I needed to see her apartment." I wandered through the living room, stopping when I almost stepped onto the outline of a body. Not twenty-four hours ago, Marta's life had ended, right here. A sudden whiff of scent caught my attention — it was familiar and yet . . .

"What is it?" Kyle asked.

I frowned, trying to concentrate. I recognized it, yet couldn't put a name to it. The fragrance was faint, lingering only in minute traces. I let my mind drift, trying to follow the thread of memory that the scent evoked. After a moment, I shook my head. "I know that scent, but can't quite place what it is."

"What are you talking about?" Kyle sniffed, but then shook his head. "I don't smell anything."

"It's musky, almost pungent, but faint."

He inhaled again. "Nope, still don't smell anything."

I shrugged. "I have a heightened sense of smell. I can detect minute levels of cyanide, identify most floral scents if given time, and have what you might call a photographic memory for scents. If I've smelled it once, I'll recognize it again."

He let out a snort. "That's some talent.

Well, if you identify what it is, let us know. It might help us out."

"May I look in her bedroom? I'll be able to tell if what I smell is one of her perfumes by comparing it to what she has." I didn't relish going through the dead woman's things but Kyle was right. This could be important.

He led me to the back room that Marta had used for her bedroom. I glanced through the sparse scattering on top of her dresser. A bottle of Lemon Verbena spray from the shop, which I was pretty sure had been lifted. An old bottle of Chanel N°5 with just a few drops left in it. Probably a gift from long ago. Deodorant, foot powder, a bottle of inexpensive rose-scented hand lotion. Nothing remotely resembling what I'd smelled in the living room. I peeked in the bathroom, but again, the shampoos and soaps didn't match.

"Nothing. I think it may have come into her apartment on somebody else."

Kyle stroked his chin. "The murderer?"

I set down the can of talcum powder that was in my hands and turned to face him. "Perhaps. I don't know. But I can tell you that from what I'm able to find, the scent didn't originate in this apartment."

He escorted me to the door. "I hope you

can place it. We need all the clues we can get right now." He locked the door behind him and we headed for the elevator. He steered me away from Mrs. Fairweather's door. "Persia, I hope you're not still upset at me about that kiss. I don't know what came over me."

I punched the button for the ground floor. "Don't sweat it, Kyle." With a gentle smile, I added, "It wasn't so bad. At least you have soft lips." Leaving him speechless, I walked out of the building and headed to my car.

I made one more stop before heading back to the shop. The Gull Harbor City Hall housed everything from the police station to the city jail to the county clerk's office. Since Kyle hadn't returned to the station by the time I got there, I had to wait until one of the uniformed officers finished typing up a report before she could escort me back to see Trevor.

The jail was small — apparently Gull Harbor's criminal element was less active than Seattle's — and the waiting room where they'd bring Trevor to meet me was clean, if a little sparse and, for the most part, empty. After letting the officer go through my purse, I took a chair by one of the booths and waited. Within five minutes, Trevor was on the other side of the glass. I motioned for him to pick up the phone.

"Hey, how you doing?" Trevor looked like he'd lost a little weight, but otherwise seemed to be in good shape. "How are they treating you?"

He forced a smile. "Not so bad. The food's decent and they aren't beating me up. What's happening?"

"My aunt's going to drop by later today or tomorrow. Has Winthrop been here in the past day or so?" I wondered just how much the lawyer had told him about our plan to find out who Lydia's boyfriend was.

"He left a message that he'd be by later today." He gave me a keen look. "Why? What's going on?"

I cleared my throat and lowered my voice. "Trevor, Marta's been murdered. They found her in her apartment after her neighbor, Mrs. Fairweather, reported a scream. It looks similar to Lydia's murder."

"Shit. Marta? Are you sure?" He looked shocked. "Who would want to kill her?"

"Somebody she might have been trying to blackmail. Maybe somebody who

305

thought she knew something about Lydia's murder. That's why I'm going over to Seattle, to the Blue Dragon club tonight." Softly, I added, "I'm looking for Lydia's boyfriend. I know this may hurt to talk about, but we found out that she was seeing someone who worked there, and that he might have some idea of who killed her."

Trevor's entire countenance changed. His eyes narrowed and he looked like he was ready to jump out of his seat. "Persia, stay away from there. It's a dive, a real pimp joint. I think they run drugs out of there but I'm not sure."

I stared at him. "You know about the Blue Dragon?"

His expression drooped and he looked like a whipped puppy. "A little. I've never been there, but Lydia . . . yeah, she said she met somebody there."

"You know?" A mingled sense of surprise and relief swept over me. I wouldn't have to rat out the fact that Lydia had been two-timing him. On the other hand, the fact that he knew provided a stronger motive for him to have murdered Lydia.

He blinked back tears. "I know the guy works at the Blue Dragon or hangs out there or something. She wouldn't tell me his name. I get the impression that he's a member of some gang. Lydia got herself tangled up with a real winner."

I contemplated his words for a moment. "Are you sure she never mentioned his name?"

"I'm sure. She didn't want me going off half-cocked. Persia, a lot of weird people hang out there. Don't go alone."

"I'm taking a friend so don't worry." He didn't have to know that the friend I was going with was Barbara. "So do you think that her boyfriend might have been capable of murder?"

Trev's head jerked up. "What? I thought she was in love with him. I asked her to marry me and she said she'd think about it. She took off for Seattle the next morning and stayed the entire weekend. The night she returned, she dumped me. Told me that it was over, that she was seeing somebody else. She called me a loser and told me to leave her alone, to never bother her again." His voice trailed off.

I stared at his face. He was in obvious pain and I could see how much he'd loved her. Who knew what drew two people together? She was a bitch and a conniving snot, but she had some elusive sparkle that had caught Trevor's eye enough to make

307

him propose. I didn't believe he'd killed her, not for one second. Behind that façade of anger rested a broken heart and it wasn't a heart that could turn and murder the object of his affection.

"Did you tell Kyle about her boyfriend?"

His eyes fluttered to the ground. "No," he said, "but there wasn't much to tell, now was there? My ex-girlfriend was seeing somebody else. Big whoop. I didn't know his name, didn't know anything about him. And it would have looked real good for me, wouldn't it? They'd say I killed her out of jealousy."

"What else do you know about him? Spill it. Every little bit will help me find him. I already know that he was probably Lydia's dealer."

Trev's jaw dropped. "What? Her what?"

Oops. So he hadn't been aware of the drug use. "Trev," I said as gently as I could, "Lydia was using. Speed, most likely. From what I've been able to find out she got her drugs from this guy she was seeing. In fact, I'm wondering if he didn't threaten her, make her back off from you so she wouldn't accidentally spill the beans."

Trevor rubbed his forehead. The officer standing guard near Trevor signaled that our time was up. "I didn't have a clue. How could I have been so blind? Persia, listen to me. Be very careful. If he is a dealer, you don't want to get on his wrong side."

"Trev, we're doing what we can. Take it easy, okay?" I motioned to the guard that I was almost done.

"Yeah . . . and thanks. I hope you find something." Trev stumbled over his words to fit in a good-bye as he was led away. I waved, watching him as they led him out of the booth, back to his cell. He looked so defeated and so angry. What on earth would happen to him if we couldn't prove his innocence? Trevor would never last behind prison bars. I pushed back my chair. We had no other option. Barbara and I would visit the Blue Dragon and find out everything we possibly could.

When I reached the shop, Barbara was waiting for me. Aunt Florence hadn't gotten there yet, so I told Tawny that we were taking off. As we stepped out of the shop, a ray of sunlight struck me in the face and I basked in the warmth.

"I forget how much I love the sun until it shows up," I said. Sunshine was a precious resource in western Washington, an infrequent visitor that was welcomed in with open arms when it showed up.

Barbara patted my arm. "When we were in Greece, it was so sunny and brilliant I honestly thought about moving there. Well, if it weren't for Dorian's parents. To tell you the truth, I love the villages over there, although I don't think we'd fit in very well."

We climbed in my Sebring and took off for her place, where I stretched out across her bed and filled her in on my conversation with Trevor while she dug through her dressing room. "This could be dangerous, you know."

"Of course I know that," she called from inside her walk-in closet. The woman had more clothes than my aunt and I put together. "I care about Trevor too, and frankly, I think you underestimate me. You remember me from years back when I was just your babysitter. I've grown up a little since then, Persia."

I grinned. "So have I. I guess we're both big girls and we can take care of ourselves. But be careful who you talk to, and don't say anything about Trevor. And don't —"

"And don't get into trouble. I know, I know! I heard the whole spiel from Dorian last night and again this morning. He's not thrilled that I'm going, but I told him I have to get out of here now and then and do something out of character. I've become too sedate. As much as I love the big galoot, I want a little spontaneity and verve back in my life."

I sighed. I still didn't think she grasped the full significance of what we were walking into, but then again — maybe I was just being overprotective. Barbara was a decade older than I. She'd seen a lot of life and probably had a good number of adventures I hadn't heard about yet.

"At least I don't have the big hair I used to," she said from behind the door. "Remember that awful style I had when I was twenty-five and you were . . . what . . . fifteen? I copied it off Joan Cusack's character in *Working Girl*."

I remembered, but had the good graces to refrain from commenting. Barb and Dorian had taken me to see the movie. Two days later, Barb had been sporting big hair, which looked even bigger thanks to its brilliant coppery color. Dorian, to whom she'd been married two years at that point, had the good sense not to comment more than his usual grunt.

I leaned back on my elbows. "Oh, those days of pretty boys and glam. I'll take grunge and leather any day, thank you!"

"Hey, I dated one of the boys in Pussy-Dewdrops during the early eighties! Don't knock it till you try it." I laughed as her voice trailed out again. "I gave up the glam boys, though," she said, "when I met Dorian and he swept me away from the discos and the wine bars. God, look at me."

My jaw dropped as she entered the room. I'd seen Barb with big hair, but I'd never seen her decked out like this. She had poured herself into a skin-tight pair of jeans that I hadn't even expected her to own, jet black with thin white stripes up the sides, and had on a crop top worthy of Britney Spears. She'd looped a gold chain belt to hang low on her waist, and four-inch stiletto Candies sealed the outfit. Her makeup was glam, but fit the look, with a dusting of gold body glitter trickling down her neck. My best friend had suddenly devolved from a competent, on-the-go career woman to an exotic extra on the set of a Missy Elliot video.

I pushed myself to a sitting position. "What the hell? Where did you get *that?* I didn't even know you owned clothes like that!"

She leaned toward her mirror, shimmied,

and squinted at her reflection. "I have my secrets, darling. I'm married, not dead, you know."

After I came out of shock, I stammered, "Barbara, you're gorgeous. Are you sure Dorian will let you out of the house like that? You'll rock the club in that get-up."

"What Dorian doesn't know, won't hurt him. He's seen me wear this, of course, but he thinks we're going to a lounge. I didn't exactly tell him it was a nightclub." At my look, she hastily added, "It was the only way I could convince him to let me go. He's got strong opinions on clubbing."

I stood up and gently took her by the shoulders, turning her to face the mirror. "Are you sure you want to come with me, considering Dorian wouldn't like it? Look at yourself."

Hesitating, she glanced at her reflection and sighed. "Yes, I want to go. I love Dorian to pieces, but I need to get out now and then. And it's not like I'm looking for anybody else." She grinned. "Besides, who's going to have your back if it's not me? So, I look good?"

I nodded my approval. "You look great."

"Okay, then, I guess I'm ready. What about purses? Leave it at home?" She held up her Coach handbag.

"I'd switch to something less expensive."

After she found a clutch and transferred her keys, wallet, and makeup bag into it, we trucked over to my place. Aunt Florence had left a note instructing me to make sure to call her if we decided to stay the night in Seattle and she also left a packet of sandwiches for us to take on the road. I might not have my mother, but I had my Auntie. That was more than a lot of people could say.

We dashed up to my room, where I chased Delilah off the vanity and picked up the bracelet that she'd knocked off the table. While Barbara poked around my closet, I slid into a pair of black leather pants that were laced up the side. They were so tight that I could barely sit down, rode low on my hips, and set off my abs. The cropped halter top had a built in shelf bra — a necessity for my build. Black Lycra, it was on the shiny side, and fit like a glove.

"You look like your clothes are molded on your body," Barb said, snickering. "Man, you've got a good figure. I wouldn't want to take you on in a fight, that's for sure." She handed me my stacked-heel black suede ankle boots with the silver buckles on the side. I slipped on a pair of socks that wouldn't show over the tops, and then zipped them up.

After scrunching into a velveteen bolero out of the closet and swinging my hobo purse over my shoulder, I was ready to go. I tucked my Day-Timer into my tote bag along with the sandwiches, a bottle of water, and several Luna Bars. As we sped off, I couldn't help but wonder if we'd find Lydia's boyfriend. And if we did, would we learn anything helpful? Whatever happened, I just hoped to hell we weren't walking into the *"gaping maws of death,"* like the screaming chicks in a slasher exploitation flick.

Chapter Sixteen

The drive to the ferry took ten minutes, though once we merged into the righthand lane that was open only to cars waiting to board, our pace slowed to a snail's crawl. Still, we managed to arrive just in time to be near the front of the line for the three o'clock run. As we pulled into the terminal we stopped by the toll booth to pay our fee, then eased into the next open spot in one of the ten lanes where drivers and their cars waited to board.

Saturdays were always busy, though not as bad as the morning and evening commutes during the week. While Sand Bar Software employed fifty or sixty Gull Harbor techies, there were still quite a few chipheads who lived on Port Samanish Island and commuted by ferry over to Seattle, Bellevue, and Redmond in order to work at one of the numerous high-tech companies making their home in the Northwest.

As we waited, the ferry eased into the dock. With two full decks for loading cars, and several decks above that where passengers could walk, look over the railings, and get a bite to eat at the vending machines, the Klakatat Ferry was named after some creature that supposedly haunted the northwest woodlands.

The ferry settled at the dock, the gates opened and a line of cars began to disembark. Able to hold over two hundred vehicles and almost twenty-five hundred passengers, the Klackatat was one of the jumbo-class category of ferries that served the Puget Sound inlet.

My cell phone rang and I flipped it open. It was Aunt Florence.

"Persia, are you on board yet?"

I glanced at my watch. "No, we still have another moment or two before boarding. Auntie, while I've got you for a moment, I went to see Trevor today. He sure could use some cheering up. It would be nice if you could get some of his friends to go visit him." The line started to move. "I've got to go. I'll call you later from Seattle."

"Be careful! Please, both of you." She was trying to sound brave but I could hear the worry in her voice.

"Auntie, don't fret. We'll be home before you know it." I flipped the phone shut, tossed it to Barb, and put the car in gear.

Barb dropped my phone in my purse and grinned at me.

"She's nervous, isn't she? Well, I don't blame her. You might not think I'm taking this seriously, but I know perfectly well what goes on in some of these clubs. I just had to get away from the bakery for awhile." She sighed. "Persia, am I old? Do I look old to you?"

I glanced over at her as I eased the car into line. "You're kidding. You look around my age. Why?"

She shrugged. "I feel old. Midlife crisis, maybe. I'm forty-one. I have a successful business and a wonderful husband. So why am I getting so antsy for adventure? I feel like I've been in a rut lately."

I guided the car onto the ramp and we ended up almost at the bow of the boat. We gathered our purses and made sure the doors were locked. "Do you want to go topside?"

"Sure. The stairs?"

I glanced at her, surprised. Usually I had to bully her into taking the stairs instead of the elevator, which always struck me as odd because Barb was hyperactive and could never sit still.

"Over there," I said, and pointed to the nearest stairwell. We climbed three flights to the top and emerged to a magnificent view. The pilot house sat in the middle of the deck. From there, the captain steered and supervised the vessel. Enclosed passenger cabins graced each end of the ferry, with stairs leading to the viewing platforms atop them. The wind was nippy, and most people had stayed inside the cabins, or on the enclosed deck below. I motioned to Barbara and we scampered up to the platform facing the bow. Nobody else was there and we had an uninterrupted view of Puget Sound. Even though the day was overcast, it was lovely and I remembered, once again, just why I'd made my home here. A loud horn signaled our departure, and the ferry pulled out from the docks and headed across the water at a surprisingly fast clip. At maximum speed of eighteen knots, the water churned up from the bow as we drove a wedge through the inlet.

"Oh God, it's so beautiful," I said, letting the wind stream through my hair.

Barb nodded, silently staring ahead. From where we stood, we overlooked the car decks. Several people were milling below, near their cars, walking out to the end of the boat's prow until they were staring almost straight down into the waves created by the ferry's passage. I leaned against the railing and closed my eyes, listening to the churning of the water as we chugged across the Sound.

After a moment, I took a deep breath and asked, "Barb, are you happy with Dorian? Really? I've never heard you talk this way before. I thought you loved being married." She was beginning to worry me. Barb had been ecstatic when Dorian proposed and, at thirteen, I'd been her youngest bridesmaid. Now, after eighteen years, was she getting cold feet?

She stared at the skyline. "I love him, I'm happy with him. I don't want a divorce or anything like that, if that's what you're asking. I just feel old. Men don't turn their heads anymore when I walk into the room. It would be nice if somebody showed an interest — it's not like I want to have an affair. I just want to feel attractive."

I heard her loud and clear. Barbara wanted to feel desirable. She wanted to feel appealing enough to make a man wonder what he might be missing. I sighed. She had no idea how pretty she was. I thought about Debbie, and Juanita. It seemed none of the women I knew felt good about their looks. While I understood this on a gut level, I'd never fully played into the game. I intimidated a lot of men, but also got more than my share of attention, a lot of it from guys I wouldn't let touch me with a ten-foot pole. But perhaps I'd feel different in ten years, when the glances my way slowed down and I began to see little lines on the corners of my eyes.

"I don't have an answer for you, Barb. I think maybe you need to do something for you, though. Take a class that makes you feel alive. Do something that Dorian doesn't want to do. You two hang out all the time together at work and at home. Maybe you just need to create some space where you can focus on your own needs."

She shrugged. "Maybe. Dorian seems to think we need to do everything together. It's not possessiveness, it's just the way he was brought up. Family is important, and even though he was glad to leave Greece, he carries that upbringing with him."

We fell into a companionable silence as the ferry rippled across the water. Shorelines of other islands were visible in the distance, heavily wooded patches of land rising up from what were once mountain valleys. The inlets and bays of Puget Sound had once been above water, caught in the clench of glacial ice floes that stretched across upper North America during the last ice age. When that epoch came to an end, the floes melted and the ocean level rose, giving birth to Puget Sound, the collective name often not only given to the actual Sound itself, but to Hood Canal, Admiralty Inlet, the Saratoga Passage, and numerous other waterways that spun off from the Strait of Juan de Fuca where the long arm of the Pacific Ocean crept in to infiltrate Washington State.

The channels in the Sound allowed the wind to whip strong storms through and, depending on which direction a storm was coming from, some communities were clobbered while others remained un-scathed. Port Samanish was in the perfect position to bear the full brunt of a lot of the major wind and rain storms that raged through the islands.

Barb and I watched as the ferry ate up the miles. Some twenty-five minutes into the ride the Seattle skyline came into view, the docks jutting out into the water amidst seafood restaurants and marinas. In some ways I missed the city, with the skyscrapers and Space Needle and Seattle Center. I did *not* miss the steep hills that had put me to the test on my morning runs. I found out the hard way why Seattle was known as the "little San Francisco" the first time I went out for my morning jog up Queen Anne Hill. I never tried that route again.

The Klakatat Ferry eased into port. As it docked we headed back down to the car and a charge of electricity raced through me. The city was so much more fun now that I didn't have to worry about finding a job here or paying rent.

I loved the quirky area surrounding the Port of Seattle. The docks, ferry terminals, Maritime Museum, and seafood restaurants all blended together in a cacophony of noise and bustle. The wharf was home to fascinating and just odd attractions, including the Imax Dome, the Maritime Museum, and Ye Olde Curiosity Shop, where the shrunken heads were real and the fudge delicious.

When Auntie came over to visit, she always wanted to go to Ivars' Acres of Clams for lunch, and then on up to Pike Place Market — the marketplace mecca of the northwest — where the fish throwers tossed gigantic salmon from one to another in a show that delighted tourists and locals alike. Yes, I had fit right in with the city in so many ways, as much a misfit as everybody else.

At the deckhand's signal, I started the car and we eased off the ramp into the docking area. We followed the arrows out of Pier 52 and turned right onto Alaskan Way, driving along the waterfront until we reached Yesler Way, which led us directly to Pioneer Square, where the Radiance Cosmetics Boutique was situated.

"I love Pioneer Square," Barbara said, peering out of the window. "It's got such character."

"That it does," I said. And it did. Pioneer Square was the oldest and funkiest part of the city, where the pavement on the roads was interspersed with brickwork. Glistening skyscrapers nestled against old, rundown taverns, and the streets were crowded with tiny specialized shops.

I signaled and made a left turn. Damn it! Wrong street. "Shit! I should have gone up two more blocks. Now I'll have to circle around again. I can never remember which street goes which direction."

The layout of the streets had driven me crazy when I lived here, patchwork and meandering like the plans had been designed by an architect drunk on cheap wine. Roads often ran one-way part of the time, then would suddenly switch direction on the other side of a main cross street.

After another half-hour of traffic gridlock and wrong turns, I finally got going in the right direction and we found a parking garage near the building that housed the boutique. For five bucks an hour, they'd better watch my car, I thought, as I stretched my legs, listening to the traffic and voices, the hum of electricity as it zinged through the wires, the blaring of horns.

"I am not wearing spikes to hoof it over to that boutique," Barb said, switching to her pumps. "I'll put them back on when we head for the club."

"Good idea." I was used to wearing stilettos, though I hadn't as much since I moved. All my boots were stacked heels, sending me soaring over six feet tall. I liked the feeling.

After making sure the car was locked, we took off up First Avenue. The street was divided in the center by a landscaped island that ran for several blocks. Cafes, consignment clothing, import goods, Persian rugs and carpeting, antiques and collectibles, crystals and bookstores, Pioneer Square had it all. We crossed Cherry, and a half-block later, saw the stairs and a ramp leading down to the bottom floor of the Bellos Building. The stairs led into a long hall, where we turned left. As we passed a Starbucks, Barb tapped me on the shoulder. "I need caffeine. Can we stop for coffee?"

I grinned at her. "You junkie. Tell you what, I'm only going to be a few minutes. Why don't I meet you at Starbucks after I'm done? Then you can enjoy your fix without hurrying."

She thought about it, then nodded. "Sounds good. I need a buzz more than I need to look at makeup." As she headed into the coffee shop, I continued down the hall. At the end, a door opened into the Radiance Cosmetics Boutique, identified by an expensive and subdued sign in shades of ivory and pink. The shop was devoid of customers. I glanced at my watch. Five-twenty. This shouldn't take long.

As I entered the shop a hush descended, broken only by the soft hum of elevator music. Five counters served for skin care, eyes, lips, cheeks, and nails. A podium guarded the entrance, and behind the podium stood a young woman elegantly coiffed in a pinstripe suit with a skirt so short that I could see the tops of her thigh-high stockings. She hurried over to greet me.

"How do you do? I'm Nadia. May I help you?" she asked.

I glanced around; a few years ago I'd

pulled a stint in a boutique much like this one. Oh yeah, that had been fun, all right. Not.

"Hi, I'm Persia Vanderbilt. I'm from Gull Harbor, on Port Samanish Island." I paused to see if the name of the town registered. It did — a flicker of recognition passed over her face. "I was an acquaintance of Lydia Wang's," I added.

"Oh!" She sucked in a deep breath. "So you knew her?" Her eyes narrowed. "Were you a friend of hers?"

I paused, considering the best direction in which to proceed. By the tone of her voice, I had the feeling that Nadia hadn't been one of Lydia's fans. Nothing surprising there, considering Lydia's lack of diplomacy with those she considered underlings.

"Not really. She was a client in our shop over there — Venus Envy, a bath-and-beauty shop that my aunt and I run."

Nadia smiled. "Venus Envy! I've heard of your shop. You make some wonderful bath products. A friend gave me your Lavender Blue bath salts and I just love them — in fact, I was planning on asking her to pick me up a few more items next time she's over in Gull Harbor."

A thought crossed my mind that we really needed to get a Web site up and move into mail order. I fished one of my cards out of my purse and handed it to her. "Just call me and I can take a credit card order by phone."

"That would be great! Now, what did you need?"

I sighed. "To be honest, I wanted to ask you a few questions about Lydia and Radiance Cosmetics, if I may. I'll buy something to make sure you get your commission — I know how these jobs are and I don't want to get you in trouble."

She rolled her eyes. "Don't sweat it. Nobody else is here this afternoon — there's a big to-do at Westlake Center and everybody's at our shop over there. But I'm not sure I can help you."

"Maybe you can, maybe not." I pulled out one of Winthrop's cards. "I'm helping out Winthrop Winchester, a lawyer defending a suspect in Lydia's murder who also happens to be a friend of mine."

She shrugged. "What do you want to know?"

"I was hoping that you can tell me about Lydia's interactions with the company. Did people respect her? Was she friendly? Did she ever show up with any men that weren't connected with Radiance?"

The phone rang.

"Excuse me," Nadia said, holding up one hand as she hurried over to answer it. She spoke in low tones for a moment, then returned, shaking her head. "Sorry for the interruption. Is this an official question? Can you keep it off the record that I answered?"

I nodded. "I'll do my best to keep your name out of things. So, was Lydia a regular at the boutique?"

Nadia's eyes flickered and she snorted. "Oh, she made it a point to come in every week for a makeover, all right. *Before* she won the contest. Afterwards, she showed up once or twice but that was it."

So Lydia had been cultivating favorites? "Was anybody here on the judging committee for the contest?"

Again the scornful smile. "No, most of the judges were from HQ, and most were older men. Lydia made it a point to get to know them, though. That much was apparent at the contest, which we were all required to attend."

So Colleen had probably been on the mark with her accusation that Lydia had slept her way to the top. "Do you know who the judges were?"

Nadia rattled off a few names, then said, "But if you're looking for a murderer, look somewhere else. None of those men have the guts to kill anybody. Their wives would make whatever time they had left a living hell. Anyway, whether Lydia slept with any of them didn't matter. That wasn't why she won."

"What do you mean?" From what I'd seen of the lineup, several of the contestants were clearly more beautiful than Lydia was, and they had to have better personalities. If she hadn't slept her way to the top, how had she won?

"Lydia was the only one who fit the uniform, if you know what I mean."

I didn't. "Explain, please."

"I'd get my butt fired for telling you this, but then again, I get paid shit wages and I'm thinking of moving to New York anyway."

I had the feeling that Radiance Cosmetics was only a blip on her resume, and I'd bet dime to dollar she wanted to be an actress and was just biding time until her "big break."

"You headed to Broadway?" I asked.

Her eyes lit up. "Oh yes, that's all I've ever wanted."

"I can see you on stage — you're beautiful." I meant it, too; she was a lovely young woman. Take her out of the Ally

McBeal suit and put her in a flowing Elizabethan gown and I could see her in a production of *Romeo and Juliet* or some other classic. She was perfect for the young ingénue.

She debated another minute and I didn't press her. "You promise you won't say where you got this information?"

I raised my hand. "I give you my word."

"Okay. Radiance Cosmetics has a culture gap. We draw a lot of upper-crust white women, and we've broken into the African-American market with the new Yolanda line for darker-skinned clients. But the one market Radiance hasn't been able to crack is the Asian line. The head honchos want to break open the market. They want it bad. And Lydia Wang was their ticket in. She was gorgeous, Asian American, from a prominent local family, and would have been the perfect spokeswoman."

"But why the contest? Why not just hire her directly?"

"The contest built her name through all the publicity, without having to pay her anything near what they'd normally pay a model. I'll lay odds somebody from Radiance knew her beforehand and encouraged her to enter. Lydia was stupid in that regard. She thought she was such a hot shot and getting so much money, but it was really jack shit and they got away with it. Except for one problem. She's dead and now they have to play by the rules and offer the crown to the second-place winner."

"So Colleen just lucked out. She would never have won the crown, no matter how beautiful she was." That was news, and my guess was that Colleen didn't have a clue in the world that she was assuming the title by a stroke of good fortune. Bad fortune, if you looked at it from Lydia's perspective.

Nadia laughed. "I'll tell you this. That girl won't last longer than a couple of months. They'll run her so ragged she'll beg to be let out of the contract and then Radiance will sue her for the rest of the money, and they'll start searching for a new face. This has been a disaster. The new China Veils line was originally supposed to come out next month, but one thing after another has happened. Now they've lost their model and this is going to set them back again. We've had so many people asking for it, and they told us to lie and say that it's almost ready. I'm fed up. They expect us to spend all our money to look as good as we can but will they reimburse us for anything?"

As she shifted the conversation, I agreeably went along. "I hear you — a few years ago I was doing pretty much what you're doing. I couldn't wait to get out that door every evening."

"I bet you have fun working at Venus Envy," she said.

"Yeah, drop in some time and I'll blend you up a custom fragrance. No charge, in fact — as a thank you for talking to me."

She beamed at me then, a genuine smile. "Hey, I remember something else about Lydia!"

"What?"

Nadia lowered her voice. "She was here a month or so ago, I think it was. I don't know what she was doing — some bigwig from HQ was here talking to her. Her cell phone rang and she moved aside to answer, but I could still hear her. She got into an argument with whoever it was, and then I heard her say, 'You do that and we're both in deep shit. Don't you dare lay a hand on him, Jin, or I'll rip your heart out and feed it to the pigs.' Who do you suppose she was talking about?"

I stared at the counter, thoughts churning in my head. Who indeed? But the name sounded odd.

"Jin? Are you sure it was Jin and not Jim?" Could he be Lydia's boyfriend?

"No, it was Jin all right, because I remember thinking how unusual it was." She nodded emphatically.

Hmm. Had Lydia been trying to protect Trevor because this guy had threatened him? Or was Jin somebody else, somebody we hadn't figured into our equation yet? After a quick thank you, and a purchase of two tubes of lipstick that I really didn't need, I headed out the door toward Starbucks. If Lydia had been trying to protect Trevor, then we might be in more danger than I thought and would have to tread very lightly at the club.

Chapter Seventeen

"If it was Trevor she was talking about, maybe he was in danger and Lydia was trying to protect him. That could be why she was killed. By framing Trev, the murderer took care of both problems at once." Barbara slipped her iced triple caramel macchiato into the cup holder, then reached down and pulled off her shoes, changing back into her stilettos.

"Good thinking, Sherlock." I grinned at her. "But we still have to figure out who Jin is."

Barb shrugged, taking a long sip from her whipped-cream-topped drink. I eyed the cup and shook my head. I loved my tea, would tolerate coffee upon occasion, but the sweet drinks were a bit too much for me unless it was a milk shake or fruit juice.

"I don't know . . . it's too easy," I said. "But then, murder isn't always rocket science and crimes of passion are seldom thought out very well. At least we have a name to go on."

"Speaking of gin, I could go for a nice martini right now," Barb said.

"Yeah, I want a drink, too," I said. "It's been awhile since I cut loose."

Right about then, a stupid driver swerved in front of me, blabbing away on his cell phone. I honked and yanked my attention back to the road.

"Idiot! What the hell was he thinking?" Barb glared out the window at him. "Jeez, it's just not safe on the road anymore."

"I know. I wish they'd outlaw talking on those damned things while driving. It's dangerous." I shifted gears and we headed up a hill.

Barb nodded. "Anyway, regarding Jin. Could he be your man with hidden secrets that Bran was talking about?"

I shrugged as we topped the hill, and flipped on my right turn signal, pausing at the light to make sure the way was clear. "I don't know, but we're going to find out, I hope."

"You like Bran, don't you?" Barbara grinned. "I think somebody's got a crush!"

I blushed. "Hey, he's better than a good share of the men I've met in my life. And he likes to climb — that's always a plus by me."

"And he's handsome and tall and —"

"Oh, stop it!" I said, laughing. "Now you sound like a school girl." I flashed her a smile. "You know, Auntie always did have a knack for picking odd friends. No wonder she and Bran crossed paths."

"When do we hit the club? It's seven o'clock now."

I calculated the distance to the Blue Dragon and factored in the inevitable gridlock and traffic jams. "Let's stop for a leisurely dinner before we head over there. The bar at the Blue Dragon opens at nine, the shows don't get going till later." I pulled into the parking lot next to Coco's Restaurant.

As Barb opened the door, she flashed me a quick grin. "Why do I feel like I'm headed to my last supper?"

I winced. "Don't even say that." But I was thinking the same thing.

The area where the Blue Dragon was located was in the south side of Seattle, near Beacon Hill and Rainier Valley. Long known for their ethnic diversity, the two neighborhoods had also managed to achieve the reputation for being the gang-filled, crime-ridden seedier side to the Emerald City. But while south Seattle wasn't free of problems and both poverty and crime abounded, the area wasn't quite as bad as the media liked to portray it.

I turned onto Northwest Navarro Street and eased my way down the pothole-laden road. The buildings here were gloomy — dark and dirty, more like huge metal warehouses rather than inviting businesses. Industry was the name of the game in this part of Seattle, and only a few miles away stood the massive Boeing complex where lumbering airships made their way down the assembly line. Unfortunately, Boeing had cut back drastically in the past few years, and unemployment rose as the company had laid off tens of thousands of workers. Tempers flared toward the aerospace giant in this part of the world.

Up ahead stood a tall building — old brick that looked like a brownstone converted into a commercial space. Flashing neon blue, a sign in one of the first-floor windows read: The Blue Dragon. The "O" had burnt out, and it made it look all the more uninviting. I eased my Sebring into a parking lot in back of the building. Dimly lit, it was probably a third of the way full and I found myself wishing for the first time since I'd bought the car that I had chosen a less conspicuous vehicle.

"Lock it up good. I'll put on the Club." I

hauled out the antitheft device and fit it through the steering wheel. I locked it into place, slid the chain — on which I kept on the keys — around my neck. "Let's just hope we don't have to beat a hasty retreat."

Barb gave me a knowing look. "I was just thinking the same thing. So, are you ready? I promise, I'll let you take the lead."

"Sounds good," I said. "By the way, don't drink anything unless the bartender pours it and gives the glass directly to you. A lot of Ecstasy floating around, a lot of roofies and other date-rape crap out there."

She shivered and followed me as we hurried to the door, wincing against the biting wind that had sprung up. A bouncer — tall, dark, Asian, and gorgeous — was leaning next to the door. He gave us the once-over, then nodded us in.

I leaned close to Barb as we entered the club. "They only start keeping track of who they let in after midnight, when the real players come out of the woodwork. Until then, it's pretty much like any other lounge. Now stick with me and don't gawk."

She poked me in the ribs, grinning. "You really do think I'm lame, don't you? Hon, I was club hopping by the time I was fifteen.

I know the ropes, even though I am over the hill."

"Um hmm . . . I know that. I just don't want your blood on my hands, because if anything happens to you, I'll have to answer to Dorian and he would not let me see the light of another day, no matter how strong I am."

The door opened into a large room with a bar running along the left side, a cluster of tables in one section, booths against the back wall, and a small but well-defined stage. The walls were black, and the colored lights bouncing off the walls gave me the feeling I'd just entered the world of film noir. A few tables were taken, and several seats at the bar were full, but we appeared to be among the early wave of patrons.

I glanced around the room, looking for potential exits. A discreet sign pointed out the way to the restrooms down a hall, and I noticed several unmarked doors scattered around the room. I peeked down the hall and saw an emergency exit door at the end, just past the ladies' room.

Motioning for Barbara to join me, I headed to the bar and took a seat. The bartender gave us a long once-over. He wasn't smiling. He finished wiping up the counter where he was working and then said, "What will it be, girls?"

"I'll have a Bermuda Rum Swizzle," I said, hoping they'd use authentic Falernum instead of grenadine. Some people couldn't taste the difference but I could, and I could peg it on the first sip if the bar was using a nonalcoholic version of the syrup. A side effect of my heightened sense of smell was a heightened ability to taste, which could be good or bad depending on the food.

Barb cleared her throat. "A Cosmopolitan, please."

As he mixed up our drinks, I took a closer look at our fellow barflies. Men, women, a few whose genders were hard to identify. The light was dim, the walls dark, and those who seemed familiar with the place wore an attitude of "don't intrude, don't bother us, you don't belong here." The music was loud, but not overpowering, and seemed to run to the techno-dance music I hated. I loved good techno-pop, but some of the stuff trying to pass for it now was ear-splitting. Nobody was dancing yet, and it seemed like a good time to have a look around and see if I could locate Jin.

"I'll be back, I'm going to work the room and see if I can find out anything."

341

The room was sparsely filled at this point, mainly with a few lounge lizards scouting the bar for conquests. One of them swept his gaze over me and pushed himself off his bar stool. Oh great. Just what I needed.

He sauntered up to me, drink in hand, and I could see his comb-over wasn't doing its job. "Hey baby, you must wash your clothes in Windex because I can see myself in your pants."

Like I hadn't heard that one before. "Back off, or you'll know what it's like to have your balls used for batting practice." I shouldered past him and, disgruntled, he returned to the bar.

I headed toward a bank of vending machines that stood near a booth that had five people — four men and a woman — sitting in it. As I dug through my purse for change, I listened in on their conversation.

"So I'm like, 'What do you mean, I gotta pay full price?' And he's like, 'Honey, even if you was my granma, you'd be paying full price' . . . it sucks. I can't believe that he won't cut me a deal. Jus' like I'm not a regular customer —"

Out of the corner of my eye, I saw one of the men glancing at me. I studiously ignored them, studying the array of candy bars available. As I plugged my change into the machine and waited for the Snickers bar to drop, I pulled out my cell phone and pretended to punch in numbers.

I counted to five and then said, "Donna? Is that you? Lee Ann said you wanted to talk to me. Whassup?" As I listened to the nonexistent voice on the other end of the line, I kept one ear cocked toward the booth. They must have decided that I wasn't a threat, because as soon as I settled into my "phone call," they started talking again, though at a bit lower volume.

"Anyway, tonight I'm gonna tell him that either he starts cutting me deals or I'll find a new source. He isn't the only game in town, even if he's the cutest."

One of the guys snorted. "Cute? Don't even think about it. He'll take your money and break your heart, and probably give you something skanky while he's at it. Now, if you want a real man, well baby, you just have to say the word."

She giggled and scooted out of the booth. "Potty break. 'Scuse me boys, I'll be back in a few minutes."

I counted to the beat of four after she headed into the bathroom, said a quic' thanks and goodbye to the silent phr and casually wandered after her, eati'

Snickers. I wasn't sure she was talking about Jin, but it sounded promising. Of course, if I was wrong, I'd look like an idiot, but I'd never let that stop me before.

The bathroom was brightly lit in comparison to the rest of the club, and had a mirror that ran the entire side of one wall. There were three regular stalls, a handicapped stall, and a vanity below the mirror with four sinks. Pale pink roses in bud vases stood between the wash basins and, all in all, it was cleaner than I expected.

I waited until the girl was in one of the stalls and went into my act.

"Damn it!" I noisily searched through my purse. As she opened the door and started to wash her hands, I upended my purse on the counter. "Jeez, I hate it when I forget things." I gave her a quick grin and shrugged my shoulders to include her in the conversation.

She snickered. "I know, my purse is like a black hole. What are you looking for? Do you need a . . . you know . . . if you started, I've got a spare." She held up a tampon.

"Thanks, but no, that's not what I need." I glanced around the room, making sure we were alone, and prayed she wasn't a cop. "Actually, I forgot something at home, you know. I was hoping to have fun tonight, but I guess I left the damned baggie on the counter."

The girl, who I could tell was about nineteen or twenty, gave me a long look, her eyes narrow but not suspicious. She looked high already; her pupils were dilated and there was a bead of moisture on her upper lip. After a second's hesitation, she shrugged and seemed to decide I was harmless.

"Don't worry, there's always somebody around who can fix you up. Just wait for a little while." She gave me a big smile and held out her hand. "I'm Mandy."

I took her hand. "Hi, I'm . . . Rose. And thanks. I'm so stupid, but maybe I'll get lucky. Say, do you know if Jin will be in tonight? If he is, then . . ." I stopped in midsentence, letting her fill in the blanks.

She picked at her teeth in the mirror and pulled out her lipstick, a fuchsia so bright it made me wince. Mandy would look a lot better in a coffee color or a neutral, with her two-toned hair and fake tan.

"Jin? He'd better be, he's scheduled to go on for his first show at ten-thirty and there will be a lot of disappointed ladies by then if he doesn't. He does three shows a night on weekends."

Disappointed ladies? What the — ?

"Yeah, I guess so, huh?" I decided to play along. Too many questions and she might get suspicious.

She shook her hair, decided that she looked fine, and headed toward the door. "Well, he *is* the best dancer they have." She giggled, then whispered, "He's also got a great . . . you know! I just wish he'd use it on me!" With another giggle, she headed out of the bathroom, leaving me open-mouthed.

Barbara was looking bored when I returned to my bar stool but good to her word, she'd nursed her drink, downed a handful of peanuts, and kept her eyes open. I glanced over at the booth. Mandy had three glasses in front of her, it looked like she was drinking tequila sunrises. Her friends were scarfing down buffalo wings and some sort of pizza.

In whispered tones, I filled Barb in on what I'd learned. "So it seems that Jin's a dancer, and he goes on at ten-thirty. Oh, and apparently he's hung like a horse, according to Mandy-girl over there."

Barb snorted. "I'll keep that in mind, thank you."

I ordered another round of drinks and a plate of nachos to keep the booze from hitting us too hard. "Nurse it slow, we want

346

to be able to drive after this."

The bar began to fill up; a number of women started filtering into the club, young and old alike, but all of them dressed like they belonged here. A few drag queens sauntered in with the crowd. I had the feeling we'd managed to hit ladies' night at the Blue Dragon.

At that moment, a swarthy-looking man sauntered up. He gave us a little bow and said, "Madam, would you dance with me?" in a Russian accent as he held out his hand to Barb. Probably fresh off one of the barges in port.

She coughed, and I pushed her out of her seat. "Go dance, have fun, I'm fine here." With a look that said she was going to kill me as soon as we were alone, she took the sailor's hand and sashayed out on the dance floor, which had picked up in action. Forty-one-year-old baker or not, she gave the rest of the dancers a run for their money, whirling with such grace that for once, I envied her petite nature. I could dance, but that woman could *shimmy*.

After the song was over, Barb landed in her seat, laughing. She waved at the Russian and he winked and went off in search of new prey.

"Oh, that was fun," she said. "I haven't

danced like that in years — but don't you tell Dorian! I promised I'd be on my prim and proper behavior tonight. And to him, that doesn't include dancing with strange men, regardless of how innocent it is."

Her face was flushed and I could tell she was enjoying herself. This was the Barbara that I remembered from our younger days. She'd been footloose and fancy-free until she was twenty-three and happened to fall into the arms of a certain young Greek god.

"He asked me to go home with him, so I let him down easy. He was very nice, though, and he dances like a dream."

I caught her gaze, wondering if I'd made a mistake by bringing her. "Are you sorry?"

She shook her head without a second's thought. "Don't sweat it, Persia. I don't want to go home with anybody but you." At my look, she added, "Well, you know what I mean. To Dorian. This is just different. It's exciting and gives me a little oomph in my life. But no, I'm not thinking of an affair or of running off anywhere. I love my home, and I love my business, and I love my husband. Even if he is a stodgy old stick-in-the-mud sometimes."

Every word rang with truth and I relaxed. She just wanted some innocent fun with a touch of intrigue. I'd have to talk Dorian into doing something spontaneous for her birthday.

As we were sitting there, a man walked by. He was short, probably no more than five foot seven, and he must have weighed all of one hundred and fifty pounds, but he was beautiful, truly beautiful in every sense of the word, with delicate features, precisely trimmed eyebrows and pencil thin mustache and goatee. Neatly dressed in a narrow black suit, his jet black hair was caught back in a braid, not a single strand out of place.

As he passed, I caught a whiff of his after-shave. It struck a bell and I closed my eyes, trying to place it. And then, I knew where I'd smelled it before — on Lydia, the day she came in for her custom fragrance. I'd thought it was perfume she was wearing, but she must have gotten some of his after-shave on her by accident. As I watched him head into one of the unmarked doors, I knew that he had to be Jin.

I nudged Barbara. "That's him — the guy that just passed. Come on." I slid off my stool and, with Barb following me, headed for the door through which he had passed. No one seemed to notice and we slid through without a problem.

The hall into which we stepped was painted a bright white in contrast to the bar, and the lights were sterile and antiseptic. It led past three doors, then turned to the right. I noticed the door nearest the bend closing and figured that was probably where Jin had gone. Before someone found us we hurried down the hall and knocked.

"I just got here, so hold your fuckin' horses —" Jin stopped short as he yanked open the door, staring at us. Obviously, he'd been expecting somebody else. "What do you want?"

I drew myself up to my full height so that I towered over him on my stacked heels. "I need to talk to you about Lydia Wang."

He examined us quickly, then stepped aside so we could enter the room. "Who the hell are you?" he asked, jerking his head toward the sofa. "Sit down, but make it quick."

I glanced around. Standard dressing room, bare with costumes and makeup scattered around. Mirror that was lit too brightly, the air thick with his cologne. "My name is Persia Vanderbilt. As I said, I need to ask you some questions about Lydia." I consciously moderated my voice so that I didn't come off as obnoxious or pushy. Jin struck me as a man who wouldn't look kindly on being pressured.

"Questions, huh?" He stared at me and I met his eyes with a steady, unblinking gaze. "So, Lydia told you about me?"

"Yeah, enough." A lie, but Trevor needed all the help he could get and if it took telling a few falsehoods, I was up to the task. "The thing is, I'm working with a lawyer to find out more about her murder."

Jin dropped into a chair, a pained expression crossing his face. "Lydia's dead? You're joking — you have to be joking. I just talked to her on Monday afternoon!"

Oh shit! He hadn't known? But if he really was in the dark about her death, then he couldn't have killed her. And his voice told me that, unless he was a stellar actor, he truly hadn't known. I slid onto the sofa next to his chair and took a deep breath.

"I'm so sorry to break it to you this way. Lydia was a customer of mine. She died in my store. As I said, I'm working with a lawyer to find out everything we can about her death. You see, one of my employees was accused of the murder and we're trying to prove his innocence. I honestly thought you knew."

Jin shook his head, staring at the floor. "No, I've been out of town since Tuesday morning. I had no idea she was dead."

Chapter Eighteen

"Lydia was murdered? I just can't believe it." Jin shook his head, then looked up at me, not acting like a bereaved lover at all. Oh, he looked shocked, but not devastated. "Who are they accusing?" A cold twinkle sparkled in his eye, one that made me uneasy.

I took a deep breath. "Trevor Wilson, one of my employees."

Jin spat out an obscenity. "Bullshit, Trevor's a wimp. Lydia could have whipped his butt blindfolded."

I gauged his reaction. No smell of fear, no smell of anger. Maybe he'd be able to help us more than I hoped. I motioned for Barb to join me on the sofa. "Trevor was framed," I said. "We're trying to pinpoint who might have it in for him. Like a jealous lover."

I could practically see the lightbulb flash on over his head. "And you think the 'other man' might be just the place to start." He arched an eyebrow.

I nodded, with just a slight upswing of my lips. "I suppose you could say that." I had the distinct feeling we were playing cat-and-mouse. I wasn't about to end up the rodent.

He shifted position, crossing his legs. "Ladies, I can offer you the names of nine potential suspects with far more to gain from Lydia's death than myself. In fact, I had a lot to lose."

Barb and I glanced at each other. I knew she was thinking the same thing I was. If he was Lydia's dealer, then he'd lost a steady source of income thanks to her murder. On the other hand, if he thought he was going to be exposed, might not it have seemed more cost effective to lose one client rather than lose his freedom?

"Nine suspects? How about names?" I asked.

He leaned forward. "There were ten finalists for that beauty contest, with a big payoff for the winner. Don't you think one of those girls might have wanted her dead? Think about it . . . if the winner cannot fulfill her obligations . . ."

"Then the runner-up will assume the crown." Colleen Murkins? True, she was assuming the position of spokesmodel now that Lydia was dead, but did she have what it took to be a killer? "What makes you think that Colleen is capable of murder?"

With a snort, he said, "Because Colleen had already threatened to blackmail Lydia. That little tart has nerves of steel, I'll tell you that."

"Blackmail? What on earth for?" But even as I said it, I knew. The drugs. Allison knew about them and somehow Colleen had found out and threatened to expose that fact to the papers, which would have forced Radiance to cancel Lydia's contract.

"We know she was using. I assume Colleen found out?" I didn't mention that I knew he was her dealer. No sense in pushing the envelope.

Jin snorted. "Practically every contestant in that contest was using, including Colleen. Lydia kept it tame compared to some of them. Diet drugs and speed, as much as she could get her hands on. She popped pills like a sugar freak pops candy, mainly to keep her weight down. That wasn't what Colleen found out. No, she was on to something else, something that would have ruined Lydia's career with Radiance Cosmetics and on the beauty circuit for good. The scandal would have dishonored Lydia's family, a double whammy."

If it wasn't drugs, what could it have been?

"Plastic surgery?" Given Lydia's vanity

and her nature, it made sense. And since Radiance Cosmetics passed itself off as the "natural wonder in beauty," they'd never allow a model who'd been nipped and tucked in all the right places. It would ruin their image if word leaked out.

"Uh uh." Jin gave me a secretive smile. "Lydia was all natural in that department. Besides, Eurasian eyes are too obvious and Radiance wasn't interested in hybrids. No, Colleen found out who Lydia's boyfriend was, and snapped a picture of them in the act. One worth a lot of money."

What the hell? "But, *you're* her boyfriend. And while I'm at it, I might add that you don't seem very upset considering you just found out your girlfriend was murdered!" I leaned forward, shaking my head. "For someone who was supposed to be in love with her, you don't seem all that devastated."

Jin leaned back, his face impassive. "Obviously, your information is out of whack."

"Apparently. So, are you going to tell me who her boyfriend was?"

He winked and gave me a secretive smile. "Maybe I will, maybe I won't." As he ran the length of my body with his gaze, I felt like he was undressing me, exposing every inch of my skin.

"Knock it off," I said, restraining an urge

to wipe that smirk off his face. "I appreciate what you've told us so far, but I'm not a slab of meat. I know what you're thinking right now."

With a snort, he said, "I doubt that, or you'd backhand me first and ask questions later. I don't like to be goaded, woman. So don't push me."

We stared at one another for a moment as I forced myself to calm down. Whether or not I liked his attitude, we still needed the information he could provide. "So if you weren't dating her, then who was? We thought you scared her away from Trevor."

Jin cleared his throat. "Not me. Trevor isn't a bad kid, though he's a hick. I warned her to cut him loose if she wasn't going to shape up, or they'd both be hurt because of her habit." He leaned forward and I had the feeling he meant every word he was saying. "Listen to me, I liked Lydia, but she wasn't my type. I like my women to have brains. She was a friend, and a customer. I got her the speed she wanted — at least I could get it clean and not cut with some other crap." He was biding his time, I could see it in his eyes — he'd tell us what we wanted to know, but at his own pace.

"The reason we thought you were her boyfriend is that she told her friends she was dating somebody who worked at the Blue Dragon."

"Somebody who supposedly hit her," Barbara said. She'd been watching from near the door. "Do you know anything about the bruises she brought back from Seattle a few weeks ago?"

He glanced at her. "You think I did that? No dice. Regardless of what you think, I cared about Lydia. I cared enough to let her use me as a cover. The fact is that yes, she did have a boyfriend in Seattle, but she wanted to keep his name on the hush. She got herself into deep shit, deep enough that there was no way out."

I perked up. It sounded like he was ready to spill the information we needed. "How so?"

Jin crossed his legs and pulled out a cigarette, lighting it and blowing a perfect ring before he spoke. "One of the judges knew how much she wanted to win. She met him through her uncle, or something. So they struck a deal before the contest. He'd see that she got the crown if she gave him whatever he asked for, but she had to be at his beck and call whenever he wanted. He likes to rough up girls, if you know what I mean. He has a very active imagination."

I shivered. From what Nadia had said,

the judges already knew that the contest was rigged in Lydia's favor. The pervert had used that knowledge to get her into bed and when she was there, had abused her. "You got a name for him? Sounds like he needs a visit from the Karma Police."

"No, what he needs is a visit from one of my buddies," Jin said and his voice was cold enough to strike ice. "Colleen spied on them a few weeks ago and managed to snap a picture of Lydia screwing the judge. I guess Colleen figured she had more to gain through blackmail than by going to the company. After all, if Radiance ran a new contest because of a rigging scandal, she might not win."

"How do you know Colleen found out?" Barbara asked.

He shrugged. "Lydia called me on Monday, shortly before noon. She was really upset so I caught the ferry and hurried over there as fast as I could. Apparently, she'd had a run-in with Colleen in some store. A little while later Colleen phoned her and threatened to spill everything if Lydia didn't pay up."

I closed my eyes; the scandal would have destroyed her family's reputation. "She would have lost the title, as well as any dignity she had."

"That's about the size of it. And that title meant everything to her, it was her ticket to the top. Colleen hadn't made any demands yet, but it was only a matter of time. I couldn't stay because I had to get back here by seven-thirty." Jin pulled out a small notebook and flipped it open. I could see it was a calendar. "That was the night that I danced a double shift."

A double shift? "What time did you finish up?"

He smirked. "Why? Wish you could have been here?"

I let out a long, slow breath. "Don't overhype yourself — it's not becoming."

Jin gave me a slow smile. "You aren't that different from me, Persia Vanderbilt. You should hang around more often. We'd probably end up friends."

Right. Like hell we would. "So you never threatened Trevor?"

"Trevor? No. But I did threaten to gut the S.O.B. who bruised her up. She got upset, told me not to touch him or she'd rip out my heart. I guess she was afraid that he'd blacklist her if I went after him."

Ah . . . the mysterious phone call Nadia had mentioned. "Back to Monday night. What time did you work?"

He stood up and stubbed out his butt in

an ashtray. "I was on stage at eight and I didn't finish till almost midnight. Then I went clubbing with some friends. I got home at two in the morning and the doorman can vouch for that. The ferries don't run that late, so there's no way I could have gotten over to Port Samanish Island. I left town to visit my mother Tuesday morning and got back today. So you see, my dear, I couldn't have killed Lydia Wang. And if you'll excuse me, I have to change for my performance. If you like, you can stick around while I dress."

Silently, Barb and I left the room and headed back into the bar which had filled to capacity since we left. Any desire I had to return to the nightlife of Seattle had been squelched by this little encounter.

"I just want to get the hell out of this seedy dive and never come back," I told Barbara. Jin had answered a lot of questions, and raised a few more, but my distaste for the man was so strong that I wanted nothing to do with him or the people who came to see him. "Do you mind if we head out?"

Barbara shook her head; the same look of disgust I was feeling was plastered across her face. "Let's go. We can make the ferry if we leave now."

We drove back to the ferry terminal without incident. Lost in my thoughts, I couldn't think of much else besides the insecure young woman who had pumped herself full of drugs in a desperate attempt to stay thin, traded her body for a beauty crown, and ended up bludgeoned to death in my aunt's shop. The trip home was far more somber than the ride to Seattle had been.

Auntie was snoring away in the rocking chair by the time I got home. She'd been waiting up for me, even though she denied it when I woke her up to let her know I was home.

"Thank heavens you're home, Persia Rose! I was worried about you."

"I love you too, Auntie. I found out some important things that Kyle will want to know. But right now, time for bed. There's nothing we can do this late." I threw my arms around her, feeling suddenly protective of the woman who had taken me in, raised me, and now was acting like any concerned mother.

She nodded. "I've got news for you, too, but it will keep. Best get a good night's rest first, Imp." Refusing to say another word, she padded up to her bedroom. I followed after making sure the lights were out and the doors latched.

I woke late to broken patches of blue sky, but when I flipped on my radio, the weatherman said that we were due for another round. "The storm season isn't over yet, folks, so fasten your seatbelts and batten down the hatches. Even though this morning started off with blue skies, she's going to blow rough tonight."

Opening my window to let the crisp scent of freshly rain-soaked cedars and firs filter through the room, I contemplated what we'd learned. Jin hadn't killed Lydia. Kyle would be able to establish his alibi easily enough, that much was certain. And now we knew that Lydia's "boyfriend" in Seattle was a cover for her assignations with the contest judge. I had the feeling that her breakup with Trevor had come right after the beating, perhaps at the insistence of the judge.

As I moved through my yoga routine, I wondered what kind of mindset it took to subject oneself to degradation and abuse in exchange for a beauty crown. If Lydia was willing to get the title by cheating, then she must have wanted it pretty damned bad.

"Persia! Brunch!"

My aunt's voice startled me and I realized

that I'd been sitting on my stability ball for the past five minutes, doing nothing but thinking. Lazy, I thought, but gave it up for the day. The rest of my routine would have to wait. I was too preoccupied.

"Be down as soon as I have a shower," I called over the edge of the banister. Ten minutes later, I joined my aunt at the table, where I gave her a full rundown on the events of the evening. She listened gravely, nodding, but I could tell there was something else on her mind.

"Auntie, is something wrong?" I poured us both another cup of tea.

She bit her lip, eying me thoughtfully. "Well, yes, in a manner of speaking. You had a visitor last night. He left you a message."

"Who?" I asked, but immediately closed my mouth. I knew who, I didn't have to ask. Elliot. "That scum! What does he want now?"

Auntie wrung her hands. "Oh Persia, I wish I didn't have to tell you this. You're not going to like it and I don't want you to do anything stupid." She began to fiddle with the hanging ivy next to the kitchen table. Caught up in a wire mesh basket, the plant trailed fronds almost to chin height. If she let it grow any lower, the cats would have gotten into it.

I took a deep breath, trying to keep calm. It must be bad, whatever it was. "Okay, let me have it. I promise I won't go buy a gun and shoot him."

She gave me a smile then. "Honey, if it would help matters any, I'd spring for the bullets. But violence isn't the answer. Okay, here it is: Elliot has decided to move to Gull Harbor. He's gone and rented one of those sleazy dives down on Arborville Avenue — the Gate 'n Lion? You remember — the place with the huge statues of the stone lions that used to belong to the library before they replaced them with horses."

I stared at my plate. "Elliot? Move here? Oh God, take me now!"

Count to ten, don't say another word until I count to ten, I thought. *Let it flow in, let it flow out. You give your opponent power if you let him unbalance your emotions.*

There had to be something I could do. I wasn't about to move, nor would I allow him to disrupt my life. I had to think this one over carefully. In the meantime, I was going to have to find a way to cope with the knowledge that he was living in the same town as me.

Auntie seemed to be waiting for an explosion. I shook my head, on the verge of tears. "I hope to hell he falls in the water and drowns or that he gets himself thrown in jail again. He's a bane around my neck. Think I'll just call him Albatross Man from now on. Al, for short."

She rested her hands on my shoulders and kissed the top of my head. "Maybe it won't be so bad. You can avoid him. I can put a stop to him hanging out at the shop. It will be okay, wait and see."

But we both knew she was wrong.

I called Kyle after brunch but he was gone and dispatch didn't know when he'd be back. After leaving a message that I needed to talk to him, I glanced at the clock. Almost two. Time to get ready for my date with Bran. I slipped into a loose pair of cotton jeans and a long sleeved polo shirt, then tied my shoes. For real climbing, I'd use boots, of course, but for the rock wall down at Gardner's Gym, sneakers would work just fine. My hair went into a braid and then I coiled it up and pinned it on the back of my head. Digging through my gear, I finally found my knee and elbow pads, along with my helmet and gloves. Even on practice walls, safety counted.

I was headed downstairs when the phone rang and I heard Aunt Florence answer. As

I rounded the corner, she called me into the den. "It's for you. It's Daphne Stanton, Bran's sister."

His sister? I reached for the phone. "Hello?"

In a clipped voice, each word uttered with precision, Daphne said, "Persia? I'm calling for Bran. He's not going to be able to make it."

So he'd set his sister to making excuses? I sighed. "I hope he's not ill —" I started to say but she broke in.

"Actually, he's managed to acquire a broken leg. He was working on his boat and a gust of wind put too much pressure on one of the ropes. It slipped and nearly dragged him overboard. He caught himself but in the process his leg snapped and he's in the hospital right now."

I stared at the floor, feeling a wave of shame. My first thought had been that he'd flaked out on me, not that something might have happened to him. I blushed, even though Daphne couldn't see me. I had the feeling she knew what I was thinking.

"Good God, is he going to be okay?"

She murmured an affirmative. "He'll have to stay in the hospital for a week or two, until they're sure it's mending right. It was a nasty break. But he wanted me to let you know so you wouldn't worry."

I grabbed a piece of paper and a pen off the roll-top desk. "What room is he in? Are you talking about Samanish Island Hospital?"

She gave me his room number and phone number and then with a cheery "Have to run," she said good-bye.

I stared at the paper. I'd been looking forward to our date, but now felt both worry and relief. Worry for Bran, but relief because I had too much on my mind to focus on a first date right now. I picked up the phone and put in a call to the hospital. Bran answered, sounding a little woozy.

"Hey you," I said. "How are you? You up for a little company?"

"Persia! I'm so glad you called!" His voice shifted into a cheerier mode. "My doctor told me no visitors today — I'm pretty out of it on pain meds, but you could come by tomorrow. They say I'm going to be in this damned cast for a good two months. The break was bad and this means that I'm not going to be able to lead my summer classes or take the boat out on tours." He sounded frantic rather than doped up.

"We'll think of something. Trust me, we'll make sure you don't lose the season's business." I paused, then added, "I'm not going to keep you on the phone long because I don't want to tire you out, but I just wanted to check up on you. I don't like being stood up, you know," I said, forcing a smile into my voice. "I expect a rain check on that date."

"Really?" he asked, and his voice set my heart to fluttering.

"Yes, really," I said, suddenly feeling shy. "I'll drop by tomorrow. Meanwhile, until then you get some sleep."

"Persia — wait! I wanted to ask you a question."

"What is it?" Please, oh please, don't make it something serious, I thought. I had enough on my mind already.

"Your name . . . it's so pretty. Why did your mother give it to you?"

I laughed. "My family has an old tradition. Every woman born into our family is named after the town or country of her birth. My mother was named Virginia, because she was born there. Auntie was born in Italy — in Florence. And I was born in Iran, so my mother named me Persia since that's a whole lot prettier, but technically still the country. If I ever settle down and raise a family, any daughter I have will be named in that manner. It's one of the few links to the past that I have left. Now be a good boy and go to sleep."

As I replaced the receiver, I thought about his brilliant eyes and luscious voice. Chemistry, I thought. We had chemistry. Even though I couldn't smell them, I was pretty sure my pheromones were saturating the room.

Auntie wandered in and I told her what had happened. "Maybe you should go buy him some flowers or a card or something to take with you," she said. "I happen to know he has a penchant for oatmeal cookies."

"Oatmeal cookies, huh?" Since I couldn't bake, it was off to the store for a shopping spree. Flowers, cookies, a card . . . maybe this dating thing was going to be fun after all.

The aisles of the Shoreline Foods Pavilion were clear — it seemed that I'd hit during the less-than-popular shopping hour. I'd buy the cookies at Barbara's, but for flowers and a card, the supermarket would do.

As I turned the corner to head to the produce section, I saw Colleen and Debbie poring over the squash. Something caught my eye. Debbie looked different, but I couldn't put my finger on how. I watched them from the next aisle over, thinking about what Jin had told me. So Colleen had attempted to blackmail Lydia. Blackmail was bad, but murder catapulted matters into an entirely different realm. Just because Colleen might rat Lydia out didn't mean that she was capable of killing her. The question was, did she have the stomach for it? Could she willingly snuff out a life? I didn't want to think so. I hoped not.

After a moment, I called out to them and they looked up. Colleen nudged Debbie and whispered something but Debbie shook her off, staring at me with that frightened Bambi look. And yet, there was a difference. She held her head higher, her shoulders straighter. Her clothes were smooth and wrinkle-free. Debbie didn't look like she hated herself anymore.

"Hey girls, haven't seen you at the store for a few days."

"We've been busy —" Colleen started to say, but Debbie cut her off.

"Nice to see you, again, Persia. I'm sorry we don't have time to chat, but we're on a tight schedule. We're going to a movie tonight so we need to fix dinner early." She tried to push past Colleen, who gave her a queer look.

"Deb, we live across the street from the theater. What's the big rush?"

They lived across the street from the theater? Uh oh, alarm bells. "You live across from the Delacorte Plaza?" I asked. That apartment complex seemed to be the central hub of activity, and none of it very pleasant.

Debbie nodded, a little too fast. "Yeah, we're roomies, you know — share the rent to make our paychecks go further!" Her laugh was a little too forced.

I gave her a blinding smile. Kill 'em with kindness. "I don't think I ever caught what it is that you do."

Colleen reached for an acorn squash and as she did so her purse slid off her shoulder, spilling items willy-nilly all over the floor. I leaned over to help her pick up a few of the things that had rolled near my feet. Lipstick, a small day planner . . . a stun gun?

"You carry a stun gun?" I said, staring at the sleek black weapon in my hand.

She shrugged. "My father wanted me to have some sort of protection now that I'm living on my own. I told him I don't need it but — you know fathers."

Actually, I didn't, I thought as I handed it to her. I'd never had a father figure. And then as the scent of her perfume enveloped me, I froze. I knew that scent. I remembered it all too well.

"Nice fragrance," I said, casually turning away to finger the onions. "Where did you get it?"

"Don't you remember?" Colleen said, laughing. "You brewed it up for me the first week you started at the shop. I love it."

A custom blend, which meant she was the only one who had a bottle of it. And that meant . . . I stared at the array of squashes for a moment, contemplating something too horrible to wrap my mind around.

Debbie interrupted my thoughts. "I'm a cashier."

"Huh?"

"You asked where I work. I'm a clerk at my father's shop. Harcourt's Hardware — maybe you've seen it? It's right down the street from your shop. I'll take over when he retires."

Harcourt's Hardware? "Your father is Murv Harcourt?" He not only owned the best hardware store in town, but he was also the local locksmith. I had to have him come bail me out when I left my keys in the car one evening. Keys . . . And then, it all clicked. Every painful detail. I had to get out of here.

"Gotta run! Later." I headed for the front of the store, quickly maneuvering the cart into the stand by the door. Shopping for Bran would have to wait. I needed to find Kyle, and I needed to find him fast.

Chapter Nineteen

By the time I reached my car, the storm broke in earnest. I raced over to City Hall, speeding around the corners, clipping a curb here or there. As I pulled up in front of the police station and leapt out of my Sebring, a deluge of water poured from the heavens and thunder echoed across the island. Thank God I kept the top on the car up most of the time. The radio was right — we were in for a gusher. I just hoped Auntie had bought extra fuel for the generator.

The station was bustling as I entered the lobby and walked up to the reception desk, which was actually an enclosed booth. A bullet-proof window separated the dispatch officer from anybody who might have an eye on shooting up the joint. She looked up at me and smiled — Katrina Tennyson had been in my junior high class and we had occasionally eaten lunch together.

"Persia! I heard you were back in town. I'm sorry I missed you last time you were here, but I was on vacation. What can I —"

"Hey Katrina — good to see you, too.

Listen, I need to talk to Kyle. Chief Laughlin." I glanced down at my feet where the rain that had beaded up on my jacket was dripping off to form a puddle. The marbleized linoleum was littered with several trails of water drops. Apparently, I wasn't the only one who had gotten caught in the squall.

She shook her head. "No can do, I'm afraid. Unless it's an emergency, he said he's not to be disturbed. I can page one of the other officers for you, but it may be awhile. There have been a lot of minor accidents today and we've got most of the beat officers out directing traffic where the lights have gone out."

I leaned close to the glass. "Katrina, it's important. Call it an emergency if you like, but I can guarantee that if you don't let me in to see the Chief, he's not going to be happy. This relates to Trevor Wilson's case."

Her eyes flickered over my face. "Okay, but if he bites my head off, it's on your shoulders." She sighed and picked up the phone, punching the intercom. "What should I tell him?" she asked me, covering the receiver with her hand.

"Tell him Persia's here, and I have that evidence he asked for."

Within less than a minute, Kyle came striding around the corner and motioned for me to follow him. As we entered his office, he whirled.

"What have you got?" he asked.

"Too much for my own good. Kyle, I know who killed Marta, and I'm pretty certain it's the same person who killed Lydia. I'm just not sure how to prove it." As he pulled out a chair for me, I sank into the soft leather and began to spell out everything that I'd learned.

"Persia," he said after I'd spilled what I knew, "I'm going to have to talk to the judge and see if I can come up with reasonable circumstances for him to grant us a warrant."

"But that could take awhile." Colleen might bolt before we could prove Trevor was innocent.

"Tough. I go by the book." He glanced out the window. "Storm looks like a rough one."

"Kyle, don't you care about Trevor?"

"Of course I do, but there's nothing I can do to speed up the process. And don't you do anything stupid, either."

I grumbled, scuffing the floor with my toe. "Damn it, Kyle, you frustrate me so much sometimes."

With a sigh, I asked him if I could use his phone and put in a call to Jared, asking him to put up a notice that my self-defense course was canceled for the evening. Surely nobody in their right mind would be foolhardy enough to drive all the way to the Gull Harbor Community College in this gale; but you never knew with people.

Jared laughed. "That won't be necessary. You must not have got the call from Admin. The college just sent out a notice to KZRR Radio that all evening classes are cancelled." He paused and I could hear someone speaking to him in the background. "Rod says to say hi."

"Right back at him." Rod was Jared's partner and together they made a witty and funny couple. I never felt like a third wheel when I was hanging out with them and they never pulled any drama-queen shit on me. "I have to run. Thanks for the favor. I owe you one."

"You owe me several by now," he said.

As I hung up, I noticed Kyle watching me out of the corner of his eye as he dug through a cabinet in the corner of the room. A potted palm tree sat next to it, the brilliant green contrasting vividly with the rust-and-blue patterned carpet. He cleared his throat.

"How's Jared doing?"

I gave him a long look. Maybe it was time to confront an issue that should have been long buried in the past. "Why don't you ask him yourself? Honestly, Kyle, this little feud you two have going is stupid. I can't believe you're still mad at Jared and me because I went to that dance with him. He's your cousin, for God's sake. Get over it."

He did a double-take. "Is that what you've been thinking all this time? That I'm still miffed over something that long ago and that minor? Boy, you really do have a good opinion of yourself!" Kyle leaned against his desk, laughing. "You just made my day, Persia Vanderbilt."

Not sure whether I should be insulted, I folded my arms across my chest. "And what's so funny about that? You haven't give me reason to believe anything else." Pausing, I shook my head. "All right, so if it's not because of the Harvest Dance, then why? Why are you and Jared still on the outs? He won't talk about it either and frankly, this feud's pretty pathetic."

Kyle sucked in a deep breath and gazed into my eyes, his expression somber. "You really don't know what happened, do you?"

I frowned. "What are you talking about?"

"About six or seven years ago Jared got married."

"Married! Jared? He never told me he'd gotten married." I couldn't believe what I was hearing.

"Yeah, I guess he was trying to pass. He used the girl to hide behind because he knew his father was a bigot — Uncle Norris never has been too progressive. Anyway, Jared married a girl named Alexandria and then got caught sleeping around. With a guy. The girl was humiliated. It was bad any way you looked at it. For her, for Jared. I'm still pissed at him because he knew he was gay all along. You just don't use people that way."

My jaw dropped. "Jared didn't tell me any of this."

"Not a big surprise," Kyle said, reading my mind, "Considering he adores you. Jared's father won't have anything to do with him, though his mother still talks to him. I'm ticked at him because I've seen him do this over and over again — he doesn't think. He uses people and then when they get hurt, he's all sorry and apologetic. It's just not right."

I sighed. No, it wasn't right. And I wasn't sure what to think about the whole thing. "I'm sorry. I never knew any of this."

Kyle shrugged. "Yeah, well, now you do.

So you'll forgive me if I don't spare any love for my cousin. Okay," he shut the cabinet door. "I'm going over to the judge's chambers to talk to him. You want to wait here?"

Yeah, wait here for him to come back empty handed. "No, I guess I'll go home."

He squinted, staring at me for a moment. "Persia, you know I can't search an apartment without cause, and your word just isn't enough to go on. Neither is your ability to remember scent. I'll talk to the judge, but that's all I can do."

"What you need is proof, right?"

"Get that look off your face. Now promise me that you'll go home like a good girl and I'll call you when I've talked to Judge Lansburg."

"Whatever." What we needed was to find Aphrodite's Mirror. Find the mirror and we'd find the killer, and I was pretty sure I knew where it was. I slipped into my jacket and, with Kyle guiding me out the door, headed off to catch a killer.

I could pull this off, I kept telling myself. I was skilled in self-defense . . . everything would be all right. All I needed to do was get a glimpse of the mirror and it would make things easier for Kyle to get his warrant. I didn't know what Colleen's car looked like, but I knew Debbie drove a little red Kia and it was in the parking lot.

After all, if I didn't break-and-enter, then I had every right to report whatever I saw to the police.

The apartment complex looked as bleak as ever. I stared up at the building, thinking that so much had happened here behind these pasty walls. I checked on the mailboxes until I came to 307A, which had both Debbie and Colleen's names taped on it. I took the stairs to the third floor and headed down the hall, feeling a nervous flutter in my stomach.

I came to a stop in front of apartment 307A. This was it. No turning back. I summoned up my courage and pressed the doorbell. No answer, but I could hear a faint rustle inside that told me somebody was home. I rang the doorbell again. Finally, the door opened a crack and Debbie peeked out.

Her expression shifted from bored to alarmed. "Persia! What are you doing here?"

Bingo, I thought. She was afraid. "I thought I'd drop in while I was in the building. Is Colleen home?"

Debbie shook her head and whispered, "She's out right now. You'll have to come back later, please. I'm really busy." She paused, then asked, "What are you doing here?"

I turned a brilliant smile on her. "I'm friends with Andy Andrews. He lives on the fifth floor but he wasn't home, so I thought I'd look you up and apologize for running off so rudely at the supermarket. I just remembered that I had to pick up my skirt before the dry cleaners closed."

She nodded, still looking nervous, but the glint of fear in her eyes had faded a little. "No problem. I've had days like that."

"Say," I added, "I hate to ask, but could I use your bathroom? I've got to pee and I can't wait much longer." When all else fails, resort to threats of wetting your pants. Kyle would laugh his ass off over that one.

She bit her lip, then nodded, moving aside and opening the door. "Sure. Down that hall, second door to the right. But please, make it quick. If Colleen catches you here, she'll . . ."

I sauntered into the room and glanced around, looking for anything out of the ordinary. "She'll what? She wouldn't get mad at you for just letting me in, would she?"

Debbie backpedaled as fast as she could.

"No, it's just that . . . she wouldn't — I mean . . . She just doesn't like unexpected company."

And I don't like liars, I thought. And Debbie was lying through her teeth. "Second door on the right?"

She nodded and at that moment, looked so young and so fragile that I wondered if I could be wrong? On one hand, for Trevor's sake, I hoped I was right. On the other, I prayed that this was all some bizarre co-incidence. The thought that Debbie had helped Colleen kill two people was more than I could stomach.

On my way to the bathroom, I passed an open door. I glanced in and froze. The room was a very messy bedroom, deco-rated in shades of bubblegum pink. And on the wall, next to the bed, rested Aphro-dite's Mirror. Bingo!

I could feel Debbie's gaze on my back and I forced myself to continue into the bathroom, where I shut the door. There was no lock. I turned on the water full force and then flipped open my cell phone, punching in Kyle's number. When he came on the line, I said, "Tell the judge that the mirror is here. I'm in Debbie's apartment right now — invited, by the way. Get your warrant and get over here."

"Goddamn it, Persia! What did I tell you about snooping around?" Kyle's voice thundered in my ear. "Get the hell out of there now, do you hear me?"

"Yeah, yeah . . . just get over here soon." I waited for a moment, then flushed the toilet, turned off the water, and quietly opened the door. I could hear whispering coming from the living room.

"She saw it, I know she saw it!"

"Quit whining. I'll take care of this. Everything will be okay. Don't I always make everything okay?"

Forewarned, I stepped out into the hallway to find myself facing Colleen. She leaned against the wall, a sly smile playing across her lips. Debbie stood off to one side, fidgeting and twisting her hair around her finger.

"Why, Persia. How nice to see you," Colleen said. "Whatever brings you to our little abode?"

Colleen's right hand was in her jacket pocket and I had a sneaking suspicion that she wasn't playing with a set of keys. "I was in the neighborhood —"

"Cut the crap. We know why you're here, don't we, Debbie?"

Debbie swallowed. "She might mean it, Colleen. She said she was visiting Andy Andrews —"

Colleen whirled on her. "Honey, I love you, you know that, but sometimes you are dumber than a fencepost. Persia knows about Lydia. I saw it on her face at the supermarket." She turned back to me. "You figured it out, didn't you? When Debbie mentioned her father's shop, you knew."

I eyed her quietly. "Whatever are you talking about, Colleen?"

"Don't play stupid, Persia. You're not blind." She locked the door behind her. "I know why you're here. What tipped you off?"

If I could keep her talking maybe I'd be able to distract her and get out of here. At least I didn't see a gun anywhere.

"When Debbie mentioned her father's locksmith business, I remembered that I'd left my purse out on the counter the day Lydia was murdered. That evening, I found my keys in the pocket of my jacket. But I always put my keys in my purse. I thought that I'd just had a brain fart, but when Debbie mentioned her father was Murv Harcourt, I knew."

"Pretty bright," Colleen said.

I edged my way toward the door, but she still blocked it. I stopped, considering the window. Three stories. Too high for a safe jump. "What did you do? Lift the keys out

384

of my purse while I was at lunch, go over to her father's shop, and make copies?"

"Don't tell her!" Debbie's eyes were wide. "Don't say anything or we'll go to jail."

"Shut up," Colleen said without even looking at her. "Nobody's going to jail." She withdrew her hand from her pocket and I saw that she had a sleek black plastic rectangle in her hand, with two metal prods on the end. Oh shit! Her stun gun! I'd forgotten all about that.

"What are you planning on doing, Colleen? Killing me, like you did Lydia? With Debbie helping you?" I took one step back, willing myself into that quiet calm space that I always entered before an Aikido tournament.

"No! I didn't do anything to Lydia. I didn't know it was going to happen." Debbie was crying as Colleen stepped toward me, her gaze locked on mine. "It wasn't my fault!"

I flashed a quick look in Debbie's direction. "Maybe you didn't hit her, but you were there. You stole my keys and you made a copy of each one at your father's shop. Then all you and Colleen had to do was wait until we closed and try each one to find the right match. Isn't that the way it happened, Debbie?"

Colleen's eyes narrowed. "Don't let her get to you —"

Debbie dropped to her knees, tears streaming down her face. "It's true, it's all true. I copied your keys. Colleen told me to. She said we'd steal the mirror because I loved it so much. I wanted that mirror. I feel better every time I look in it." She hunched over, hiding her face in her hands.

I backed up another step. "So Colleen, you promised Debbie the mirror to get her to steal the keys? I'll bet you had it all planned out. You called Lydia and told her to meet you. She thought it was because you were going to demand a blackmail payment."

She stopped then, looking startled. Good, I'd thrown her off guard. "How'd you find that out?" she asked.

"I have my ways. I know that you tried to extort money from Lydia. But I think you planned on killing her all along so you could take her place. You probably started out just thinking about money, but the opportunity to get rid of her arose and you took advantage of it."

Colleen let out a high-pitched laugh. "Miss Lydia the all-high-and-mighty. Miss Lydia the bitch queen. Where's her crown now, huh? I'll tell you where it is! On my head! And Debbie's got the mirror. And everything's going to be just fine once, I —"

At that moment, she leapt forward, the stun gun held out in her hand.

I jumped to the side as much as the narrow hall would allow, bringing my leg up to block her attack. Her arm flew back and I heard a nasty crack as her hand hit the wall, but she managed to hold on to the stun gun.

Colleen shrieked as she whirled. I couldn't pull back far enough to get away; the wall blocked my retreat. She nicked my arm with the stun gun and pressed the trigger.

It was as bad as grabbing hold of a downed power line. Rocked by the intensity of the shock, I let out an earsplitting howl as I fell to the floor and my muscles contracted uncontrollably. Twitching, I rolled over on my side, unable to do more than focus on breathing as the current worked its way through my system. The next moment, I saw Colleen bearing down with the stun gun again. I screamed in reflex, panicked that the next shock might stop my breathing altogether, although I knew that stun guns weren't supposed to do any lasting damage.

"Stop it! Stop it! Not again, Colleen. I can't go through this again." Debbie's voice rang out from somewhere near my feet, but my nerves were too scrambled to allow me to lift my head.

Colleen paused, in my line of sight just enough for me to see that she had turned around to look at Debbie. "Damn it, don't fall apart on me now. Don't you see? She knows. If we let her go, we're dead meat."

"Better that than live with another murder on my conscience." Debbie's voice had turned defiant and I silently cheered her on. Maybe she had a backbone after all. "It's all your fault — you couldn't be happy with second place. You had to have it all, even if it meant killing Lydia to get what you wanted."

Way to go, Debbie, I thought. Keep her busy until the shock works its way out of my system — which would take another five to ten minutes if the gun was similar to the ones I'd trained with. My only hope was that Debbie could keep her talking long enough for me to recover the strength to fight my way out of here.

Colleen smirked. "Give it up. You hated Lydia just as much as I did. Look at the way she treated you! And Trevor, don't get me started on him! He acted like you weren't even alive. I did you a favor when I pinned her death on his shoulders."

"Trevor isn't like that! Lydia had him fooled."

"Oh yeah, the hunk couldn't help himself, slobbering over the beauty queen." Colleen turned back to me, leaning down to stare in my face. "Persia, I'm sorry you got mixed up in this, but I can't let you go. You understand, don't you? Debbie and I will leave town after I finish up with you. Oh hell, I'll be back in a minute."

I heard her say to Debbie, "Watch her. If she moves, hit her again with the gun. You know how to use it, so don't get all squeamish on me."

As she disappeared from view, I noticed a tingling in my fingers again. The numbness was wearing off. I focused my energy on slowly clenching and unclenching my hands. My grip was nonexistent, but at least I was moving. As my toes began to tingle, I realized that within a moment or two I'd be able to stand up, but I also knew I'd be dizzy as hell so I had to make every second count.

I took a slow, deep breath and shook my shoulders to get the blood flowing. I kept waiting for Debbie to notice and shock me again, but apparently she was off in her own little world, because she said nothing.

Colleen reappeared, holding a long knife in her hand. "I couldn't find anything else," she said with a cheery smile. "But this is sharp so it will all be over fast."

I sucked in a deep breath as she brought her arm up, the blade pointing straight down toward my heart. As it began to descend, I forced myself to twist to the side, rolling as hard and as fast as I could. The knife slammed into the floor next to me — I could feel the swish of air as it hit the carpet and stuck.

"Shit!" Colleen stumbled back a step. I pushed myself to a sitting position and fumbled for the knife, trying to grasp the handle with my weakened grip as I awkwardly pulled myself up, using the wall for support.

"You've got the gun! Get her!" Colleen screamed, waving frantically at Debbie.

Debbie stood there, uncertain, her gaze flickering from Colleen's face to mine, then back to Colleen's. As I watched, as if in slow motion, Debbie brought the gun up and turned it my way. Then she whirled, catching Colleen in the side. Colleen screamed so loud I thought she was dying. She convulsed and fell to the floor. Debbie looked over at me, panting.

"No more," she said. "No more."

Just then, a pounding on the door was followed by Kyle's voice. "Open up! Police!" The cavalry had arrived.

Colleen had broken her arm when she fell and the paramedics strapped her onto the stretcher and took her away, an officer riding shotgun. Debbie limply submitted to handcuffs, and as a policewoman led her off, she glanced back at me.

"I never meant to hurt anybody. I didn't want any of this. I just wanted to be liked. I tried to get Trevor off the hook."

"You made the phone call and left the note, didn't you?"

She nodded, sniffling. "Yeah, I couldn't stand to see him in trouble. I love him."

I stared at her silently, not sure what to say. Debbie had gotten railroaded into something bigger than she could control, but she had the chance to put it right and she hadn't. As far as I was concerned, she was as guilty as Colleen.

Kyle helped me over to the sofa, where I submitted to an EMT who insisted on checking me out. Once he proclaimed me fit, just a little shell-shocked, and told me to avoid driving for a day or so, the paramedics packed up and left.

I looked at Kyle as his men swept through the apartment, beginning the long search for evidence. "Don't let them break the mirror," I said, though I knew that I never wanted to see it again.

"We'll be careful," he promised.

I leaned forward, resting my head on my knees. I still felt nauseated from the stun gun attack. "Those things are legal?" I finally asked, pointing to the gun that was now in an evidence bag.

He nodded. "Yeah, they pack one hell of a punch, don't they?"

"Sure do," I said. I looked up and saw that he was holding out a bottle of water for me. I took it and drank slowly. "So, Colleen murdered Lydia. She and Debbie stole my keys while my purse was sitting near my counter, they made copies, and somehow they lured Lydia into the shop and Colleen killed her."

"Why did Colleen do it? All of this violence just for a beauty crown title?" He shook his head. "I don't understand people."

"There was a lot of money attached to that crown, at least in Colleen's eyes. And a lot of self-validation. You'll piece together the rest. When you question Debbie, remember she's not very strong emotionally, Kyle. Be careful with her."

"Why?" He gave me an odd look. "She helped with — or at least kept quiet about — two murders. What makes you care about her feelings?"

I shrugged. Something in Debbie reached out to me. A longing to be accepted, a feeling that she didn't belong anywhere. I didn't understand it, but I couldn't deny feeling sorry for the girl. "She saved my life at the end. She turned the stun gun on Colleen instead of me. By the way, what took you so long?" I grinned at him.

Kyle let out an exasperated snort. "You wouldn't have needed us if you'd kept your nose out of things like I told you to! I'm just glad I followed my gut and got my ass over here when you called." He gave me a long look, then draped his arm around my shoulders as we headed for the door. "So Colleen's perfume tipped all of this off."

I nodded. "The minute I smelled it at the grocery store, I remembered that I'd smelled it before — in Marta's apartment."

"That's one hell of a nose you've got there," he said. "You ever want a job as a bloodhound for the station, give me a call."

"You might say that I've got a nose for murder!" I said, laughing.

He snorted. "Right, just don't let it lead you into trouble again."

Chapter Twenty

By morning, the storm had blown itself out and we were treated to clear skies and a crisp breeze coming off of Puget Sound. Auntie, Barbara, and I were walking along Lighthouse Spit, a long, narrow strip of land that stretched into the water. At the very end stood a lighthouse that was still used by the harbor. It was open to the public, and next door, the Lighthouse Café took advantage of the tourists who came to snap pictures of the beacon.

I was feeling shaky, but better. The shock of the stun gun had worn off, but every muscle in my body ached as if I'd had a full-fledged iron workout and hadn't bothered to stretch out afterward. Auntie had insisted that I go to the doctor even though the EMT had pronounced me fit, and I'd submitted to a thorough exam and come out with flying colors.

Barbara, of course, had been properly horrified. She and Dorian had come over for dinner and brought with them every delicacy they made in their bakery. Auntie and I had looked at the pile of goodies and threw caution to the wind, digging in for all we were worth.

This morning, though, I just wanted fresh air and a long walk. As we silently passed the lighthouse and came to the edge of the beach, Barbara pointed out a long driftwood log where we could sit and watch the tide as it flowed quietly into shore. While they sat on the log, I stretched out on the sand and leaned back, letting the sun beat down on my face. The air was warm enough to bask in, and it looked like we were due for some nice weather for a change.

The sound of the gulls echoed as they soared over the water, looking for clams and oysters. Come low tide, they'd feast as the waters rolled out, leaving a smorgasbord for the critters who frequented the shore.

I sighed. "When's Kyle supposed to show up?"

Auntie reached over and patted my shoulder. "He said he'd be here by nine. It's only eight forty-five."

But he was early — showing up five minutes later. He joined my aunt on the log, and we all turned to him expectantly. Finally, I spoke up.

"So? Did Colleen confess?"

He nodded. "She didn't have to, considering everything we got on tape, but I guess she's praying for an easier sentencing. She confessed to both murders. She exonerated Debbie — at least from the actual crimes. Debbie's still an accessory, but I have the feeling that by the time this is over, she may end up in a mental hospital rather than a prison. She's losing it pretty quick."

Auntie clasped her hands. "I just can't get over it. Those girls . . . they're so young. To do something so horrible, what could they be thinking?"

Kyle shrugged. "Well, we know why she killed Lydia, and we found out what went down with Marta. Apparently, the old girl went over to borrow some coffee and she stopped in the bathroom while she was there — just like you did, Persia. Debbie's bedroom door was open and Marta saw the mirror. If she would have kept quiet she'd still be alive, but she put two and two together and tried to blackmail Colleen. Colleen gave her all her savings — that's where the five thousand dollars came from, but Marta wanted more. So Colleen killed her."

"I heard that Radiance Cosmetics is dropping their China Veils line. It was on the news this morning. Of course, they have no comment about Colleen yet — their PR department is going to have to scramble on that one." Barbara chuckled. "Talk about what goes around, comes around. They rigged the contest and look what it did for them."

Kyle grinned then, and he looked almost happy. "Speaking of rigging contests, if you like their makeup I suggest you stock up on it now. I reported the whole seedy mess to the Attorney General, and I also told them about the judge who insisted Lydia sleep with him. Mr. Wallace Clifford Dover isn't going to be keeping his job as a lawyer much longer."

I gasped. "Wally Dover? Oh my God, he's one of Seattle's highest profiled attorneys. I didn't know he was one of the Radiance judges."

Kyle snorted. "Well, his fame train just jumped the tracks. And his money. His wife owned stock in Radiance Cosmetics, that's how he got on the judging committee. But that's a fraction of her wealth. Now he's losing his job, and when this scandal hits the papers, you can be sure she'll take her fortune and walk. I have a feeling that Radiance Cosmetics isn't going to be around much longer. Not when their customers hear this whole sordid story."

He had a good point. People wanted to trust the companies they did business with and Radiance had been so corrupt that they'd never keep their clientele.

"Have you let Trevor out yet?"

He reached over and patted my hand. "Yes, Persia, thanks to you, Trevor's a free man. I let him out of jail this morning, and apologized to him."

"What I still don't understand is why Colleen pinned the crime on his shoulders." Auntie said.

Kyle spoke up. "Trevor was just in the wrong place at the wrong time. Colleen witnessed the argument between Lydia and Trev, and it fell together in her mind right then. It was easy enough for her to grab his hammer out of his truck while he was off eating lunch. And Colleen was the one who called Trevor, pretending to be Lydia to get him alone so he wouldn't have an alibi."

I stared at the water as the waves crested gently against the shore. Trevor had given his heart to Lydia and look what it had gotten him. Love . . . one of life's greatest gifts, and one of its greatest banes. Which reminded me. Elliot was moving to town. Shit, what the hell was I going to do about him?

Kyle interrupted my thoughts. "Persia, can I talk to you for a moment?"

He walked me down to the water's edge. "I know I've been acting pretty snotty to you. I think I've realized why. I was looking at a picture of Katy today — she was my wife. You know, you remind me of her. You were both strong women, both brilliant."

I just nodded, letting him talk.

"Thing is, when she died, it felt like my gut had been ripped out. And when you came home, I think I felt guilty because I found myself attracted to you. Anyway, I'm sorry. It's not your fault."

I didn't want him to be attracted to me, but I couldn't be rude. Couldn't shake off his confession like it meant nothing. I touched his arm. "Kyle, everything's okay. It must be hard. I never met Katy, but from what I've heard about her, she was pretty special."

He smiled then, a broad smile that lit up his face. "Yeah, she was. I'd like to tell you about her sometime. Would you consider going out to dinner with me? Not a date — I promise. Just two old friends, having dinner together."

Not a date. That was good, because the last thing I needed was to get involved with someone like Kyle. Good friends? Yes. Lovers? No. Besides, my mind was still on Bran Stanton, who I found intriguing and altogether delicious. But dinner with a friend? That I could do.

"Sure thing. I'd like to hear about Katy. Bring pictures, okay?"

He let out a long sigh of relief. "Thank God. After that stupid mistake with the kiss, I was afraid to ask. You pack a good punch, lady. You know that?"

I snorted. "Of course I know it. And I'm proud of it."

We rejoined the others, where Kyle said a quick goodbye and headed off to work. I linked arms with Auntie and Barbara and we strolled along the shore. The waves were crashing and the constant susurration of the wind sounded like wind chimes and voices mingling into a melody fresh in off the ocean. Barbara said something silly — I don't remember what it was — and we all laughed.

We stopped at the foot of the lighthouse, and Auntie turned to me and gave me a fierce hug. "I am so glad you came back to Gull Harbor, Imp."

As I stared out at the ever-changing dance of the waves, I knew it was true. I was home. Regardless of ex-boyfriends moving to town and local beauty queens getting murdered in our shop, regardless of anything else that might happen, I was home.